Ice Moun̄   ̄ ̄s

The Adventures of John Grey
Book Six

Frederick A. Read

A *Guaranteed* Book

First Published in 2009 by
Guaranteed Books

an imprint of Pendragon Press, Po Box 12, Maesteg
Mid Glamorgan, South Wales, CF34 0XG, UK

ISBN 978 1 906864 03 3

Typeset by Christopher Teague

Printed and Bound in Wales by
Print Evolution
www.print-evolution.com

www.guaranteedbooks.net

Chapters

Foreword

The trials and tribulations endured by John and his two very good friends have finally brought them to a crossroads both with their current shipping line owners, and their own survival within the Merchantile Marine service.

This was at a critical time for John who had worked hard in his pursuit in following his dream of becoming a Chief Engineer.

His private life was to suffer yet another fatal blow as will be apparent within these pages, but will he and his ship survive their own perils during an unexpected voyage to the bottom of the world, visiting the 'White Continent'?

Chapter I
Hello There

The weak spring morning sunlight tried to warm John's face as he walked across the road from his still sleeping cottage, he felt elated on going back to sea again, after several weeks at home, recovering from his last ordeal of a voyage.

The antiquated single-decker bus rattled and squealed its brakes when it stopped for him to board.

"Morning Admiral. Off on your jaunts again I see?" the bus conductor asked breezily, noticing the gold rings on John's tunic.

"Maybe, but I don't know where yet. Just give me a single to the Black Man, please."

John replied civilly not wanting to enter into a conversation with the man.

"Right ho Admiral! That'll be one and sixpence, but we go past the docks if you want to stay aboard, in which case it's an extra tuppence."

"No, that's okay. I've got to call in somewhere first."

John held out his money then took his ticket and put it into his top pocket ready for the customary visit by some officious ticket inspector.

He rubbed a hole through the steam on the window so he could watch his onward journey, and watched the houses and streets slowly pass him by in a long procession.

The bus was empty by the time John got off at his stop, and because his suitcase was light he decided to walk slowly along the street and enjoy the fresh air before entering his shipping HQ.

The reception desk clerk was giving verbal instructions to several messenger boys before he turned and spoke to John.

"Just getting the 'go-fors' sorted for the morning. Now what can I do for you sir?" the burly man asked civilly as his moustache twitched with what John took to be a smile.

"I have a letter telling me to report to the shipping office, and

1

see the purser of the SS *Inverary*."

The clerk took the letter off John and proceeded to look down the lines of the big book in front of him.

"Ah Yes. SS *Inverary*. Captain Daniel Freeman. He hasn't arrived yet, but the *Inver* office is just along the corridor to your left, so you might as well wait there." the clerk said off-handedly, and giving the letter back nodded in the direction. John picked up his suitcase and made his way to a glass-panelled door with gold and black engraving on it proclaiming that it was the *Inver* line office.

The room was smoky from several pipes and cigarettes of the men waiting in line before in front of a hatchway where a bespectacled man was seeing to them.

"Next! Sign your papers here, and here." the man demanded in a high pitched voice.

John looked around the room and seeing a door that said 'Officers Only' on it, decided to go through it, rather than wait his turn. The room was neat and tidy with fresh air coming through the open windows, and a few fellow officers sitting quietly around a large table.

"Hello there John! Didn't know you were back, how are you?"

"Hello Bruce, nice to see you again. What news from that big Board of enquiry about the *Inverlaggan* that we were supposed to attend?" John replied shaking his friend's hand.

"That is still to be conducted due to certain diplomatic and legal wrangles, but we've got nothing to worry about. In fact, according to my calculations, we're all in for quite a few hundred pounds each as an interim payment, subject to re-scrutiny, and the usual claw back penalties from Belverley and co, of course. Never mind that for the moment, I gather you had a bit of a rough time a while back with those coastal tankers. You'll have to tell me some time, but sit down here and take hold of this mug of tea, its delicious." Larter invited.

John sat down and started to drink his tea, when two senior

officers, indicated by the oak leaves that decorated the peaks on their caps, came into the room.

"Morning gentlemen. I'm Captain Freeman, and this is Chief Engineer Chapman." the tall and much slender one of the two announced, whilst looking around the room.

"It looks as if we've got our compliment of officers Frank, so we might just as well get them bussed and onto the ship. She should be alongside now, so let's get going."

John didn't recognise any of the other officers, but Chapman came over to him and offered his hand.

"You must be my 2nd, Engineer John Grey! I've heard a lot about you from my cousin Happy Day."

John stood up and shaking Chapman's hand politely, merely nodded in agreement.

"Pleased to make your acquaintance Chief. Hope Happy is well?"

"Yes, and thank you for asking." Chapman replied, then went back to stand beside Freeman.

"We shall be boarding the *Inverary* en bloc, but make sure each of you have signed your articles and papers for the voyage before we leave, you've got 20 minutes to do so. We'll be on board before the crew gets there." Freeman announced then left the room with Chapman.

"You're the boffin Bruce, any ideas where we're going?"

"Down to Cape Town I believe. Let's hope we make it this time." •

"Sounds like a direct route. But then the *Inver* line is famous for that." a person with a Welsh accent said from behind Larter, and then introduced himself.

"I'm 3rd Engineer Ken Morris." he said and offered his hand in friendship.

"I'm John Grey, and this is my old pal Radio Officer Bruce Larter." John responded.

• See *Fresh Water*.

3

This introduction prompted the other officers to introduce themselves around the room before everybody filed out and made their way to the main entrance.

The men that John had seen earlier were lounging around with their baggage or talking in small groups among themselves, and assumed that these would be the crew signed on for the *Inverary*.

As the bus arrived at the dockside they could see that the ship was about to be tied up alongside.

John looked at his new home and decided that it was much bigger and roomier than his previous one.

He looked up at the squat, smokeless, buff coloured funnel with three black coronets painted on it, declaring that it belonged to the Three Coronet shipping line, commonly known among the crew as the Triple Crown line.

"Here we are again John. Just like old times."

"Yes Bruce, pity we don't have Andy to make it complete." John said quietly.

"Still talking to yourself?" a very familiar Scottish voice whispered from behind John, which made him flinch with surprise.

"Well beat me with a wet woodbine. Hello there Andy you old Haggis Yaffler." Larter said with a mixture of surprise and pleasure.

"I see you're still up to your tricks John?" Sinclair said, taking hold of and shaking John's hand. This was not the usually accepted protocol between Officers and crew, but it was a special greeting between three friends of many voyages together.

John felt himself shiver at the strange feeling he had, as he shook Sinclair's large hands again whilst standing next to Larter. The years had instantly rolled back to their very first meeting almost at the very same spot.[•]

* * *

[•] See *A Fatal Encounter.*

The *Inver* line ships were mostly large bulk freighters, licensed to carry up to 40 passengers, instead of the more usual amount of 15 to 20 passengers. This is in contrast to the slightly smaller ships of the *Lea* line, which, although carrying much less gross cargo weight, could take more than 60 passengers. The *Inver* line part of the Triple Crown fleet were the workhorses of the fleet, ranging from 20-35,000 tons and all between 400 - 500 feet long. Thus enabling them to attract more revenue per bulk cargo as opposed to the smaller Lea ships whose main revenue mostly passengers with their baggage and light loads of cargo obtained.

John took his turn to step onto the ship, and was traditionally greeted by his Chief engineer.

"2nd! Your cabin is a double one, for reasons I will explain later. Get into overalls and meet me in the engine room in one hour." Chapman said civilly, greeting John again.

John had been on these type of ships before, so knew which way to go to get to his cabin. Once there he took time to unpack and get himself familiarised with the ships layout that was depicted on his cabin wall, before making his way down to the engine room.

The engines of this ship were steam turbines. Which meant that they were quieter than the diesels of the Lea line ships, but not as dependable as the sceptics would have it.

"We have a 2nd Engineer due for promotion to acting chief, who is joining us for the ride down to Cape Town, so I request you take over the Outside Engineers' duties as well as your instructional ones."

"Does the 3rd know of this?" John asked with surprise.

"All I'm doing is re-allocating engineering duties so that I can get optimum performance from my officers and men. I need you on the deck for a while and for the 3rd to remain in the engine room until such times as we get a qualified 4th engineer on board."

"Very well Chief!" John agreed with a nod, observing the stokers who were coming down the ladder past him and onto the decking below the control platform.

Chapman waited until the stokers were down and settled before he spoke to them.

"I'm Chief Chapman. The officers standing behind me, will, no doubt be known to you later." Chapman commenced, as he started to issue orders and instructions to despatch men all over the engine room and other destinations.

John spotted a familiar face among the men and nodded to him, who smiled back as he recognized John. It was stoker Dawes. The briefing by Chapman went on for a little while longer and concluded with everybody engaged in some chore or another.

John went up onto the main weather deck with Morris following along behind him.

"This is my second voyage on this bucket 2nd, and I'll be glad of some engine room watch-keeping again." Morris volunteered.

"All you need to do, is take me on a conducted tour of your responsibilities, and show me your inspection and repair schedules." John said quietly.

"Haven't got any of them. Not sure what is required, but I know what's what and when to repair them."

John gasped at this revelation, because it went against the instructions that Happy Day had given him and against the personal regime he set for himself during his time as a 3rd Engineer.

"It seems as if you are in need of help. How long have you been a 3rd?"

"This is my first as Acting 3rd, because on the last voyage on this ship, I was only the 4th."

"Thank you for being honest. Maybe you'll take the trouble to make yourself available to me for extra instructions and how to do things the right way if you want to get on."

"Sounds good to me 2nd, but I'll have to sort out my watch-keeping pattern first."

"I'll speak to the Chief about that, Ken. As for now, lets get this hand over inspection done with, as its nearly lunch time I fancy." John said evenly, following Morris around the decks.

Morris took John around the different deck machinery, some of which he saw was slightly different from his previous *Inver* ships. During his round he met up with Sinclair who was instructing some able seamen in the wheelhouse.

"What ho Bosun! Where's your mess-deck on this?"

"Hello 2nd. There's nothing for'ard on this crate, we're all in the aft end. All behind like a Hottentot, even a Phattie if you like." Sinclair responded jovially.[*]

"A much better layout than the *Inverlogie* too." Sinclair added with a pronounced nod.

"Yes Andy. It does seem you're right." John agreed.

"Our stokers are aft with the odds and sods too!" Morris added.

John smiled and nodded.

"At least we've got a bigger and better bit of metal between us and the briny, even though the *Inverlogie* was a much newer ship." he said, and waved to them before he left the compartment.

"Right then Ken. Go and get yourself spruced up and I'll see you in the passengers lounge. The skipper is giving a briefing after dinner, so be on the ball." John advised.

John went to his cabin to refresh himself too, and met the other 2nd who was getting his gear unpacked by a steward.

"I'm Acting Chief Engineer Phil Cooper." the man said amiably."

"But on this voyage I'll be temporarily as the 2nd. Hope you don't mind!"

"Hello 2nd! Yes, the chief did explain the score. You carry on." John replied courteously, then turned to the steward and asked him his name.

"I'm Dovey, your steward 2nd." the steward replied indignantly.

"Hello steward. Hope we have a pleasant trip." John said quietly,

---

[*] See *A Beach Party*.

seeing that the steward was miffed at not being recognised.

"You lot have the skippers briefing after lunch, so that'll give me time to get your stuff stowed properly." Dovey announced with less gruffness.

"Working your passage to Cape Town, and then where Phil?" John enquired as both men walked the short distance to the passengers lounge.

"I'm joining the *Inverkeithing* at Durban, for onward passage to Brisbane then join some ship at Brisbane. By all accounts, we've still got one of our cold store ships down there that still needs seeing to. I shall be its new chief Engineer, and should be there by the end of next month with a bit of luck. I won't hold my breath on keeping my deadline anymore, as this line is famous for being long overdue into destination ports. But then, I expect you know that by now John."

"The ship you might be referring to, and if I'm right, was my old one that was almost done for out in the Pacific. If you bump into a 3rd by the name of Blackie Blackmore, then please tell him I said hello."

"If you know that scoundrel then I'll be pleased to send on your regards. He still owes me a noggin or two. Hope he's learned a few new tricks of the trade by the time we meet up."
John nodded his head and grinned

"And a few more if I've shown him right." he replied happily and entered the saloon together.

The saloon was spacious if sparse with its leather bound furniture, with a crystal chandelier glittering above him seemed to cheer the place up and give it some luxury.

The individual tables had been joined up to make one big table and each chair had the place name of each man to show where they would sit. John was third chair down from the top on one side, and saw the names of the deck officers on the other side, all in descending order of rank to the bottom where the junior officers sat. He looked at the distance between where he first sat at such a table and to where he graced it now.

'Such a short gap between the places of the chief and 4th, yet such a big one to bridge professionally' he mused then felt a hand on his shoulder.

"Having a scotch John?" Larter asked, and offered John a large glass of liqueur.

"Thanks Bruce. Just like old times what? Oh and by the way, here's your lighter. You must have dropped it earlier."

"Thanks John, I've been searching everywhere for it, as always. Anyway, lets hope we have a better voyage this time." Larter said pocketing the lighter.

"Amen to that. I've already had a job change given me, so I'll be able to pop by and see you on my rounds as usual."

"That's good John. Must go now, here's your 3rd coming." Larter said and went to sit three places down the table from John.

Freeman and Chapman came into the saloon and placed themselves at the top of the table, before Freeman conducted the customary 'welcome on board' speech.

The stewards served the food, which to John was cold and unappetising, but he decided to eat some of it just for politeness.

The meal was a hushed and rushed affair, much to John's secret approval, as he toyed with his almost empty whiskey glass.

"We should get another drink now before the skipper starts, so get us a large one from the bar when you've finished, Ken." John whispered in Morris's ear.

Morris had finished his meal so did as John requested, then they sat with recharged glasses waiting for Freeman to continue his briefing.

"We are sailing for Cape Town, via Lagos. We will have passengers and some special cargoes for each port of call, but mostly we'll be carrying engineering machinery, lathes and the like, and railway engines for the colonials.

The ship sails in two days time, so each of you are advised to get your personal and departmental stores sorted before we leave. Should any of you not wish to complete the voyage then see the purser here to make your alternative arrangements.

The doctor will give out the necessary jabs and medication to those not in medical compliance, and see that your department crewmen comply with this. I don't want another plague on this ship.

I will hold my final voyage briefing before we sail. Due to the vast amount of pre-voyage work to be done on the ship, there is no shore leave until I'm satisfied with each department." Freeman concluded, then picked up his briefcase and left with Chapman following behind him.

Chapter II
Footprints

John managed to sort out a timetable for his instructional periods with the two new juniors on board, and to keep an eye on Ken Morris. He liked Ken because he was such a laid back person that almost nothing fazed him, yet he seemed to have the appetite to learn at almost the same rapid speed as himself. This apart, and another reason for John to keep an eye on him, was because of his much talked about wayward antics and capers, that always seemed to bounce back and get him into all sorts of trouble.

"Ken. Get the two juniors mustered in my cabin in half an hour and I want to see your journal then." John ordered.

"But I've not finished it yet John." Ken moaned.

"Never mind, I want to see if when we sail later today, you're ready to take over the shift." John said sharply, trying to produce his own work schedule ready for Chapman's inspection. Without this paperwork, the ship could be deemed un-seaworthy and prevented from sailing by the Lloyds Shipping and Insurance board.

Morris and the two junior engineer officers arrived at John's cabin for him to look at the juniors efforts to surmount their classroom training and take on the reality of life in a real engine room. He also looked at Morris's book, then stated that it was not quite up to the mark and needed more detail, which would only be got through actual watch-keeping.

"On the whole gentlemen, its not too bad, but you do need to pay extra attention to your duties and ask more questions than you've been doing recently. We'll leave it for now as we've got the skippers sailing briefing in twenty minutes. Get yourselves cleaned up and suitably dressed. See me in the saloon. Morris, you get the drinks for us all if you like." John concluded, but smiled at Morris who nodded his head at John's request.

"Afternoon gentlemen." Freeman greeted, taking up his position at the top table again.

"It seems we've got an extra stop in Southampton, but only for extra passengers. I'm pleased with the work you've all done over the last two days, and lets hope we have a good voyage. This is a trial run to test company backup and support, but it's only to Cape Town and back, so we'll be taking it slow and easy and be back in about eight weeks.

We sail on the tide, so get your men organised. I want this ship working as it should." Freeman said loftily, picking up his cap and leaving the officers to themselves.

John stood up and going over to the steward, asked him what the skipper meant by that.

"It means 2nd. That our last voyage was a disaster between one thing or another. The other being that the National Seaman's Union and the Dock Workers Union held us up several times due to industrial action. If it weren't for the skipper we'd still be the other side of the Black Stump."

"I missed all that palaver as I was on shore. But lets hope all does go well."

Dovey simply nodded and handed over a glass of whiskey and soda to John, before he entered the transaction down into a book.

John looked at this familiar book, which was the 'Mess Tally' for each officer on board. This was paid at the end of each voyage, and everybody was eager to have the receipt, which stated 'Paid Up'. Without that, the person concerned wasn't allowed anything else on tick until it was.

"Coming on deck now 2nd?" Morris asked politely then started to leave the saloon.

John downed his drink, grabbed his cap and followed Morris out onto the main deck.

"We'll be sailing in about one hour judging by the engine readiness state. Better you go below and get ready for your own duties. I usually stand up on the foc'sle when entering or leaving harbour. That way, if any capstan or winch seizes up at a critical time, I'm on hand to see to it. Something for you to remember Ken."

12

John said quietly, watching the sailors untying the gangway and preparing to slip from the dockside.

"Yes I heard about that. Sounds a good place to be, at least you get a good view of the place at the same time. I usually positioned myself below the outboard bridge wing." Morris replied holding onto his cap to prevent it from blowing away with the stiff breeze.

John stood on the foc'sle watching the seamen slipping the ship from its berth, as the 2nd Deck Officer shouted his commands cursing the men who were too slow to react to the ship's needs.

He looked back and up to the lofty bridge and saw Freeman wave and heard his shout to get fenders over the side to protect the bow from bumping against the solid stone of the dockside

He felt a large bump travel up through his feet and his legs, as the ship thumped into then bounced back off the dock. He decided to step back a few yards to get out of the way of the deck officer who swore and cursed at the men.

'It seems that bow plates are twelve a penny these days. But I'd better take a look at the damage in case.' he said softly to himself, and waited until the ship was in mid-stream and making its way down the channel of Belfast Lough.

The damage was seen to be minimal, but John went down into the for'ard compartments to check on the structures, just in case there was something untoward there, but he found that all was fine.

The ship sailed down the silent water of the lough and entered the Irish Sea for its downward passage to Southampton.

John stayed on deck making sure that the Deck Officers had their winches and other deck machinery secured properly before he finally left and went into the ship superstructure to make his report to Chapman.

"2nd ! How is my bow?" Freeman asked, passing John on his way.

"Just a few slight dents, but the compartments seem okay captain." John replied casually.

"Very good 2nd. I was a bit concerned, but put in your report anyway." Freeman advised and concluded the brief conversation.

The lounge was buzzing with passengers talking and generally relaxing when John entered it at the same time as the First mate.

"Ladies and Gentlemen. I'm First mate Brown. You are requested to pay attention, as I shall be doing lifeboat drill in five minutes. We are obliged by law to conduct such drills and you, as passengers must obey our instructions. Do not be alarmed, as luckily its only pretend this time, but we must be prepared just in case." he announced over the shrill voices of children, who were playing on the carpet covered steel deck.

The announcement lulled everybody into silence as they waited for their drill to commence. John had never had the chance to witness such a procedure before and decided to stick around and see just what was what.

Brown blew his whistle just as the ships foghorn blasted out.

"Everybody is to take a lifebelt and put it on like thus." Brown said, and proceeded to demonstrate how to put the bulky cork lined jacket over his head. He watched the passengers don their life jackets, with other Deck officers assisting those who got muddled up.

"Right everybody. We'll go up this flight of stairs and onto the lifeboat deck. From there we will show you where your own special lifeboat will be in such emergencies." he continued.

All the passengers trooped up the wooden stairs and out onto the windy part of the ship where the funnel was letting out volumes of black smoke. This started to make some of the passengers choke and some of the children cry for their parents.

"It's only smoke from the funnel. But the lifeboats you will get into are the ones in front of you. You will see some like it on the other side of the deck, which can be used as well. Plenty for all as you can see."

"Yeh, yeh! We've seen the bloody things, now lets get out of this damn smoke." a man's voice shouted, which amused John, who waited for the response.

"It can get a lot more smoky than this for real, folks. Just put up with it for a moment until you see one of the lifeboats being lowered."

Brown signalled to the davit operators to start lowering one of the large boats over the side, and watched it come down level to the deck.

"As you can see, the boat is now level with the deck for you to step into it. Once you've sat down, the boat will be lowered into the sea for you to escape. Each boat will have three crewmen to look after you from there." Brown said as he started to cough with the smoke.

"I think that will be all now. Go back to the lounge and take off your lifejackets, where you'll get a nice drink to clear your throat from the smoke."

"About ruddy time too!" came the same Yorkshire voice from behind the crowd of passengers.

John went over to the crewmen who operated the davits watching them struggle with the winch.

"Problems with it?" he observed.

"Yes 2nd. One of the davits is off-line and tends to get stuck half-way out on its arc. We had a landing craft on this one for our last voyage, but its now on the other side with the skippers private motor launch."

"Landing craft? er, er…." John asked with an enquiring look.

"I'm leading seaman Kirk, and this is my oppo Knocker White." Kirk said quickly to help John out.

"We carry two small landing craft to ferry stores and the like when we're anchored off anywhere. The skipper likes to use his motor launch rather than the motorised whalers. That way he can get ashore much quicker and easier."

"I see. So we'll have to keep an eye on the other ones too. But who operates the other davits, as I saw nobody but you two, Kirk?"

"There's two more of us for the other side and that's it. But we only come here for the passenger drills."

"Very well. You can leave the repairs with me, I'll get it fixed later on." John replied then walked over to the radio office just for'ard port side of the funnel, and attached to the back of the bridge.

He knocked on the door before entering the compartment room, and saw Larter with his 2nd Radio Officer with earphones on their heads, intently listening to morse code, writing down what they heard. He stood for a moment looking around the array of radio equipment, with several postcards adorning the bulkheads.

Larter finished his writing, then after a moment operating his morse key, he took off his earphones to look over at John, and burst out laughing, then kneeled down onto the deck and started to sing.

"I'll walk a million miles for one of your smiles, my ma-a-am mee." he joked, pointing to a small mirror on a bulkhead.

John looked into it to see how black he was from the smoky funnel, and realised that all the passengers were probably just as sooty.

"Shades of past voyages, eh what Bruce?" John smiled, then went over to a small sink to wash himself.

When he finished sprucing himself up again, Larter introduced him to the other Officer.

"Jock! Meet an old friend of mine, John Grey. John meet Jock Wallace."

Wallace was a large well-built man who held out a sturdy hand to greet John.

"Pleased to meet you John. What brings you to our neck of the woods?" Wallace asked politely.

"Just started my upper deck rounds. That's a nice accent Jock, what part of Bonnie Scotland are you from?"

"I come from Cumnock, why do you ask?"

"Just curious, only we have a mutual friend who hails from Fraserburgh."

"Oh you mean the Bosun, Andy Sinclair. Aye, he sold me his

Triumph Bonneville, very reasonable price too. That's it under the flag locker over there." Wallace said with pride then went over and uncovered the black and chrome motorbike

"But it's playing me up a wee bit, must get it sorted soon." He added.

"Hmm! It's a 650cc engine. But I'll have a look at it for you later on, when it's quiet." John promised, then told them it was time for him to move on.

"See you in the lounge for supper John." Larter said, as John shut the door and went back out onto the soot-covered deck, where each step he took left a smudged foot-print to mark his track.

The ship sailed peacefully down the choppy Irish Sea and round the tip of Cornwall at Land's End and passed to where many a vessel had come to grief on the sharp jagged rocks of The Lizard, that stretch out into the English Channel to catch unwary mariners.

As the ship sailed up the Solent towards the great seaport of Southampton, she passed a very large liner that John had been watching from his vantage point on the foc'sle. Three very large red and black funnels, which towered way above him, topped the vast black and red coloured hull and he craned his neck to read what ship it was.

"*Hmm. Just as I thought. RMS QUEEN MARY. Probably on her way to New York. I'd like to be her Chief, but no such hope at present.*" he muttered to himself and stood in awe at her vastness seemed to slip silently past him before it slowly and steadily diminished in size as she sailed away.

The ship docked and started to take on board more cargo and passengers, while John finished his deck rounds. It was almost evening before he managed to get into the saloon to have his supper.

Just as he finished his meal and got up to go over to the bar for a smoke and a drink when he saw a face in the crowd. He stopped in his tracks so sudden that the lady who was slightly behind him and going the same way, almost bumped into him.

"My apologies!" he offered to her, who accepted it gracefully.

He felt his pulse race and his stomach seemed to be in knots as he looked right into those very brown eyes surrounded by little freckles on a little nose that he first knew, oh so long ago. John went straight over to the seated woman and taking hold of her hands, pulled her up swiftly towards him

She gasped in surprise at the sudden motion, but when she looked up to see who it was, she flung her arms around him and started to kiss him passionately and fervently for several moments.

"John! It's you! Let me look at you." she said hoarsely as she stopped kissing him and looked into his blue eyes.

"We are together again, yes?"

John held her close again, whispered her name and kissed the blonde curls on her head. The world seemed to stop still and completely silent during those moments he held her.

"I thought you had gone away somewhere. But yes dear Helena, we're together again as betrothed lovers." John said gently, kissing her again.

He heard cheers and clapping come roaring back into his ears when he saw the other passengers watching them with pleasure on their faces.

John recognised another face and went over to the woman.

"It's good to see you too Stella!" he said spontaneously and planted a kiss on the woman's upturned face, struggling to catch his decorum again.

"Then meet my husband, my two children are playing over there, dear John!" Stella replied gently, taking hold of and stroking John's hand.

"Ruud, this is the John Grey I told you about." she said to her husband, who stood up and shook John's hand vigorously.

"Pleased to meet you." he said warmly, embracing John, continental style.

"I'm glad you were on board that time otherwise I'd be without my Stella and the children too." the man said in English but with a prominent Dutch accent.

John smiled at the man whilst looking over towards the children who were too busy to notice him.

Helena pulled John down beside her and giving him her drink, reached over for another one for herself. He sat there not drinking from the glass but drinking in her stunning beauty and the memories of them when they loved the long voyage nights away.

As the evening wore on, the two circles of people started to intermingle, but the officers made certain that John was not disturbed from his company.

The First Mate came in briefly to announce that the ship would not be sailing until the following morning, but any visitors must be off the ship by midnight, then left.

John and Helena walked out onto the passengers' small promenade deck and found a secretive place where they would be alone.

The night was mild, and the cloudless sky was lit up by a full moon, with millions of star galaxies twinkling down upon them, as the bond of love was being renewed between two young people.

"John. It's time we loved again. Your friend the Bruce said we can use his cabin, and he'll sleep in yours." Helena whispered, taking John's hand and placing it upon her breast. John looked down at this voluptuous female, slipped his hand around her waist and gently led her towards Bruce's cabin.

As they passed one of the lounge windows, he saw Bruce looking his way who gave him a nod as if to say, 'get going'.

John took his time, as he quietly and gently led Helena over those mighty tidal waves of passion that they had shared almost several lifetimes away, but the memory of his encounter with the beautiful young Polynesian girl Telani and her sisters made him more attentative to her needs.

Their lovemaking was unbridled and unfettered and kept drinking from the cup of sheer pleasure delighting in renewing their knowledge of each others bodies, before falling into the abyss of sleep.

"John, Helena, its time to get up, the ship will be sailing soon after breakfast." Stella whispered, trying to wake up the entwined love-makers.

John woke up with a start, then gently disentangled himself and started to get dressed.

"Thank you for coming and telling us Stella, I have some duties to see to before we sail. Tell Helena that I hope to see her later on today." He whispered, then pecked Stella on the cheek and left them.

John went back to his own cabin and was changing into his overalls when he heard Larter whispering to him.

"You lucky git, and to think that it's me that seems to get all the luck round here." Larter said, then added.

"She gets off in Cape Town to see her Aunt who runs a tobacco plantation up country somewhere."

John smiled slowly at the information, brushing his long black hair back.

"Thanks for the lend of your cabin. I'll probably need it again during the three week voyage, any chance?" he whispered back Larter chuckled softly and teased John by pretending to blackmail him, but both knew it was only fun.

Both officers got themselves ready for the day ahead then went into the lounge where they had an early breakfast. As the lounge was empty of passengers, the officers took the time for a few minutes quietness and a smoke before starting their duties.

Cooper came over and talked quietly to John for a while but only discussed engineering problems and watch-keeping duties for Morris. John was in two minds to tell Cooper about the occasional sleeping arrangements but decided not to instead he'd have a word with the steward.

The dawn crept slowly over the inky waters of the harbour as the ship drifted slowly away from its berth and made its way downstream again towards the busy English Channel.

This was her proper start to a 10,000mile voyage down the entire length of the Atlantic Ocean.

CHAPTER III
Soap Suds

John was on deck fixing the lifeboat davits when Brown the First mate and another Deck Officer were making their rounds.

"2nd. We are heading for a storm in the 'Bay', be good enough to ensure the boat is secured properly when you've finished with it. We've got extra lengths of cordage on the for'ard cargo deck if you need it."

"If that's the case First mate, then you'd better send a party of men to secure the rest of them, as I've discovered that the existing cordage is rotten and the securing hawse wires are rusted right through each one of them.

"It can't be! I had them all renewed and secured before we left the dock." the junior deck officer protested.

John shrugged his shoulders.

"Oh well. What do I know about sailors work." he sighed and threw a length of rusty wire and shredded rope at the feet of Brown.

Brown stooped down and picking up the articles, examined them closely for a moment then turned to the other officer.

"Get all off-watch sailors on deck. I want every lifeboat, Carley float, cargo deck coverings, and other items with lashing, re-tied and lashed with new cordage. Do it now." he barked, throwing the rotten rope at the rapidly departing officer.

John finished his repairs on the davit and started to move off to carry out other minor repairs, unconcerned about the furore he created.

"I hope you'll make this finding in your round report 2nd." Brown called out as John left.

"Nope! It's none of my business if you let shoddy workmanship get by you. It's your department, not mine." John replied, and took no further notice of Brown who was ranting and raving to himself.

* * *

The seamen were crawling all over the tarpaulins re-roping and re-tying down the deck cargo, and ensuring the chocks, cradles and other securing devices were correct to prevent the cargo from disappearing over the side.

This activity was repeated within the cargo holds as well, as it is potentially very dangerous for any cargo to get loose and move about with the ships corkscrew movements.

John was in the for'ard hold when the storm broke, and had to brace himself from time to time against the heavy machinery that was the cargo, when he noticed water seeping through an overhead deck plate join.

He couldn't see any daylight from the area, which would indicate a hole, so he ran his wheel spanner across the riveted area and found that one of the rivets actually broke and fall into his hand in two rusty pieces. He took several minutes to examine closely the whole ridge where the deck plates were riveted together and discovered that the rivets were stressed and the plating buckling with the overhead weight. On going onto the main weather deck and being drenched into the bargain, he worked out where the area was for him to see what was bending the thick steel plates.

Looking under the tarpaulin of the deck cargo he discovered that it was a large locomotive with a full load of coal in its tender coupled to it.

His mind was swiftly working out the stress load when a large wave sloshed itself over the side of the ship and deluged both him and the engine. The instant waterfall sluiced itself away through the deck scuppers would have taken John with it if it wasn't for his safety harness he wore, that was lashed to a deck eye-bolt. Seeing another wave coming over as if to try its luck with him, he swiftly unbuckled his harness and raced to the safety of the bridge ladder. He saw his tools being swept into the scuppers and disappear over the side, and blessing himself realising that that could have been him too, made a rapid ascent up to the bridge.

"Captain!" John said brusquely, striding over to the captain who was by the chart table.

"2nd. What can I do for you?" Freeman asked, holding onto a stanchion to steady himself.

"We have a weight distribution problem on the for'ard cargo deck. Come and I'll show you." John stated, going over to the bridge window and pointing down to the deck below them.

"What's wrong with my cargo this time 2nd? You've already got my sailors re-rigging and re-tying everything that moves thanks to you spotting some duff rope work on the lifeboats." Freeman snarled, peering out of the window.

"That locomotive and its tender are too heavy for the deck plating. I've discovered that the deck itself is weak and should have been removed and replaced during your last docking period. The rivets are shearing or ripping the metal apart." John said evenly, pulling out the snapped rivet pieces and handing them to Freeman.

Freeman looked at the offending pieces of rivet for a moment, then down at the locomotive.

"It's probably some left-over rivet from the dockyard, and that locomotive is secure and won't leave its blocks." he said with a shrug of his shoulders trying to dismiss it as nothing to worry about.

"Not only am I the Outside engineer Captain, but I'm a 2nd engineer and qualified enough to offer my suggestions to you." John stated angrily

"Unless we shift that cargo to a safer place, it'll make an even bigger hole, especially right through the belly of the ship. Then what will you do?" John added.

Freeman called for the steward to bring his Sou'wester and after putting it on whilst John stood in an ever increasing puddle dripping from his overalls, he beckoned John to come with him down onto the deck.

Both men scrambled around the rigging and lashings of the cargo as the water swished around their legs, before Freeman signalled to John that they were to go back up onto the bridge again.

"It seems that you're right 2nd, but there's nothing we can do until the weather abates somewhat, or we call into somewhere to re-load it. In the meantime, ask the chief to come and see me." Freeman said in a more pleasant manner.

"Captain. If we shore up the decking immediately under that loaded area, it should give us a breather until such times as we do shift the load."

"That's exactly what I had in mind, 2nd. Now better get yourself dried off or you'll catch pneumonia. Messenger! Get me the First mate." Freeman commanded.

"I shall put it in my rounds report this time, Captain." John responded and sloshed his way down the steel ladders that led into the passengers and officers quarters.

He met Helena on his way, who was alarmed at the state of him, so shepherding him into her cabin, she stripped him naked and pointed to the shower cubicle.

"Now get in there and warm yourself up with some clean hot water. I'll be there to dry your back." She said wickedly, gently taking hold of his manhood then led him slowly into the shower.

Before he knew it, she was as naked as he, and he felt her gentle hands glide over him as she lathered his entire body in scented soap suds, especially his naughty bits which received special attention.

"Helena. We are good for each other, but what are we going to do about our future together?" John whispered softly, feeling his manhood grow, under her gentle and teasing caresses.

"Oh John." she said gently, then knelt down, kissing his manhood until it was large and rampant between her shower moistened lips.

"We have talked about this several times before when you visited me for a while at my home. We only have each other as I cannot have children, ever since that collision." she said sadly then raising herself up, started to weep gently in his arms.

"Hush dear one. As long as we have each other that's all that matters. We can always adopt as many as we want to." John said, gently kissing her tears away.

Helena gave a wistful smile and looked into John's eyes as she entwined her body with his, and when the two of them were joined as one, they rocked gently with the motion of the ship to bring them both to an orgasmic crescendo.

Shortly after they took it in turns to dry each other and were lying entwined in each others arms on the bunk, Stella came into the cabin accompanied by her children.

John went to cover them both up to be decent in front of the children, but Stella laughed and told him that the children were used to seeing naked bodies, as naturism was part and parcel of their upbringing.

"In that case, why undo their mothers teachings." John laughed with bravado, whipping off the bedcovers again and continued to lie in his lover's arms in gay abandon.

Stella made everybody a cup of tea, but John had his laced with a miniature bottle of whiskey.

"For medicinal purposes" Helena said happily.

After a brief chat John looked over to the cabin clock and realised he needed to get his rounds done.

"Sorry my dear, but I must go now. I'll see you later after my rounds he said, wrapping a towel around his waist, then grabbed his wet overalls, entered the empty passageway and slipped into his cabin before someone else could see him.

"There you are John." Cooper said with surprise, seeing John's attire.

"Making use of the passenger shower system I see." he said with a wink, then added.

"Better get yourself dressed and see Chapman, he wants to see you before you start your rounds."

"Thanks Phil." John replied appreciatively, feeling a warm glow come through his stomach, putting it down to the whiskey-flavoured tea.

Within minutes he was properly attired and stepping into

Chapman's cabin where he saw Brown sitting down, looking over a detailed drawing.

"John! We've got a problem with the for'ard deck cargo that's about to break through and plunge into the cargo hold." Chapman commenced.

"Yes I know. I reported it to the captain some" he started to say, then looked at his watch to realise with surprise that he had managed to steal three brief but magic hours with Helena.

"Three hours ago when I finished my for'ard rounds." He concluded

Brown looked up at him and frowned.

"But how did you know? It was the captain who told us." he asked in bewilderment.

"Quite simple. The same way as I found out about those rotten rigging and wires, First mate."

"Well never mind all that. Here's the proposed remedy." Chapman stated, referring to the drawing Brown was holding, and went on to expound his theory and method of recovery.

This went on for a little while, whilst the three men discussed other ideas and suggestions.

John liked this 'brain storming' method of planning, as it meant that each person involved came to a mutual agreement and an understanding as to who was going to do what.

As the plan was about to be put into action the ship sailed out of the storm and into some much flatter water to swim through. This meant that all they had to do was shift the deck cargo around with the aid of the derricks and winches, with lots of grunting and sweating bodies to finish it all off.

Freeman came down onto the deck inspecting the reshuffled cargo declared that it was a job well done. It was so well done that he could now cancel the hastily arranged stopover in Gibraltar, only just around the corner of the Spanish mainland.

"Rats and double rats!" John heard some sailor mutter, which was followed by someone whispering that they should have not done such a good job to be diddled out of a run ashore. He smiled at their misfortune but realised that he could have had a few hours ashore buying Helena a nice 'rabbit' (gift) from the well-stocked bazaars Gibraltar was famous for.

For the next ten days on her way to Lagos, the ship made a steady progress down the coast of Spain and crossed the mouth of the Mediterranean Sea before she skirted the coast of Morocco. As she went south she was getting into much balmier weather and calmer waters that approach the equator. This was the part of the voyage most sailors enjoyed best as they left the angst of the cold northern waters behind them, and got into the routine of any respectable cruise liner, or even any other ship for that matter as long as it was peaceful.

There were lazy hours off watch enjoying a cool beer watching the dolphins and flying fish play racing or 'tag' with the ships bow as she carved a white ribbon of wake behind her.

John had his machine maintenance under control and was able to conduct his rounds as and when he felt like it, and he even found time to fix Wallace's bike for him. But most of his past time was spent in the company of Helena, and occasionally with Stella and her family.

His special arrangement with the steward cost him a 40 oz bottle of brandy, but was worth it as he was able to enjoy Helena's private attentions without any awkward situations or questions cropping up.

Chapman was sitting up on the foc'sle one morning, enjoying the sea breeze created by the forward motion of the ship, when John strayed past him whilst doing his rounds.

"Morning John. Haven't seen much of you since we left the 'Bay." he greeted.

John sat down on one of the capstans near him and looked out to sea.

"Been busy, between one thing and another. The air conditioning is playing up but I've got Morris onto it as extra instructional duties." he said nonchalantly.

"Bit much for him, surely? Even though he was looking after it on his last voyage."

"I was only a 4th under the guidance of Happy Day during my instructional days, so it means nothing to me. He'll either get it done or he won't see his 3rd rank confirmed."

"Ah yes, Happy did mention about your exploits. Just as well we've got you on board, as I'm not too keen on that Phil Cooper. He has strange ways that man."

"Well, I'm not the one to judge him Frank, but he must know his stuff to become the next chief on the fridge ship he's about to join."

"Weren't you on one of the new fridge ships too? We've only got three of those big ones at the moment, but isn't he joining the one you were on?"

John looked up at the cloudless sky and around the blue ocean until he finally looked at Chapman.

"I'm not sure what you're talking about, Frank. I don't think of past voyages, only the ones I'm on now." John lied, and got up slowly to continue his rounds, adding

"Must press on. You'll be looking for my daily report soon."

"Not to worry too much on that score. All I ask, is for you to tell me only when there really is something to report, just as your own regime dictates too, I understand." Chapman smiled pleasantly.

"Thanks for that Frank. With luck, you won't hear from me until we reach Cape Town." John stated and finally left the foc'sle.

It was nearing time to approach their first port of call, and the crew were getting land happy again, eager to spend some of their money on the one commodity they lacked whilst sailing in the hot climes of the tropics, women and lots of them.

The ship entered the very busy port of Lagos, which is the chief port and at that time, was the capital for the ex British colonial African country of Nigeria.

Nigeria is on the west coast of Africa with a big contrast of weather, from the arid north bordering onto the Sahara desert, to the tropical rains way to the south. Due to the delta of its principle river, the Niger, there is a very large population of farmers and rich agricultural lands. But the country is also rich with such a diversity of products, both natural; such as gas, oil, timber, mineral ores and man made items like agricultural machinery, radios and metal products.

The British influence to its infrastructure and everyday life is such that the official language is English although there are several local languages including Yoruba and the widely spoken tongue of the Huasa tribes.

This would be home for the ship over the next few days.

CHAPTER IV
Funny Mood

"**H**ere we are in busy Lagos. I've been here a few times, what about you dearly beloved?" Helena asked, standing close to John, taking in the hustle and bustle of the docks.

"This is my first time. Maybe when I've completed my rounds, we can go sight-seeing with the bus trip the purser has organised."

"Ruud has a work colleague living up-country and is taking Stella and the children to meet them. It will give us time to be just the two of us again, what do you say John?"

"Sounds good to me. Give me an hour and I'll see you in the lounge." he replied, kissing her on the tip of her nose before he left.

"He's a good man Helena. Make sure you don't lose him this time." Stella said softly as they both watched John walk swiftly away from them.

"I haven't told him yet that I'm going up-country with you to stay with our Aunt when we get to Cape Town. That's why I'm spending as much time as possible with him."

"Well you'd better tell him before we get there, because he loves you like mad and it might harm him if you don't."

"He'll be alright dear Stella. He's got his job to do and is ambitious enough to try and reach the top and I appear to be just his little concubine during this voyage."

"How diabolically cynical of you." Stella rebuked angrily giving Helena a slap on her bottom.

"You always manage to lose your men quicker than you get them dear sister. John Grey might not be as tall or as muscular and handsome as my Ruud, but at least he is loyal to you, which I can't say the same about you to him."

"The men in my life have nothing to do with you Stella. He already knows that we will marry some day, but that I can't have the children he wants me to have. So all that is left for me is to feel a good man inside me, and that's precisely what I'm doing, getting some of the action before the rest of my body goes." Helena said sadly.

"But you're supposed to marry him, if only to make an honest woman of yourself! He is by profession, a Sailor, but when it comes to the final say, both of you must forsake all others and keep yourselves for just each other."

"Yes, I know all that, but…" Helen started to say when the children came towards them which stopped the conversation dead.

Chapman was on deck with a team of welders when he saw John coming across the for'ard cargo deck.

"Going ashore John? Because I need you to supervise this welding operation, as the 2nd is required in the engine room."

"Where's Morris? He's next in line for hull and deck repairs." John replied swiftly and tried to walk away.

"He's got a team to supervise the air conditioning and ventilation systems, and I've got to see the Dock Superintendent about our evaps. So it looks as if you're nominated."

"I'll be there in 10 minutes. Who's the welder? If it's not Dawes, then you'll have to get someone from the shore-side ship repair unit." John said angrily, going swiftly towards the lounge to where Helena was waiting for him.

"You're not changed John, coming in your overalls are you?"

"Helena my dear, I've just been given a rush job to do and won't be able to go ashore until its done." John said apologetically.

"Not to worry, I'll be with the purser and some of the other passengers to keep me company. You see to your bits of metal. You men are all the same!" Helena said with disappointment and stormed off angrily towards the gangway to join the departing trippers.

* * *

John went back onto the for'ard cargo deck and had the men work furiously for hours before he was satisfied with the result. The men were soaking wet with their own sweat, panting hard in the afternoon sun.

"Can we have a breather 2nd. Maybe slake our thirst with some gophers, 'Harry Limers' (limeade) or something?" Dawes pleaded, removing the thick protective visor from his head.

"You and your team have done well Dawes. I'm satisfied with it so you can get everything returned to the engine room and take the rest of the day off. I'll see that you get an overnight stay if you want." John relented.

"That sounds good to me 2nd. We've certainly earned it." Dawes said appreciatively as John left the men to clear away the equipment.

The bustle of the ship and the rest of the port had subsided, with the last stragglers making their way home in the evening sunlight, as John stood on the bridge wing smoking his cigarette.

"Evening John. Tried my bike out today. Whatever you did for the engine worked because it went like a good'un, so thanks again." Wallace said jovially, arriving alongside him.

"Where's Bruce, still ashore?"

"Yes. He went over to that ship behind us to see if he could bum some signal pads. He knows the Radio Officer on it. I've got the duty anyway." Wallace volunteered.

"Have you been ashore here before Jock? What's it like?"

"Came here on one of the *Bay* tankers last year. We went to that island over there to take a load on board. We were here for days because the skipper forgot to clean and ventilate the tanks first. Got my feet under the table with an ex-pat's Nigerian missus until I got found out. I've just come from there and tested my bike at the same time, but they've moved up country somewhere."

John smiled at the audacity of the man.

"It seems that this place has a habit of coming between man and his mate, jungle or not."

"You're right enough there John. But just wait 'till we get to Cape Town. Lots of spoilt, rich white females just gagging for it, especially from us officers. What will you be doing when we get there, we've got a week before sailing back?"

John looked at the smouldering butt of his cigarette as he reflected on his answer, but decided he'd just say that he really didn't know.

Wallace saw the look on John's face and decided to leave the topic there, instead telling John to cheer up, he excused himself and left for the wireless office.

The lounge was quiet as most of the passengers had left and the new ones had not arrived to join the few going on to Cape Town.

"Hello steward. Can I have a scotch and soda please?" John asked quietly in an attempt not to break the silence.

"Certainly 2nd. On the tally or cash?" the steward asked, looking John's name up in the mess book.

"I've paid up for this part, so start again if you please." John said, pointing to his nil balance on the sheet.

"Wish all officers paid their bills as promptly as you, and yours was pretty hefty too considering you were, entertaining guests, shall we say." the steward responded with a knowing wink.

"Well, just keep it coming. I'm on my own now by the looks of it." John said dejectedly.

The steward sensed that something was up, but decided to let the matter drop by offering John one of his cigars from his own personal stock, which he always kept under lock and key.

John thanked him and went to sit in one of the deep cushioned chairs puffing on his cigar as he went. He drank several glasses more and smoked another cigar before he realised that it was nearly midnight, and Helena had not come back on board even to enjoy her favourite glass of wine from the well stocked bar. He doused the last of the cigar into the ashtray and left his empty glass on the table as he went through to the cabin compartments on his way to bed. It was the first time he had slept in his own bunk since leaving Southampton, and although it was a warm night, he felt it as cold as winter without his lover lying next to him.

The following morning was again sunny and bright as John finished his favourite breakfast of freshly baked rolls with lashings of butter and thick slices of bacon wedged in the middle. The morning was still early so he decided to go for a stroll along the upper deck to clear the whiskey fog from his brain. It was then that he noticed the fleets of lorries chugging along in a long column just like a train. As the multi-coloured, ramshackle lorries stopped at each ship also in their own long line along the harbour wall, so the dock cranes started to bob and weave to the efforts of the stevedores toiling away, both on the ship and ashore.

This was a familiar sight to him, yet every time he watched such a scene, it appeared to be different somehow, and always took his mind back to the first occasion in Barbados, which seemed to be several lifetimes away now.

The morning wore on as John conducted his upper deck machinery inspection standing for a while to watch the large locomotive and its' tender being reloaded onto his newly re-inforced deck plates.

"Seems to be holding well 2nd!" Dawes said appreciatively and moved over to stand by John.

"Yes Dawes. You and your team did well. How would you like to come with me and see from the under side?"

"Sounds a good idea, but there are a lot of animal hides and the like, full of maggots and disease carrying fleas, that will invade our clothing as soon as we enter the compartment."

John was surprised by this revelation and asked Dawes to tell him more.

When Dawes had finished his observations on the different cargoes, which had become the 'bug bear' of the rest of the crew, John was certain of one thing.

"Untreated hides must be the reason why the mid-ships

superstructure is alive with maggots and wind-borne insects. And the reason why the Air Conditioning Units (ACU's), vents got clogged up so quickly. It also confirms a mystery I was able to solve on a ship I was on a while ago."

"Well knowing you, 2nd. You'll come up with something to please the guv'nors."

The two men talked for a little while before they went below into the for'ard cargo hold.

John had to go there for the machinery that was kept in these large open spaces, and had seen for himself the enormity of the problem Dawes had spoken about. This set his mind on another round of problem solving, which he was glad of if only to distract his attention from the sudden disappearance of Helena. The two men parted company and went their separate ways, as John decided that it was time for him to complete his rounds and maybe go for a spot of lunch before going ashore.

"Hello 2nd. I'm pleased with your work on the for'ard decks." Freeman said, approaching John at his dining table.

"I've discovered another problem that will need attention once I've sorted out the technical details." John replied.

"Oh 2nd! Nothing horrendous this time I hope?"

"The air purification and ACUs are being swamped with fleas and other wind-borne insects that are infesting our cargo holds. Have you had a similar load on before, such as copra?"

"Yes. On our last voyage, we had several hundred tons of copra. But the holds were supposed to have been disinfected with the DDT gas. Why you ask?"

"Unless the ship is deloused properly then we'll have to re-install new air units or ventilation trunking on board. Our next port is Cape Town, perhaps we can do it in the Naval dockyard there and delouse the ship completely, Captain."

"Hmm! I see what you mean 2nd. Well leave it with me. Have yourself a run ashore this afternoon, but we'll be sailing early tomorrow morning." Freeman said thoughtfully and carried on with whatever his mission was.

"Thank you captain." John replied slowly, finishing off his after lunch cigarette.

John walked over the gangway and onto the dockside where a taxi was hovering around to pick up a fare.

"We're off to a decent pub down the road John, are you coming?"

John looked into the cab and saw Sinclair sitting in the back with a couple of sailors.

"Hello Andy, haven't seen you much this trip! Yes, glad to be along."

"Make room for a real Engineer!" Sinclair commanded, for the men to bunch up and make room for him.

The cab went swiftly through the gaily-coloured streets, dodging wayward vehicles driven by their drivers who had no road sense. It arrived at a long wooden building with a cast-iron railing as its veranda, and almost naked women leaning over a balcony watching out for new 'flesh' or the last of the big time spenders.

"I'll get out here and walk for a while. I'm not in the mood for female flesh just now, just a cold beer." John said and started to walk away from the men, but Sinclair held his arm.

"You can always have a cold beer here John, they serve chilled Double X, and the only bar in the whole country too. Besides, not even we would come here unless we wore at least a treble rubber on our truncheons." Sinclair said persuasively, and smiled at John, who ceded to the suggestion.

The place was alive with music, dancing and lots of noise from several sailors from different ships, all inter-mingling and getting to know their fellow seafarers.

"We'll sit here, John. This is my favourite spot." Sinclair suggested.

They quickly sat down and were served promptly by several scantily dressed young girls, who were black all over except when they smiled to show perfect sets of white teeth.

'No change here either. Black and white. No difference, just the country.' John thought, and taking hold of his cold beer took a large swig from it.

"You never said you've been here before, Andy?"

"Aye, several times. I'm the 'Yard of ale' champion in Lagos, and this is where they hold the challenges." Sinclair said, pointing to a picture of him holding a large barrel of beer.

"That was my prize. A barrel of what you're drinking now, and a free afternoon upstairs.

Well worth the ten bob entry fee." Sinclair said with a huge grin on his face.

"There's two challengers over there, warming up. Judging by what I see, they've no chance. But I must be there to witness their attempt." he added, pointing towards a group of men.

"In that case Andy, we'll just go over and take a closer look." John stated, and picking up yet another full glass of Guinness, strolled over to the noisiest table in the bar.

"Whey hey man! Get it doon ye! Yer'v got'a beat 11 seconds ye know." a burly, ginger bearded man said in a broad Geordie accent.

"Right! He's ready. Get the Landlord and the gubbins. We'll show who's the fastest." another man shouted, and beckoned the manager over arranging the championship attempt.

Everybody got off their seats to form a big ring in the middle of the bar room, clapping and cheering the two contestants, just like watching the start of a boxing match.

The two contestants had their 'trainers' fan them with the large bar flannels to keep them cool, whilst the barman filled each 'Yard of ale' glass and held them until the men were ready.

"Right then. I'll count down from 3 to 1. On 1, you'll start drinking. Any spillage or help from anybody else will disqualify you. Are you ready?"

The two contestants gripped their long glasses and held them to their mouths, ready to start drinking when the count got to one.

John looked on just as eagerly as the rest of the onlookers, but more so, Sinclair, who was heckling them, trying to make them spill the drink or stop.

"C'mon you're a bunch of wassocks! You'll have to do better than that." Sinclair shouted, as one of the men spilled some of the beer down his face and onto his shirt.

"Ha! One down and one to go!" Sinclair chanted, as the rest of the men counted out the seconds loudly.

"Nine seconds, ten seconds, eleven seconds." Everybody chanted.

The second man finally finished his ale, then wiped his face before belching most of what he drunk back up onto the floor.

"Have to do better than that Geordie!" Sinclair teased, stepping around the pool of vomited beer, taking the glass from the man.

"Now I'll show you just how it's done." He said and waited until the barman refilled the glass.

"Two pints in less than 10 seconds is the target. Now watch this." Sinclair said, starting to drink on the count of one.

He shook the last drop from the glass tube, into his mouth just as the count got to 9 seconds. When he handed the glass back to the barman, everybody cheered Sinclair, who went over to the two despondent men.

"Never mind lads. Maybe if you're in Cape Town you can always try and break my 1 pint in six seconds."

"Hang on a minute, you're the one in that picture. No wonder we didn't stand a chance." one of them said but without malice, and shook Sinclair's outstretched hand in mutual friendship. Such is the way of seafarers.

John was feeling the heady mix of whiskey and Guinness so decided that it was time to go back on board. Sinclair said he was ready too, and said so long to the others who had lustful ideas concerning female flesh on offer upstairs.

The cabin was cool and refreshing from the tropical heat, as John stripped off his sweat soaked shirt, and prepared himself for a quiet evening on board.

He felt it strange not to have Helena in the shower with him, even though it had taken some getting used to again after months of separation due their job commitments.

When he entered the saloon to take his supper, he saw Stella and her family sitting in the lounge with a group of other passengers. Within moments he saw Helena talking to a young man wearing a bright orange waistcoat and smoking a large cigar, but decided to satisfy his hunger first before his curiosity as to who it was.

"Hello John! Did you miss me?" Helena whispered gently into John's ear as he finished drinking his coffee.

"You know I did! What was that outburst for yesterday Helena, I did not deserve it?" he replied, turning his head as Helena came around to sit in front of him.

She took his hands and stroked them and looked shyly at him.

"A girl likes to be at her best for her lover. Yesterday and today was nature's way of telling us to have a rest, if you like. Most women get funny moods during those times."

John kissed her blush red cheeks.

"I suspected something but when I saw that 'Satsuma' you were talking to over there, I hoped it wasn't him. Never mind, it certainly has given us a bit of a rest. So get ready for part two lover girl." he replied softly, then stood up and hugged her gently, much to the astonished look on the face of the cigar smoker.

CHAPTER V
Cold Satsuma

The ship sailed out of the busy harbour, in the early hours of the following morning, with John standing bleary-eyed at his usual spot on the foc'sle.

'I must lay off the booze if I'm to keep Helena happy in the bunk'. he avowed to himself starting to feel nauseous from the smell of the animal hide cargo that was coming out of the cargo ventilation shaft. Fortunately everything was secured and lashed down for the long leg down the African continent to Cape Town, so John could leave his post and get up-wind away from the rotten smell.

"Chief! We've got a load of Freon bottles in the after cargo hold. If we seal off the for'ard section with the hides in it, we can create a fridge to that compartment with the Freon to keep the cargo fresh and all of us from being overcome by the fumes."

"But I thought we had the air purification plants serviced in Lagos, 2nd?"

"Yes we did, and Morris did a good job too. But I feel this is beyond the efforts of even that." John replied swiftly.

"I'd better speak to the captain and let you know. In the meantime John, we've had another 4th join us before sailing. Get him organised instructional wise, and tell him to come and report to Cooper for engine room watch-keeping." Chapman advised, then went off to the engine room.

John was on the bridge talking quietly to Sinclair reminiscing over old voyages, when the 3rd mate told him the skipper wanted to see him in his day cabin.

"Grey! The chief and I have a plan that involves some of your 'tween deck pumps and other machinery." Freeman commenced and explained what he wanted help with. Chapman explained the technical details except for things that only John knew concerning the new method of refrigeration that didn't involve ammonia.

"I can make it work for you Captain, if you don't mind losing a good third of your Freon cargo. You'll have to insulate the other sides of the bulkheads, and seal them off in case of escaped gas.

And the entire hold will have to be sealed preventing anyone entering it, otherwise they'd perish there." John said at length, and this was greeted with approval from the other officers.

It took them several hours to reduce the offending compartment to nothing more than a large fridge, and a few more hours adjusting the cargo and living spaces ventilation system.

"The ship has benefited from your knowledge, 2nd. Now we can enjoy the rest of the voyage. Maybe our passengers will tell me soon enough, as they are quick to notice these things. " Freeman said pleasantly, completing his final check on the work.

The second half of the voyage from Lagos was another ten days of John and Helena getting into various grips with one another, interspersed with John's duty to the ship and her master.

Tradition has it that on the last full evening at sea all the passengers have a little farewell party before everybody lands ashore to go their own separate ways into the world again. Officers were encouraged to join in, even though most knew by then, that John had already done so since leaving Southampton. As long as it was discreet, nobody minded, was the unofficial view.

"Looking forward to your new ship Phil?" John asked when both officers were getting ready for the evening.

"More or less. I've been told that I've got a few days ashore first. This part of my journey was the easy part. I'm joining the one in Oz as its chief, and I've got the dreaded promotion board to sit before I leave Cape Town." Cooper replied.

"According to Bruce Larter, Belverley and Invergarron will be there, so you should be alright. No sweat."

"Thanks for your confidence John." Cooper concluded as both men stepped out of the cabin and made their way to the passenger lounge for the evenings bash.

John went over to Helena who was sitting and talking with Larter.

"My my John! How handsome you look in your tropical uniform. You all look so wonderful." Helena said delightedly, patting an empty seat next to her.

"Here, sit a while lover. I'm talking to your good friend the Bruce."

"Evening Bruce me old Scouser!" John smiled, planting a kiss on Helena's neck.

"None for me John. I'm trying to give it up thanks." Larter said in mock horror, and smiled, as the friends laughed at the implication.

The evening went on well into the night, with speeches made by Freeman, Chapman, and Brown on behalf of the officers and crew, and a speech by Stella and the passenger who John had dubbed the 'Satsuma'. In fact John was impressed by the elegant oration given by him, but was glad that he wasn't called upon to speak.

John and Helena slipped away to practice more intimate holds that they discovered they could do, and did so until yet again Stella separated them gently.

"Thank goodness we're not on our way to Australia instead of De Arsburgh." she said as the lovers lay in each others arms.

"De Arsburg Helena?" John asked sleepily.
"Who's going there?"

John sensed a hushed silence and saw Helena looking fiercely at Stella.

"Stella. What about this De Arsburgh?" John asked softly.

"Hasn't Helena said?" Stella asked haltingly, not knowing whether to tell him or not.

"I haven't told him yet Stella. I was going to do it later." Helena gasped.

"Okay dear Helena. Maybe you were going to surprise me with a nice trip up-country for a few days before heading back again? And Stella has spoiled your surprise, is that it?" John said teasingly, but realised that there was something more sinister to it.

"More or less dear." Helena lied, but Stella demanded that she told him the truth.

"I'm going up there with Stella and the family, to help run an Aunt's ranch. But I'm staying to take a teaching post in a local school there." Helena blurted out, and started to weep.

"Oh is that all? I thought you were going to marry the local witch doctor and disappear into the jungle to start your own tribe." John said in disbelief.

"No it's true, John. Our country's government have financed this trip and Ruud has been sent to become the local Radio Station Engineer. The 'Satsuma' as you call him is the new Radio Station controller. We're in fact emigrating there so that the children can have a good future in a growing country. Our own as you know is still broken with the devastation of the war." Stella explained.

"Oh well. Don't let me get in your way. I'm only an engineer on a ship. But who am I going to come home to when my days at sea are over?" John asked sadly, beginning to see the endgame of a pattern of events since leaving the UK.

"I was going to tell you John, really I was." Helena gasped and started to sob onto John's shoulder.

John looked down at his lover, putting his arm around her until she stopped crying, all the while Stella was weeping gently into her hankie. He just laid there gazing at the deck-head feeling totally devastated at this news. His personal life was now at a crossroads and one that he had to face.

"And here's me thinking we had a good party last night. A funny way to end it though!" John said bravely, offering Helena a tissue to blow her nose with.

"You can always come and visit us when you're down this part of the world! Just give us a call and we'll come and meet you wherever you dock." Stella said, kissing John then left the cabin.

"Time you got packed then Helena. I'll try and see you before you disembark." John said, and kissing Helena tenderly for the last time, left the cabin to go to his own.

* * *

John stood at his spot on the foc'sle watching the massive stone walls of the harbour breakwater pass either side of the ships bow, when she entered the busy merchant dock area of Cape Town. This was normally his first glimpse of an unfamiliar port, but to him it was just a blur. The familiar nudge he felt told him he had arrived alongside in Cape Town, but his mind was in a turmoil with the devastating news about Helena. No matter how he tried to shake it off, he came back to the same conclusion.

Helena was, as of now, out of reach for him, and he would probably never see her again. Just like Princess Telani.[•]

As if coming out of a trance, he stepped across the cargo deck and waited as the passenger's gangway was being positioned. The one for the crew was already on and lashed up.

"There you are John." Larter said quietly, arriving behind him.

"Hello Bruce. I'm waiting for Helena." John stated robotically, staring at the empty wooden gangway.

"Stella has just told me what happened and where to find you. Sounds a bit of a rum do. But then that's women for you, John. We, your friends that is, have told you for years now what the score is in trying to keep hold of a woman from a different part of the world. Being at sea is one of the worst professions to be in. I'm speaking from a long history of experience." Larter said gently in a sympathetic gesture to his friend.

"Yes Bruce. You're spot on yet again. But it still hurts just the same." John sighed, watching Helena walk towards him in company of the 'Satsuma', Stella and her family.

"John." Helena gasped, seeing John standing at the top of the gangway.

John went to kiss her but she side-stepped him and said.

"I was hoping to just slip ashore and away before you arrived, to prevent us from getting upset. You've made it very awkward

---

[•] See *A Beach Party*.

for me now. Please don't make a scene."

John looked at Helena's face and the attentions the 'Satsuma' was giving her, and decided that enough was enough. He felt betrayed, needing satisfaction to calm his anger, then turned to the 'Satsuma'. Although he was much taller than John, nevertheless John's fist landed squarely onto his chin, knocking him out cold.

He turned to Helena with tears in his eyes, and said.

"I have never thought you would be the one to betray me. You must have planned this and only kept me amused during this voyage, playing me like a puppet on a string."

"Oh John. It's not like that, and you know it." Helena sobbed, trying to embrace him, but he pushed her away.

"It appears that you're now setting up shop with your fancy pants. Well you can have him, and hope you're happy." John hissed, pulling out the locket she gave him in Bermuda some years ago.

"Here. I've always worn this wherever I went. It appears you have someone else to give it to, obviously I mean nothing to you now you're starting a new life." he said bitterly, thrusting the locket and chain into her hand, and squeezed her palm tightly for her to feel the metal.

She winced at the pain of it, but John whispered into her ear.

"Your pain is nothing to what you've just done to me. Goodbye Helena, and thanks for nothing. I might look it but I'm not stupid."

Ruud stepped in between them in case John accosted Helena, but John looked at Ruud shaking his head slowly, turned around on his heel leaving the gangway with tears glistening in his eyes. Stella ran after John and managed to stop him.

"John, you are totally wrong in doing this. She likes men yes, but she loves only you. If you were ashore all the time then there'd be no problem. She was always pining after you every time you went to sea just like all sailors' wives and lovers do. Can't you just come back some day and say hello to us, after all the history we have built up between us?"

"Stella. I'm but an engineer trying to earn a living in a trade that I know. My home is where my hat hangs, and at the moment it's on this ship. I do not know where I'll end up or when I will settle down, but I was hoping it would be with Helena even though she was not able to give me children of our own. She had obviously planned her chosen future already, before coming on board. Up the jungle with fancy pants and his promise of wealth in running a radio station, rather than stay at home and wait for my voyages to end. I wish you and your family well and hope you live and prosper in these new surroundings. All I ask, is for you to remember me from time to time." John said at length, wiping his face with the back of his hand, before kissing her cheek gently, then walked away towards the engine room hatchway without a second glance.

By the time John regained his composure, all the passengers and most of the crew had gone ashore. He entered the now very empty passenger lounge and sat in a large chair with a bottle of whiskey and a soda siphon. He just sat and drank but paid no attention to anything that went around him.

"John. How would you like a nice quiet run ashore in this lovely town. There's plenty of sightseeing and plenty of decent beer ashore." Wallace asked quietly, arriving and sitting next to him.

"Not for me thanks Jock, maybe later on. I've a few things to attend to including meeting up with Belverley later. You go ahead and enjoy yourself." he replied slowly, looking into the bottom of his empty glass so Wallace just sat there with his own drink for a little while.

"Hello John! Coming ashore with some of your mates? Maybe we can phone an old friend who lives in these parts. Do you remember 2nd engineer Tansey Lee off the *Inverlaggan*? Well we could try and contact him and get a decent run ashore for old times sake." Sinclair asked, popping his head through the lounge doorway.

"Hello Andy. Jock has just asked me the same. And yes, I do remember Tansey Lee, have you brought him on board? I'd love to see him again." he responded woodenly, then turned to Wallace and suggested he go with them.

"It appears John that you don't appreciate what your friends are trying to do." Larter snorted when he too arrived on the scene.

"Hello Bruce. Not you too? Now I know what Caesar felt like."

"Come on John. Snap out of it. You've been in serious danger and lived through most of what mother nature and man has thrown your way, don't lose it all now for God's sake. What would Happy and all of the others say if they found you like this, wallowing in your own self-pity. Our old friend Tansey Lee is mentioned in the phone book, come and speak to him." Larter baited.

John sighed and stood up slowly, almost falling over the table in front of him.

"Now look here you bloody lot…" he started, then sat down suddenly onto his seat again spilling a fresh drink all over himself.

"Jock, Andy! Lets get him to his bunk. He's had enough for one day by the look of him." Larter said quickly, and leapt to John's aid.

The three men gathered around John and half-carried half-dragged him into his cabin where Larter loosened his clothes for him and laid him on his bunk.

"Have a good sleep John. Belverley and Co won't miss you until tomorrow." Larter said quietly as John fell into a drunken sleep.

"What's happened for him to be like this Bruce?" Wallace asked.

Larter and Sinclair looked at each other and at their old friend John.

"Let's just call it woman trouble. We can't get any and he's just lost another one. Andy, get Dovey to keep an eye on him, he's got to meet Belverley tomorrow." Larter answered, shutting the cabin door quietly and walked back into the saloon.

Cape Town is a settlement that has grown to a sprawling city, right under the famous geographical feature called the Table Mountain at the bottom of the massive continent of Africa. It is the first or last stop depending on which way you were going, from the Atlantic Ocean, into the smaller Indian Ocean.

It has a Naval dockyard there, which has thrived since the influence of the British Colonial days during the 18th and 19th centuries, and prior to that, at the hands of the French and Dutch colonialists.

South Africa's predominant activity is gold and diamond mining, but is also rich in coal, tin, other minerals and oil, which it uses to barter within the large family of the Commonwealth. Its people are a mixture of those countries, which dominated its past. Because of that, it has several languages, of which British is the official one. But due to the indigenous black tribal populations, Zulu, Hottentot and other local languages still surviving today.

Chapter VI
News Headlines

"2nd. Its time you were out and about. You've got a meeting to attend this morning. Come on wake up!" Dovey said and, reaching over the wakening man, opened his port-hole windows to let the light in.

John woke up quickly then groaned as the sunlight beamed into his face.

"What time is it Steward?" he croaked.

"A little after 7." he replied

"It smells like a distillery in here. What 'ave you been up to?" he continued, clattering the furniture and rattling a tray of crockery.

"Here's some breakfast for you. I'll be back to see to the cabin later."

"Thanks steward. Where's Cooper?"

"He's already up and away ashore. He says that he hopes to see you before he leaves for Durban." Dovey said informatively.

John lowered himself slowly from his bunk onto the deck, then made his way to the small table to eat his breakfast.

"Oh yes. He's got his promotion board before that, and I'm seeing Belverley after that again. Hope Tansey Lee can come to see us." he said hesitatingly starting to drink his cup of tea.

Dovey saw that John was now up and about, left the cabin by saying.

"The chief would like a word with you in his cabin before you do anything else."

"Thanks for the info Steward! I'm fine now, off you go." John replied, nodding towards the door.

"Tell the Chief I'll be there in half an hour, if you please." he said as Dovey shut the door on his way out.

"Morning John!" Chapman greeted, pointing towards a chair as John entered the cabin.

"Morning Frank. What can I do for you?" he responded politely.

"We have a change of orders from Belverley and Co. As of today we're to go into dry dock and have our hull re-inforced for a special mission before returning to Belfast." Chapman started, then went on to explain the engineering details and the extra manning that the ship would be taking on.

"So I'm to stay as Outside Engineer for the benefit of these boffins coming on board? What would I know of their specialist machinery and the like Frank?" John asked.

Chapman answered these and other queries John posed until Chapman held his hands up.

"Okay John, I surrender. No more questions if you please. Sufficient to say that we both will get to know more about everything when we have our first meeting in the lounge later today. And by the way, our proposed meeting with Belverley and his chums has been cancelled, so you can relax until this big confab is held."

"Will you need me for the docking move, or can I get ashore for a look round? I have an old shipmate to try and see from Durban. I don't know if you met him but his name is Tansey Lee." John said with a smile as he posed yet one more question.

Chapman chuckled and said.

"I was warned by Happy that you were a question and answers man, but yes I'll gladly let you ashore for a while if only to give my ears some peace. And yes I know Tansey Lee, he was a very good 2nd engineer, but apparently a very rich 'Kaffir' now. Something to do with a diamond rich area of land, somewhere up on the Namib coastline. Er 'Chantral' I think the new place is called."•

John didn't seem to take in what was said walking out of the cabin and into the lounge where other officers were sitting around drinking coffee and reading the latest newspapers.

• See *Fresh Water.*

It was the front page news headlines that stopped him in his tracks when Larter came over and showed it to him.

"Take it easy, as it's no good upsetting yourself now." Larter said soothingly, as Wallace and Sinclair also came over to him:

'BRIDGE COLLAPES INTO SWOLLEN RIVER, DROWNING SEVERAL IMMIGRANTS ON THEIR WAY TO THE NEW CENTRAL PROVINCES, AROUND THE DE ARSBURG AREA Among the passengers was the brilliant Dutch Radio Engineer, Ruud Kloggert and the rest of his family.'

John sat down and stared at the paper for a moment, then looked up to see a ring of concerned faces from his friends around him. He stood up and silently giving the paper back to Larter, walked out of the lounge and onto the deck, followed by his friends.

He fumbled to open a pack of cigarettes but they all fell onto the deck at his feet, but was quickly given one by Sinclair.

"Here John have one of my Capstan full strength you always like them." he said softly, lighting it as John put it into his mouth.

The hubbub of the noisy dockside seemed to disappear into nothingness as John stood for a moment smoking his cigarette.
Finally, he looked at his friends who were standing silently beside him, and said quietly.

"My good friends. There but for the luck of the Irish or whatever you may think go I, as I was supposed to go with them for a few days leave. Maybe Helena knew something like this was going to happen, because she kept waking up during the night talking of trains and bridges. She had a habit of predicting things that always came true in the end." he said hoarsely, as tears slid slowly down his cheeks.

His friends gasped at this revelation but kept quiet and continued their wall of protection around him.

Sinclair wrapped his large arm around John's shoulder and gave John his not so dirty hankie.

"Here John. No sense the public seeing our top 2nd Engineer in distress, its bad for their morale." He said softly, steering John back into the lounge out of sight of curious onlookers.

John wiped his cheeks, thanking everybody for being so understanding.

"Our ship movements have been altered somewhat, and there's something I have to do before we sail." he said slowly as if in a trance.

This news was new to the friends too, who looked at each other in puzzlement.

"The ship can wait. We'll help you, if you tell us what it is, John." Larter offered, which was quickly taken up by the others who also volunteered their services.

Freeman came into the lounge and saw a circle of officers standing close, talking quietly amongst themselves.

"Do I smell mutiny on board my ship? What's going on over there. Grey, what are you up to." Freeman demanded to know.

Morris was on the periphery of the group guessed what was going on, so went swiftly over to the Captain grabbing him roughly by his lapels.

"Now look here pal! Keep your big ugly trap shut or I'll shut it for you." Morris said throwing Freeman back down onto his feet then slapped him around the face with the newspaper.

"Here. Read this and inwardly digest, Captain!" Morris snarled.

Freeman grabbed the paper and read the headlines quickly, then looked over to John, then back to Morris.

"3rd engineer Morris. You're sacked! Get yourself and your gear off this ship within ten minutes. As for the rest of you get on with your work. Grey, go and wait for me in my bridge cabin." Freeman ordered in rapid succession.

John went onto the bridge and started to light up a cigarette when Chapman arrived.

"What's this about Morris, John? More to the point what's the score with you and the skipper?" he asked, just as Freeman arrived onto the bridge himself.

"I'll tell you exactly what chief! Both of you step inside." Freeman ordered, pointing towards his cabin.

"Right then Engines. First off I have sacked your 3rd Engineer Morris for accosting me in the passengers lounge. Secondly, I caught 2nd Engineer Grey in a compromising situation that I took as mutinous behaviour. Now I want to get to the bottom of this before we move down for the docking." Freeman demanded.

Chapman looked at John in puzzlement and stated that he was not aware of such goings on until he, the captain, pointed it out to him. Both officers started to debate the merits of such behaviour while John just stood by, until he shouted to the both of them.

"Now look here you two. Yesterday I discovered that my fiancée was deserting me for a namby pamby and disappearing up the jungle to start a new life with her family. Today I found that everyone of them are now dead due to a rail accident up-country. On the very engine that we carried all the way down here." John said vehemently.

"Okay so what?" Freeman asked brutally.

John stepped right up to Freeman telling him to stuff his ship right up his arse, that he, John, was going ashore to visit the accident site to see about recovering the bodies.

Before Freeman had the chance to deny John, Chapman turned to him saying what a cretin he was. He explained the reason behind John's and Morris's behaviour, and that only he, Freeman, had exacerbated this by not being diplomatic enough about the whole incident.

"So that's the reason. Why wasn't I told of these matters Chief?" Freeman asked belligerently.

"Simply this. Just because you're the captain of the ship, it doesn't mean that you have the right for everybody's private life to be known to you. What happened yesterday and today was none of your bloody business, and something that which Grey has the right to sort out without anybody else poking their noses into. Grey happens to have several officer friends on board this vessel, who he's been to sea with several times in the past. Those officers you saw with him were part of his circle of friends, which my cousin Chief Engineer Day and others would vouch for any day of the year, and that I dare say would go for the Lords of the Company too." Chapman growled at his equally ranked officer.

"I'm captain of this ship, Chief Engineer, and don't you forget it." Freeman started, but Chapman turned and cut him short by saying.

"We're in harbour now. If nobody turns up to sail your vessel back out of here, then just think who will get the blame for it. Certainly not me nor my men. I suggest that unless you recall Morris then we sail undermanned. And I also suggest that Grey be given as much leave as possible to sort out his bereavement. I for one will not have him on board before that time as he would be a total liability to me and the rest of my department."

"Are you blackmailing me Chief Engineer?"

"Let's put it this way Captain. Its your ship, but if we're undermanned and the Lords find out about it, its your career not mine nor the other two. Just think about what I've just said. Put up, or Shut up!" Chapman concluded, indicating to John that both of them were leaving.

"But! But…" Freeman stammered but was left alone talking to himself in his cabin.

"Right John. You get yourself up-country on the next plane out of here, and do whatever you have to do. But remember, we sail in three days, so for God sake get back here in time."

John looked at Chapman telling him that another officer and the Bosun would accompany him, then thanked him for his support.

"If it wasn't for my Cousin Happy Day and other friends who speak very highly of you, you'd have gone to hell as far as I'm concerned. Now get the hell off this ship before I change my mind." Chapman said angrily, but John did not see the smile on Chapman's face when John disappeared down the gangway with Larter and Sinclair.

* * *

The friends finally arrived at the scene of the accident and saw exactly what had caused it.

"It's that steam engine we brought down here, Bruce. It's a wide gauge Garrett, 12-wheel driver and too heavy for that bridge, just like it was for the cargo deck plates. Look how deep it is buried into the river bank. Even the carriages were too heavy. Someone somewhere is in for the high jump when that's discovered because the bridge and the track should have been re-inforced just as we did to our decks."

Sinclair brought a man dressed in priests robes and introduced him to the others.

"If you're looking for the victims, I have them in my parish church just down the road here." the priest said softly, clutching his open bible.

"Maybe you can help in identifying some of the bodies." he added, pointing the way to the little wooden church standing in a clearing in the wooded area around them.

They walked slowly along the rows of dead people until John stopped at the feet of Stella.

"Here is Stella. She has a husband, two children and a sister. The sister was my fiancée." John said sadly, gently touching Stella's lifeless body and stroking her head.

"In that case, we can take our time to look around. Not all bodies have been recovered yet." the priest said quietly and reverently.

John walked among the covered bodies, stopping to uncover ones that looked familiar, until he had finally identified the two children, Ruud and the pathetic looking body of the 'Satsuma'.

"There is still one missing from the group and that is my Helena." John revealed to the priest, who had already been told of the connection between them and the bodies by Larter.

"We have some more just come it, maybe she's among them." the priest responded, and guided John over to the reception area.

John looked at each body until he stopped at one still covered over.

"This is my Helena." he said, uncovering the face of the dead body.

He knelt down and kissing her cold lips took hold of one of her hands. He looked tearfully at the silver locket she had clutched in her dead hand, and carefully freed it from her. John looked around her, tenderly brushed the blond hair from her face, whispering her name and kissing the locket.

"You knew all along my dearest. That's why you pretended not to care for me. I shall keep this where it always belonged." he said sorrowfully and bent his head so as not to be seen in his state of bereavement.

The priest was standing with Larter and Sinclair, but all three saw John's distress.

"Leave him be for a while. He'll come back to you, when he's ready." the priest said holding out his arms to prevent them going to him.

A policeman came over to the waiting friends and asked them whom they were and what business had they to be here.

"See that officer over there. He's just lost his fiancée, and we're here to see that he gets back to the ship again." Sinclair said softly, keeping a vigil over John.

"We shall be burying the ones already identified, over in the parish cemetery, later on today. If you care to get your friend to come along and give me a statement just for the records, then I'll be on my way." the police officer said diplomatically.

John finally came back to his waiting friends who escorted him to the cemetery in time for the mass funeral. He had plucked a flower from somewhere to lay on Helena when she was lowered into the ground. Having whispered his last farewell to her, left the grave for others to have their turn.

When it was all over the three men walked back to a waiting bus that the local constabulary had provided to take people back to the town.

Andy and Bruce didn't say a word during all this time until they were heading back to the local airfield to catch their flight to Cape Town.

"My Nanny Stock always used to say. It's best to celebrate the life of a dearly beloved person who has passed on, rather than dwell on things. That way, as you live, so does the memory of that person." Sinclair said sombrely, offering John a cigarette.

"What are you going to do now John?" Larter asked gently.

"Nanny Stock is right. I'm going for a bloody good wet in the nearest bar. Helena would have wanted that and so would Stella. They were always having a good time and nothing ever got them down. I shall drink to that. And thank you both for staying with me." John said sadly, after his moments deep in thought.

"Now you're talking. Lets remember the good times and sod the rest. Then afterwards we can go and get poor Morris out of the pokey." Larter said almost jovially, trying to cheer things up.

"Yes, fancy that! Fancy threatening to stick one on the skipper! And in full view of everybody else. The skipper's face was a picture. " Sinclair chuckled, slapping John gently on the shoulder to make him smile at the thought.

"Aye not half. I thought Freeman was going to go bust a vessel the way he went so red. Even the first mate dropped his coffee all over himself when he saw it. Now that was a good sight." Sinclair added, as they entered the departure lounge bar.

They drank several glasses of ale, before their flight announcement interrupted them forcing them to leave and board their plane.

John looked out of the plane's only porthole and saw the disaster area away into the distant jungle, as the plane finally left the drome heading south again.

The flight took several noisy hours to arrive back in Cape Town but the three friends were glad to get back to the relative quiet, familiar surroundings of their ship.

Chapman was on the gangway when they arrived asking Larter politely how John was.

"He'll get over it once he's back at sea again, chief. He had to do what he did, as did poor Morris."

"Thanks for looking after him Sparks. We'll need all the officers we can get for this next voyage, including our demoted Morris." Chapman said.

"Demoted? That's a bit steep considering the circumstances."

"Let's put it this way, he'll never get beyond 3rd in this outfit for as long as his arse looks downwards. In fact, he was originally sacked and threatened to be beached Freeman made certain of that as the price for John's trip up country. But don't tell him that for Christ sake, or we'll lose another good engineer." Chapman whispered.

Larter nodded his head then went into the lounge to rejoin his friends.

"What did chief want, Bruce?" John asked.

"Oh nothing. Just said that he was glad we returned safely. But that you are asked to go and see him in the morning." Larter lied sitting down beside him.

"Andy said he'll see us later on once he's sorted out his gang of men. Whatever that meant. Anyway, that flight was a thirsty one, what say we have a good drink and early night. I don't know about you but I'm absolutely knackered." John informed.

"Aye, me too. The last two days have been a hard slog for us." Larter agreed, going to the bar to get some drinks.

"Your drinks are on the house, Sparks." Dovey said almost in a whisper.

"Why thank you steward. To whom do we owe the gratitude?"

"Let's put it this way. Since we came out of the dock this morning, and saw in the papers of you three up-country, we, the crew that is, held a whip round for you. Not much but you'll have free drinks all night if you wish." Dovey said, giving Larter a copy of the local paper.

Larter looked at the picture and recognised John standing over Helena's body with the flower he managed to pick.

The caption read: 'Officers from the Three Coronet Shipping Line, pay their last respects to their lost passengers who were victims of the bridge tragedy in De Arsburg.'

Larter bundled the paper under his arm then carried the tray of drinks over to where John was sitting.

"Here you are John. According to chief steward Dovey, it's all on the house." he said jovially, hiding the paper under his coat for John not to see.

"Thanks Bruce, but let's see that paper you've just hidden under your coat." John smiled at Larter's attempted deceit.

Larter sighed telling John it was an old one that he just picked up to read later.

"Well never mind. Maybe we can catch up with recent gossip and why we have a change of route." John insisted, holding out his hand.

Larter shrugged his shoulders grudgingly then gave him the crumpled paper, which John sat reading quietly for some minutes. Larter looked at his friend and shook his head in disbelief.

"That's us on the front page John!" he said with astonishment when he saw that John wasn't paying any attention to it.

"Yes. It's a good likeness. Maybe it'll be a good publicity stunt for Belverley and his cronies. I'm not interested anymore. Helena's dead and nobody can change that fact, so that's that, which just means that I've got to start all over again." John said cynically raising his glass to Larter.

"Cheers! Here's to our next voyage and to absent friends. Pity we didn't get to meet Tansey Lee. He's probably too busy making his 3rd million at the moment at least according to the Durban times. He must have gone back to our little holiday camp as he's managed to keep it's name on too, look." he said, handing over another local paper, with Lee's face on the front page.

"Come to think of it, Chapman did mention something about that. Let's have a read of it and see." John replied, then commenced to read the paper's report.

* * *

John woke earlier than normal, for some reason, but put it down to 'after funeral shock'. He rose, took a cool refreshing shower then got himself dressed for the day. As it was still early morning before sunrise, he decided to take a quiet stroll along the weather deck to have his pre breakfast cigarette.

He walked slowly over the for'ard cargo deck, to where the massive locomotive engine was stowed. An icy chill ran down his spine, followed by searing hot then numbingly cold sensations rushing through his whole body and up through the top of his head before everything went back to normal again.

In that brief moment, he saw Helena standing in front of him, smiling and waving. He couldn't hear what she was saying, but managed to read her lips, that told him she was calling his name, and blowing a kiss to him. He looked at her waving back as he held up the silver locket from around his neck. A warm and cosy glow engulfed him briefly, then her apparition faded away leaving him in a very quiet but happy mood all morning that nothing and nobody could spoil.

Nanny Stock was right after all, dear Helena. I must remain to make a new life for myself, but I'll know you'll always look after me no matter what I do now.' John said to himself, sitting down on a deck chair up on the boat deck.

Sorry John, did you say something?" Wallace asked passing him just as he spoke.

Oh nothing Jock. Just clearing a few things from my mind that all." he lied, and getting up from his chair went down to the lounge to get ready for the big pre-voyage confab.

Chapter VII
A Game of Soldiers

John walked over to sit beside Chapman and began to smoke a cigarette, when a sudden influx of passengers seemed to engulf the officers waiting for Freeman's briefing.

It was a little while before everybody was quiet when Freeman arrived at the head of another small group of people, who looked around the lounge as if they owned the place.

Freeman gathered up a large sheet of paper and introduced the strangers, enlightened his officers as to what was going on.

"We have been requested to take these Scientists and their entire staff of some 40 people on an expedition down to the Antarctic to set up an International Scientific Research Base, then onto the Falklands before returning here again. Their own research and supply vessel which should have been here some days ago, ran into difficulties on their way over from S. America. We are now their supply and support vessel until either as they finish their experiments, or we get relieved by their own special ship."

"We did not sign up for any cold water voyages. How long will it take us, and who's paying for all this?" Morris asked gruffly.

"It seems that the International Scientific Research Institute, will be our paymaster. But as it's part of the company's territory in service to the crown, they have agreed that this voyage will be taken by this ship, hence the strengthened bows and extra heating equipment installed over the last few days. The ship's superstructure was given a fresh lick of paint so that we can be easily seen between any icebergs that we may meet during our voyage." Freeman replied calmly, then continued with his spiel

"We have to take on extra Officers and crewmen for this special voyage, meaning that some of you will have to double up with your cabins, likewise for our passengers. There will be special equipment brought on board for the scientists, both cargo holds will contain all their equipment and be for their exclusive usage, so are be out of bounds to all crewmen except those on maintenance duties."

When he finished, he invited a session of questions and answers from his officers before leaving everybody to meet and become acquainted with each other.

It was only a short while before the atmosphere in the lounge became relaxed and informal, with the scientists and the officers getting to know each other. This was unlike the normal pattern of leaving the passengers almost to themselves, while the officers got on with their duties.

"Excuse me sport! Are you the Outside Wrecker, commonly known as 3rd Engineer?" a drawling Aussie voice asked as he came up to John, who nodded his recognition.

"In my case you're speaking to a 2nd engineer, but what can I do for you?" John asked, seeing a well-tanned beefy looking man standing in front of him.

"I'm 4th Engineer Clarke, detailed off to help you on this excuse of a ship." he offered jovially, with an outstretched hand. John shook it and smiled.

"Well this excuse of a ship must need excuses for Engineers, for the excuse it's been used for." he replied in the same manner.

"Oh really! And here's me thinking you Pomms needed to be shown a few things or two." was the earthy reply.

John was always tickled at the way the Australians didn't care much for protocol, and Clarke was acting pretty much the same way as Morris.

"Well, er, Aussie! Glad to have you aboard. You'll double up with 3rd Engineer Ken Morris, standing over there." John stated, pointing to Morris.

"Thanks mate. See you later!" he replied, then left to go over to Morris.

"Getting to know your new staff John?" Larter asked, handing John a drink.

"I've got another Sparker, but he'll have to sleep in the radio shack. Meet Mike Fields, he's part of the scientists team." he stated, as Fields and John gave a mutual nod of acceptance.

The midday drink and subsequent meal went well, then everybody excused themselves in order to get organised and settled for the long, dangerous voyage to the bottom of the world.

John was surprised to find that he had a scientist sharing his cabin, and that strange equipment seemed to be scattered all over the already cramped cabin.

The ship finally sailed with much pomp and ceremony, on her downward leg to the lonely island of Bouvet and beyond.

During this leg of the voyage, John took Clarke and Morris with him on his rounds. He had them installing extra heating arrangements that would soon to be used with a vengeance because the wind and the waters would get much colder as the days went by.

"The purpose of this special pipeline, Aussie, is so that we can play steam over crucial machinery and other items that the seamen might have to use whilst on deck. This is extra to the special coverings the winches, capstans, and davits have that you now see in place."

"Yeah but what about the rest of the bits exposed to the elements?" Morris asked after a little while whilst they tested the steam pipes.

"It's everybody on deck with chipping hammers, I presume." said Comerford, the 2nd Mate.

"Hello 2nd Mate. Didn't see you coming behind. Here, get one of your men to have a go with this steam nozzle for a while. Now's the best time to learn." John suggested, handing Comerford the hissing pipe.

"Aussie! Show the 2nd Mate how to operate it and what not to do with it." John commanded.

The engineers stood for a while watching the sailors play with the pipe before he announced an early stop for the day on the main deck.

"Let's get where we belong 2nd! Down the boiler room and warm up for a while." Morris suggested, but Clark responded by saying.

"Sod that! Lets all go for a wet in the lounge. Get warm inside first with a few noggins."

"Whatever you decide to do that's fine by me, but I'll be wanting you two to come and see me with your Task journals and maintenance schedules after tea time. I'll be in the forward cargo hold." John instructed, leaving the two junior engineers to their duties.

John entered his cabin to see Dovey, giving instructions to another steward as they went about tidying up his already neatly piled books.

"Hello steward, got another helper?" he asked politely.

"Hello 2nd. This is Alfie Baggs, who's part of the team we're taking. He normally looks after their cabins and shacks when the teams go out on their experiments. But because one of his scientists is sharing with you, he'll be taking over from me as I'm required for other duties." Dovey explained.

Baggs nodded in confirmation and explained briefly that he had been a ships steward long ago, and this was his chance to renew his skills again whilst on board.

"Sounds a good idea." John said quietly, sitting down to take off his heavy woollen jumper.

"Let's hope we've got warmer gear to wear on deck, as we'll be needing it a few degrees further down the chart."

"Don't you worry 2nd. We've got the latest and best stowed in a locker just down the aisle there." Dovey said with a smile as both men left the cabin, shutting the door quietly behind them.

Over the next several days, when the ship passed the island of Bouvet, the winds started to pick up and make large waves for the ship to climb over. Sometimes it was just windy or with a few squally showers, other times it was almost blizzard conditions as the level of mercury in the thermometer got lower and lower.

They had been at sea for over ten days now and were nearing the white continent where man entered at his peril, as every action he took was for survival, and the scientists were busy trying to educate the officers and crew on how to survive such conditions.

The daylight hours were getting shorter with the temperatures dropping by the hour and the seas turning brackish with icy slush, but the ship bravely ploughed her way ever south and westward, seeking her destination.

John went on deck and felt the winds were blowing a full gale and with every wave that cascaded their spray over the foc'sle, each droplet of water was falling as snow to cover the deck with yet another layer of ice.

He turned the steam hoses on full power for the sailors working on the deck, who were hard at it chipping the ice off the deck fittings, the cargo masts and any other ice-covered items.

Even they had to keep moving, otherwise they too would be icebound to the spot where they stood. Not even the pressure steam hoses they used seemed to have much effect against such an onslaught of bad weather.

"Okay men!" Brown shouted.

"That's it for now. Stow your gear and get below for a breather. Muster again in the after well deck in two hours. Leading seaman Kirk, make sure they turn up!"

"Aye aye 1st mate!" Kirk muttered as the men scrambled over the very slippery deck with indecent haste to stow their gear and get below decks.

John finished his inspections and securing the steam hose nozzle, followed the first mate quickly over the rapidly deepening snow on deck for both men went up the bridge ladder to escape the ice-cold piercing wind through their tunics.

He arrived onto the bridge to make a report and found it like an oven. Whilst he took off his heavy foul weather gear,

Brown went over to the barometer and stared hard at it.

"Ah 1ˢᵗ Mate, just the man I want to see!" Freeman purred, strolling over to him.

"I think its about time we had a change of watch on deck to clear this snow and ice."

"But Captain! I've just dismissed the watch on deck, after not the two hours as recommended in these conditions, but for four hours solid. They're exhausted and need to keep warm if they're to keep going. Besides, I've ordered them to muster on the after deck shortly." Brown said in defence of his men.

"First Mate! Just who holds the Captains rank, or quoted for the men to do this 2 hour deck watch?" Freeman snapped, then went over to one of the bridge windows and looked out of it.

"So the men finally managed a decent watch of four hours. In this weather, that four hours is only a fraction of the amount I expect from the men. Do I have to spell out your duties required in these latitudes and prevalent weather conditions in order to survive?" He snarled with contempt.

John and the others on the bridge were surprised at this sudden outburst between the two senior officers, but dared not to intervene for fear of further trouble. It wasn't John's concern what they did as long as the ship was kept afloat.

"No you don't, captain!" Brown responded angrily.

"But if the men don't have a rest at regular intervals then they'll be rendered useless for any further duties that might be required at short notice." He added.

"First Mate. Not to put too fine a point to this discussion, unless the Deck watches keep on top of things, this ship will capsize and sink with the top heavy weight, and everybody on board will perish within seconds of hitting the water. If that happens Mr First mate, then no further duties would matter, would it?"

"No Captain, but...!"

"No but's First Mate. Do as I command and everything will be okay."

Brown stood still for a moment as if to absorb the implications of Freeman's orders.

"Have you understood the seriousness and the logic of my commands?" Freeman snarled.

"Captain, I don't and never have questioned your command, but…" Brown started to say

"But what?" Freeman butted in.

"But what, I asked?"

"But, I don't understand your logic, I was about to say." Brown shouted back.

"Okay! Fair enough First mate! If, god spares us and this ship, you'll be a captain of your own vessel one day. And God help us all the day that happens." Freeman started in a condescending manner, then went into a lengthy and detailed explanation of present ship conditions, and many 'what if' scenarios as to the survival of the ship. He ended his monologue with, "So you see 1st mate, although you have some textbook knowledge of our ships present status, it's only now that you'll gain first hand knowledge of how you will survive this voyage to tell the tale."

Brown stood quite still and listened without interrupting Freeman, then took a moment to speak slowly and clearly in reply.

"Thank you Captain, but I must insist on a two hour rest period even though I had planned a watch pattern of '1 on 1 off' with a 'stay on watch' for the galley crew."

Freeman looked at his 1st mate with surprise.

"Now you're talking my language, 1st mate. I'll make a good captain of you yet." Freeman crowed.

"I'll grant your new watch system, but keep a close eye on the weather in case 'all hands on deck' is needed. According to Radio Officer Larter's latest weather forecast, this should blow over or slacken off a lot within a day or so. Now be about your business and keep me informed." Freeman said, dismissing Brown with a wave of his hand.

"Aye aye Captain!" Brown replied hastily and rattled down the bridge ladder and back into the icy grips of the winds and sea spray.

During this slanging match, John had time to write into the bridge log, the summary of his inspection report, and left the bridge almost at the heels of Brown.

"2nd engineer. Did you want to see me?" Freeman asked abruptly, observing that John had almost disappeared from sight. But John pretended he did not hear and carried on going without a backward glance.

He managed to get his two charges into their studies for a while before evening dinner time and to enjoy a well earned rest.

When he finally got back to his cabin, and after a brief chat with his fellow cabin mate, he decided to take a few hours off watch and get some sleep before his next arduous inspection.

The time seemed to slip by for John, who woke up suddenly, feeling peckish, and decided to seek something to eat. He met Dovey coming down the aisle with a tray.

"Ah steward! I've been feeling very tired and have missed my breakfast. Any chance of a roll or a sandwich and maybe a cuppa brought to my cabin?" he asked, eying the food laden tray.

"Certainly 2nd. Won't keep you a minute." Dovey replied, disappearing into a cabin doorway.

Dovey came back shortly and stepped into John's cabin.

"Here you are, just what the doctor ordered. And I mean the doctor sharing your cabin. But there's enough for the both of you. You've got a good measure of brandy in your coffee, so don't go on deck just yet." he announced quietly and put the silver tray down on the rubber sheet that covered the table.

"The brandy wasn't really necessary but thanks anyway." he said gratefully, drinking the last drop from his cup, as Dovey quietly left the cabin.

John looked at his watch again, deciding as it was still too early for his rounds, he'd have a quick nap before getting up at a more decent time.

His sleep was shortly interrupted by strange but extremely loud noises, so he got up and dressed quickly and decided that he might as well do his rounds sooner than later.

He arrived on deck to see that the ship was slowly making its way through a belt of calving icebergs.

The growling, cracking noises from the icebergs some miles away was so loud it rattled through the ship like thunder, as giant blocks of ice broke away from the massive and seemingly endless ice cliff that formed part of this white continent. John made his way to the bridge in case he had to provide any assistance that the captain might need, but stood mesmerised at nature performing in front of them. He saw that the sailors were on deck and being marshalled by the 1st mate.

"Stand by with fenders in case one bobs up close." Freeman ordered, then shouted for the lookouts to keep a good eye open for any more.

"Look there's one there, on the port bow about 200 yards away." came the warning from several of the lookouts.

"And another up on the starboard bow about the same distance."

"Captain! There's another dead ahead!"

Freeman looked at the three icebergs through his binoculars and decided that it could be just one big berg slowly rising out of the sea, with water cascading off it in giant waterfalls.

"Full astern together. Hard– a– port! Engineer Grey, get onto the foc'sle and keep a watch on my hull. You men below, get more fenders starboard side and over the bow in case we collide with it."

John arrived on deck and helped a sailor drag a large wicker fender over the bow, securing it to the anchor chains.

The ship seemed to shudder to a stop almost right at the edge of the berg. John and the sailor looked up at the towering cliff of ice above them, held their breath and the fender tightly waiting for the crunch. But sighed with relief when the ship swung herself right round pointing towards some free sea space. Both men looked at each other, then quickly over the bow to see if anything was damaged.

"That was a close thing 2nd! I had visions of becoming an instant icicle if any of that dropped onto us." the sailor said with obvious relief.

"Indeed. But better get yourself starboard side in case you're needed again." John replied, watching the stern coming round, making the ship come broadside to the towering ice cliff once more.

He then raced back up to the bridge in case he was to be despatched to some other task.

Freeman observed the rapidly changing seascape, and like the conductor of an orchestra, rattled off a series of orders to almost everybody around him.

"Helmsman. Port 20. Full ahead together. No1 get all the fenders over the starboard side. Grey, inform the engine room to prepare for a broadside collision starboard side. Sparks, take our position and prepare for a distress signal. Messenger, broadcast for all hands on deck, now!"

The gap between the ship and the mountain of ice was gone and it was now towering high above them, making the ship look like a matchstick.

Some of the overhanging ice was falling onto the deck, smashing through the cargo hold covers. Then an avalanche of ice and snow rumbled down and covered the ship making it bob up and down in the water. An up-swell of water flushed the ship sideways and away from this floating island of ice. The ship managed to shake herself clear from the ice debris, and started to bob her way into clear water and seemingly out of danger.

Suddenly a huge up-swell of water lifted the ship up, tossing her away from the iceberg like a top, The noise of screeching and tortured metal filled the air above all the other natural or man made noises.

"Bleedin' hell 2nd! Go and see what that was!" Freeman cursed as John darted away down the ladder to see the damage control team below decks.

"Captain. Chief told me that we've been peeled like a potato along the starboard side. We've lost almost a whole plate in the for'ard cargo hold. They have managed to seal off the watertight bulkheads." John said breathlessly as he arrived back on the bridge. He looked at the inclinometer and added.

"Captain we will take on a 15 degree list and more if we don't get a trim to counter it."

Freeman looking grim and pale, and the twitch on his right eye more pronounced, replied.

"Grey. We're lucky to escape with that. We could have been snapped in two or been sunk by those ice avalanches you've seen. Tell the engine room to do what's necessary but get my ship on an even trim then get down there and take charge. Send up another engineer for me, but just keep me informed at all times."

Chapter VIII
Apple Woman

The *Inverary* had been severely wounded by yet another act of nature, which man had to try and survive.

Freeman went out onto the bridge wing and looked over his wrecked ship. Several men were laid sprawled out in pools of red slush. Large blocks of ice were sticking up out of the forward cargo hatches. The radar dish was smashed under a mound of ice and snow. The upper part of the main foremast for the derricks was snapped off, and on looking aft, he saw a similar picture.

His motor launch and one of the lifeboats were smashed to smithereens, some of the vent cowlings were snapped off from deck level or lying flat. The radio aerials trailed like broken washing lines. He saw a large chunk of ice sticking out of the ships side, when she rolled beam on into another oncoming wave.

He felt a presence by him and looked around to see a panic stricken Brown standing next to him.

"Ah 1ˢᵗ mate! Come to report have you?" he asked civilly.

Brown was holding his left shoulder and breathing heavily.

"Captain. I haven't enough hands to clear away now let alone man the fenders." he said haltingly.

Freeman looked at the state of Brown

"What's wrong with your shoulder, man? Are you hurt?" he asked with mild concern.

"It's nothing compared with some of the men captain. I've got 7 dead and 5 seriously injured and the rest are like me. You can see exactly what my problems are, so can you spare me some of the stokers to help out?"

Freeman, in one of his rare moments of sympathy, and showing some of his long lost chivalry, replied.

"Sit yourself down and have a breather. I have another story to tell you."

Freeman explained about the large hole in the ships side, and having no radio or radar. Being many thousand miles away from dry land. Fuel problems, lack of food, and now the loss of some good crewmen.

"So, 1st mate. I need people like you in one piece to help me through this. For as God made smalley apples, we ain't going to make it any other way. Send me your 2nd mate before you go below." Freeman paused to stroke his growing beard, then added.

"Don't spend too long 'tween decks, its bad for morale. Go see the Doc!"

"Aye aye captain." Brown said softly and with a tired smile he left the bridge meeting John on his way onto it.

"Engineer Grey, glad you came back." Freeman said and beckoned John over to the starboard bridge wing. He pointed to a large floating island of ice rectangular in shape, which had its own miniature mountain rage on top of it.

"Do you see that? That's what caused what you now see here." he said, pointing to the offending object, then down onto the ships deck.

"You've been on deck and witnessed what has happened. But you might not be aware of the fact that we've been holed just below the waterline. Too much for an opposite trim to effect repairs, and still not enough for it not to be fixed. In other words Grey, we've lost 1 complete side plate and will lose another, and another, until we sink unless your lot does something about it. I have the chief helping me down below to save the ship, but I need you, as a fresh brain onto the subject, to start thinking up something tangible to do so."

"Thank you for placing your faith in me captain, but I'll need to go on deck and see things for myself first." John replied seeing the agitation growing on Freeman's face.

"Let me put it bluntly 2nd Engineer Grey. We're almost dead in the water now until we can get power and steerage. There's a dirty great storm about to come our way and an even bigger threat from these floating islands all around us. Our radio is u/s and our lifeboats are matchwood. In short Grey, we're in shit-street. So unless you can come up with something pretty damn quick, start saying your prayers now along with the rest of the crew." Freeman snarled and looked vehemently at him.

"I'll be back in 30 minutes captain. " John said soothingly, quickly descending the bridge ladder and going to the forward cargo deck.

Freeman watched Johns progress as he stroked his beard, but with his mind in deep contemplation.

"Reporting to the bridge." came an intrusive voice, disrupting Freeman's thoughts and startling him.

"What the? 2nd mate, what made you so late getting here? I've just watched the 2nd engineer go about his duties. What is it you want now?"

"You sent for me captain. The 1st mate will be along shortly." Comerford said soothingly as if to calm down his irate captain.

"Ah yes, so I did. Give me your deck report now as I've some work to get done."

Comerford narrated the events from the broadside onwards until arriving onto the bridge.

"Thank you 2nd mate. Very accurate indeed! I hope you'll put it all down in writing just as you've said. We've an inquiry somewhere I'll warrant, and your written account will come very handy." Freeman agreed, then went on to issue several orders for him to carry out.

"Aye aye captain. I'll report when completed."

"No! You'll report to me on completion of each order, do you understand?" Freeman corrected Comerford bluntly.

Comerford just nodded his head and left as swiftly as he arrived.

Freeman paced the width of the bridge stroking his beard whilst he continued his deliberations for a while.

"Bosun! Get yourself relieved and go below for a couple of hours. I'll be needing you bright-eyed and bushy-tailed very soon." he ordered.

"Aye aye Captain!" Sinclair acknowledged.

"Here Bones! Cop hold of the wheel, and keep lively. I'll send your winger up to be your messenger. Listen out for the engine room phone, and for God sake tell the skipper each time it rings. Have you got that?" Sinclair ordered his Bosun's mate, making sure everything was all right before he left.

"Sparks! Did you get our position off after?" Freeman called angrily, on entering the radio office.

"What's that Captain?" Larter asked emerging from under a large radio transmitter.

Freeman saw Larter extricate himself, to repeat the question in a more civilised voice.

"Yes Captain. But I got no reply. I broadcasted it blindly to several stations, but wasn't able to get a reply before I lost my power supply." Larter said evenly.

"Okay Sparks! At least you've done your best. Lets hope some bastard heard you!" he replied, looking up at the patched hole in the roof of the office and around at the electrical bits and pieces scattered everywhere.

"I have no radar which is my eyes, nor radio which is my ears to keep me in touch with the world. So how long will it be before you can give me at least my ears Sparks?"

"As you can see captain, I'm in the middle of fixing my main transmitter and I have to rig up a jury aerial to any highest point to get my signals out. The receivers are damaged but fortunately I had a spare one in my storeroom, so I'll be able to get weather reports or whatever as they come in. In short captain. Nothing sent out for quite a while, but incoming signals as and when."

"Very well. As soon as you get the receiver set up, never mind the transmitter, get on and fix some eyes or navigational aids, as I need them more just now. I don't care if you can only get me on short range radar, at least I won't be totally blind. Only then can you go back to your other work. Ok?"

"I'll be on it in about 30 minutes captain. But as all my repair stuff is up here you'll need to get what's left of the radar dish and its control box down off the top of the bridge for me to work on.

If not then it will take me days, not hours to give you what you want."

"Hours did you say? You can give me some eyes in hours?" Freeman asked in total amazement.

"You get the stuff up here and I'll have you navigating up the English Channel by daybreak Captain. I can't say any fairer than that." Larter said convincingly.

"You've got a deal. But remember, no radar and radio by daybreak tomorrow and I'll have you and your box of tricks ditched overboard with the rest of the garbage."

Larter sighed and said with sarcasm.

"Now if you'll excuse me captain, I've a real mans work to do and can't spare the time to be chatting to some stray apple woman!"

Freeman glared ominously at Larter, stroked his beard a couple of times then turned on his heel and left, swearing and muttering to himself for allowing a measly low ranking officer to upstage him.

The fit men on deck were busy clearing away the ice debris, repairing the cargo hatches, the foremast and rigging. There were stokers with welding torches spitting and spluttering as new metal patches appeared like measles all over the ship.

The moans and screams of the injured men were heard coming up from the sickbay and interspersed with heavy hammer blows thudding and ringing against metal.

Nature added to the cacophony of sound with moaning, cracking and loud sploshing noises from the growlers and calving icebergs which were near enough to the ship to be heard.

The wind was whistling and showers of heavy hailstones rattled on the ship as she rolled heavily in the deep swell.

"What a flippin' mess we're in and its going dark very rapidly, 2nd mate" John said at length, when he and Comerford stopped for a brief rest.

"At least we're still afloat. But only just. We appear to be in some sort of a 'Polinis', but unless we get moving or in the lee of one of these Ice Mountains, we'll be icebound by morning, then we can look out." Comerford observed, pointing to the water turning to ice before their very eyes.[*]

"Not if the captain or the Chief has anything to do with it. Nor me if it comes to it 2nd. So come on and lets get ourselves moving or we too will be welded to the spot by the ice."
John replied, unsticking his footwear from the freezing deck.

"Aye, we needed that break anyway 2nd. See you later in the lounge." Comerford said, nodding his head then left to do his own chores again.

The sun was casting long shadows from the berg now, leaving the ship to the mercy of the cruel night that was silently and swiftly creeping upon her.

The moment John pulled the switch for the main deck lighting, miraculously brought new hope to them all, as the light bulbs spluttered then shone brightly down upon the ship.

"Hooray!" came a big cheer out of nowhere, and a quip from some unknown comedian who shouted at him.

"Somebody lent him a shilling for the meter god bless them."
John smiled and blinked a few times getting used to the bright lights.   Then wended his way slowly along the upper deck towards the bridge access ladder. When he reached it, he met Brown coming swiftly down it.

"Just the man! I am about to do my fore deck rounds for tonight and would appreciate your company in checking certain items for me that are of a mechanical nature." He beamed.

"I've done aft and am going for'ard doing just that anyway. And yes you're welcome to come along as well." John countered.

Brown checked the new fore derrick mast and its new outfit of blocks and tackles.   The tarpaulins and covers over the cargo

---

[*] *Polinis* is the name given to an area of water that has not yet turned to brackish ice, before finally freezes over, and an area that whales and other marine mammals use as a crucial breathing hole in the pack ice above them.

hatch and other items in general. John busied himself by tapping here and there with his wheel spanner on the seams of the newly welded steel platings. Checking on deck valves or gauges. When they met up again on the foc'sle, they both checked the anchors, capstans and other vital equipment.

"Well 2nd. That's a good as it gets, under the circumstances. We've been lucky and managed to get her a bit shapely before anything else happens to her." Brown volunteered.

"Yes, it never rains but it pours. We really must have kicked the cat this time. I've got extra duties in the engine room shortly, and that should be fun and games down there too. What's your story?"

"The captain wants all officers in the lounge after supper for a round-up of what's happened so far today. So I'll expect you'll be forced to abandon your shift to someone else and attend it with along with Comerford."

"As if we didn't know already what's gone on. Everybody can see that and everybody already knows the score and what we're up against." John scoffed.

"Now now 2nd. Don't be like that. We shall be getting our heads together with some cunning plan or other to get us out of this pending doom." Brown chided mildly.

"And besides! The captain's opening his whiskey bottle tonight, and that is something definitely not to be missed. Is it?"

"Freeman opening his whiskey bottle! Well strike a light! That as they say, settles that, so count me in on that one." John said cheerily at the thought of seeing Freeman opening his famous store of best malt whiskey, and licked his lips at the thought of it.

Both men walked silently back up to the bridge, when Brown thanked John for his company on deck and hoped to see him at the officers meeting at 2000.

John nodded and went towards the accommodation space doorway, making his way to his cabin. When he entered it he saw somebody other than his fellow cabin sharer.

"Is that you steward? Can I help you?"

Baggs turned round and in the dimmed blue lighting, he could see a large white patch stuck to his face.

"Yes 2nd. I've had part of my face re-arranged today, but it only hurts when I laugh." came the doleful reply.

"I've never heard even a titter from you, all the time you've been on board. But maybe one day. What is it I can do for you?" John asked impatiently.

"I've a message from the Chief who asks you to go down to the engine room immediately you've finished your rounds on deck. He told me that half-an-hour ago and I've been looking for you ever since."

"Well thank you steward. I've just finished my rounds, so kindly do me a favour and see if you can rustle up a cuppa for me. I'm perished and want something before I go back on duty again."

"Aye aye 2nd! I'll be back in a jiffy." Baggs replied and scurried down the passage towards the lounge galley.

John struggled for a while to divest himself of his thick fur lined outer garments and his snow boots, before sitting down heavily in his chair to recover from his efforts. He put his hand inside his overalls to get his cigarettes and lighter, but felt his shirt soaking wet with sweat. After he removed the shirt and dried himself off, Baggs arrived with a large cup of steaming hot coffee and waited until John was dressed before offering it to him.

"Here you are 2nd! I've put a drop of brandy in it to help you." he said amiably.

"Many thanks for your nice thoughts. Your boss says that alcohol is bad for you in freezing conditions, as it quickly wears off. Also you'd be drunk before you knew it."

"Sorry 2nd! It won't happen again."

"Never mind steward. Besides, I've got some whiskey coming my way later on tonight and we don't want to mix my drinks, now do we." John smiled, swigging his drink.

"No I suppose not." Baggs conceded.

"But don't forget you've got to go down to the engine room 2nd! Unless you tell the chief I've told you, he'll probably give me a rocket for not doing so."

"Not to worry. I'm on my way and I'll tell him for you. Get your face rested for a while steward, and I'll see you later."
Baggs nodded his head slowly for fear of hurting himself, and left the cabin.

John felt much lighter now after wearing his cumbersome cold weather gear, or was it the brandy in his coffee? He clambered his way down into the engine room and stood in front of Chapman, as it was almost impossible to talk above the banging and drilling noises in the compartment.

"Glad you could make it John, and I'm sure you enjoyed your coffee too." Chapman smiled, tapping his lips

"I can smell it on your breath John. Better watch the skipper doesn't find out."

"Medicinal purposes as dispensed by an over zealous steward who gave me your message, Frank." John replied swiftly with a beaming smile.

"Okay John. Now you're here, come, I've got something to show you."

Both men went up a series of steel ladders before stepping into the relatively quiet and warmer sanction of the Engineers Office.

Chapman pulled out a filing cabinet drawer and removed a large roll of drawings and plans, then placed them on the small table in front of them.

"Right then John. We've got just over an hour to sort out what we're going to do with this leaking home of ours, and get it moving again."

The two men worked from one drawing to another, pointing out relevant details and scribbling down referral notes as they went along. Questions or problems were sorted out with answers gleaned from the paperwork, until Chapman looked at the brass clock above their heads.

"Well John, that's all we've got time for, as the captain wants us in the lounge in about 10 minutes. Time to go."

"I'm on watch about then Frank." John reminded him.

Chapman stuck his head out of the tiny office window and gave a whistle to some engineers standing below him. He beckoned for someone to come up and see him, who arrived at the top of the ladder breathless.

"Morris. The 2nd and I have a special meeting in 10 minutes, duration not known. I need you to take over the watch until you're relieved. Can do?" Chapman asked, but was more or less an order.

"No problem Chief. I've got some extra studying to cram in anyway and the best place is down here." Morris said affably

"Well done Morris. This will help you mitigate your recent altercation with the captain." Chapman responded and dismissed Morris before he and John went through the air-lock and out of the engine room compartments, arriving in the lounge to find all the scientists and the senior deck officers sitting quietly with some drink or another.

"I'll get the drinks John, find us a seat." Chapman offered

Chapman came back and gave John his drink.

"Lets get our workings ready for when the captain arrives." he suggested as John took a sip of his drink and settled down next to Chapman.

"Hello John!" Larter said pleasantly.

"Haven't seen you since we sailed."

"Hello Bruce, Jock!" John responded as he looked over to where the two radio officers were sitting. "Hear you managed to get our radar and radio back in commission. Well done."

Larter and Wallace gave big toothy grins.

"Yes! The skipper is splicing his own main-brace when he comes in. What have you boys come up with? Something good to match me I'll wager." Wallace asked, taking another swig from his glass.

"Nothing tangible yet sparks, but we're working on it."

Chapman replied for the both of them.

The noisy banter of the officers subsided as the bearded yet ashen-faced captain slowly came into the compartment.

"Evening everybody. Glad to see you all here." Freeman began.

"This gentlemen, if you like, is a council of war. A war that we must fight and win if we're to survive this hell of a predicament we find ourselves in."

He went on to relate the event of the day of how everyone had pulled the stops out for them to survive. The casualties sustained, the triumph of getting both the radio and radar working again by the sparkers. This drew a cheer from everybody else making Larter and Wallace beam with pleasure.

He went on to mention what still needed to be done and the need to continue keeping everyone focussed on surviving.

He asked questions and obtained his answers from all quarters including the scientists, all except from Chapman and John, whom he kept until last.

"We now turn to the cream of the shipping line, in marine engineering terms, ask them to provide us with some answers to the various questions posed here tonight. Take it from here gentlemen, the floor's all yours." Freeman said, sitting down and started to drink from his ever-full whiskey glass.

Chapman explained the damage sustained to the ship. Its loss of power; the temporary coverage to give the ship some lighting; their steerage problems and other effects, plus the need to find a way to circumvent the domino effect from the ever-increasing hole in the side of the ship.

The scientists offered ideas and answers to some questions posed to them.

As time went on, the heady smell of cigars and strong whiskey was like fire in John's empty belly. He looked into his half-full whiskey glass and saw the partially thawed ice cube slowly circling the glass.

'There's ice everywhere, even in my bloody drink' he muttered to himself and was thankful that nobody heard him.

He sat mesmerised by the swirling ice cubes and saw that a slice of lemon was resting on the top of one. The natural motion of the ship made the ice cubes bob up and down in the micro world of the glass, but the piece of lemon still remained above the liquid. After a little while he put his fingers into the glass and plucked out the cube with the lemon still stuck to it and examined it closely.

"That's it! That's it! That is what we need!" John shouted aloud.

Everybody suddenly stopped talking, looked over to see John holding an ice cube close to his eyes with his fingers.

"What's that 2nd?" asked Chapman, his voice breaking the silence.

"That's it! Don't you see Chief? The answer has been all around us all along!" John said excitedly.

"Chief, I hope your man is still in the land of the sane, and not showing any signs of being drunk!" Freeman bellowed, looking around at the puzzled faces of everybody else.

"What is it that you've discovered, John?" Chapman asked quietly, coming nearer to take a closer look at what John was staring at.

"Do you see this piece of lemon? Its stuck on top of this slightly hollow ice cube, see?

If I put it gently into the tumbler like this, so as not to displace the lemon, right? Look at the result!" John said, concluding his little demonstration, with great delight showing on his face.

"Did you see what I meant, chief?" John prompted, as a scientist rushed over at the same time as Freeman.

Freeman, Chapman and the scientist bent their heads close to the top of the tumbler and looked intently at what the fuss was all about.

"Captain! No, you Professor Lovatt. What is the ductile strength of ice?" John asked swiftly.

"I don't get you 2nd! What are you asking?" Freeman asked slowly and deliberately.

"Ahah! I see what he means captain." Lovatt exclaimed and looked directly at John.

"See what! See what?" Freeman asked angrily.

Everybody in the room remained seated to witness this drama unfolding in front of them.

"Captain. If that cube was the size of an iceberg and the slice of lemon a ship, we'd have a ready made floating dry dock to get our repairs done." John blurted out, hardly containing his excitement that was infectious to the onlookers.

"Yes captain. That is quite feasible, providing you're able to park your ship on a suitable iceberg." Lovatt concurred.

"Oh yes! Just send a few sky hooks and lift us up why don't you." Freeman scoffed and tried to pour scorn on the idea.

Another scientist came over to the group scribbling on a note pad as he arrived.

"I've made some weight ratio and ice load calculations, captain. It should work providing all things measured exactly." he announced, then asked Freeman.

"What is the current ship weight?"

"The ship is only 450 feet long with draught of 14 feet, and at 6,500 tons dead-weight. But we've got your stores and equipment on board at around 4,000tons, plus an extra 5,000 tons of fuel and stores due to the extra passengers and a longer voyage. But due to fuel and stores consumption weight loss over 12 days at sea, then the sudden weight gained from the ice, probably an extra 500 tons, maybe a round the 15,000 tons, but apart from that I haven't got a clue." Freeman said offhandedly with a shrug of his shoulders.

Two more scientists stopped at another table, muttering various formulae to themselves as they frantically worked their slide-rules.

Eventually John's little group was surrounded by all the scientists, who had their slide-rules out and asking Freeman and Chapman some pertinent questions about the ships handling, engine performances and the fuel problems. John and Chapman answered their questions with quick-fire response, until Freeman decided he'd had enough.

"Questions, questions! I'm surrounded by daft people with idiotic questions!" Freeman exploded,

"Has everyone gone mad around here?" he asked an apparently deaf audience.

The two professors eventually came back with their formulae, and showed John what they were doing. Both engineers looked at the unfamiliar formulae, but they deduced what was worked out, all of which fitted John's discovery.

Chapman looked down at the now seated and bemused captain asking him to look at what he was about to draw on the large sheet of blank papers in front of him.

"Captain! He started gently.

"Thanks to Grey, the boffins have worked out that if we were to find a suitable iceberg with a kind of ice ramp, then go full speed as if to ram it. But given a lift by the heavy swells, we would be lifted up onto the berg and skate over the ice like a Bobsleigh does. Enough to get the ship virtually beached so we could patch up that big hole of ours. All we have to do then is let go of the anchors holding us piggy back on the berg, and we'd slip gently back into the water again, fully repaired and get back on our way again. Alternatively, if our speed took us completely out of the water, we could winch ourselves back again, or even just wait until the ice melted and we'd simply re-float again. We could hold a mini launching ceremony too.

Either way, we can get all our repairs done to be almost as good as new, and still live to tell the tale."

Freeman looked at his whiskey glass for a moment, recalling what Chapman had said then slowly turned his head around to look at John sliding his ice cubes across the table.

"Grey! Come here this instance!" he bellowed.

John went quietly and calmly towards the captain and stood by Chapman.

"Its not very often I offer junior officers a drink of my best whiskey. But it's thanks to my drink you've managed to discover our salvation." Freeman said condescendingly.

"You Mr Grey can have a whole crate to yourself if we survive this."

"Thank you for your generous offer captain!" John said with surprise at this turn of events.

"No. Don't thank me 2^{nd,} thank my whiskey. Just you wait until I inform his lordships about my discovery! My very own whiskey indeed!" Freeman stated flatly and got up to fetch another bottle from the bar.

Everybody gasped with shock, talking amongst themselves about how Freeman had just stolen John's discovery, and would be taking all the glory from another mans thunder.

"John. I'm totally disgusted with what the captain has just said and done. If I have anything to do with it, it's you the lordships will be thanking." Larter stated angrily.

"Bruce. I'm used to such back-stabbing by captains. Remember the SFD incident back in Belfast, the *Fernlea* incident and others? Well this is on par." John said dejectedly.

The two professors and the other scientists stated that they would be making a formal protest over this blatant act of piracy of another mans discovery.

Chapman came over, whispering in Johns' ear.

"Remember John. The captain is God on here, and all the glory goes to him, but any of the shit for when things go wrong, gets delegated downwards to the lowest rank, and as it happens, that is you."

John looked at the departing chief, shrugged his shoulders in dismay, feeling a great rush of anti-climax to his spontaneous elation of being able to find a way for the ship and its occupants to survive.

After a little while speaking to Larter, John went over to sit by Chapman who was talking to one of the scientists. But as he arrived, the scientist got up, shook his head in pity then left the lounge.

"John, you've struck yet again haven't you!" Chapman said quietly.

"I've been told about your past escapades, but dared not to question them in case. Now I know them to be true and I'll tell Happy about it."

"The captain can keep his whiskey and I hope he chokes on it." John replied with a shrug of his shoulders

"Well, this time you've got independent witnesses who are backed by international governments. So the captains ploy will backfire on him just you wait and see." Chapman said sympathetically.

"Oh well Frank. Must get back on watch, for the last half hour at least." John said wearily.

"No you don't. Get turned in John, besides Morris is doing an excellent job on his own."

"Yes. Must thank him next time I see him."

"It's the other way round John. The whole ships crew and the passengers will be thanking you soon, I'll wager. So don't fret on that score. Have a good night in, as there's nothing doing in the engine room anyway." Chapman said cheerfully.

"Thanks anyway Frank, see you!" John said, then made his weary way back to the peace and calm of his little cabin, to rest his aching body before another day's onslaught.

Chapter IX
Flying Kites

John stepped out onto the freezing cold upper deck to start his rounds when he met Lovatt and the other professor Van Heyden, looking through a microscope at pieces of ice that were still scattered across the deck.

"Morning Grey!" they said in unison.

"We have been making various calculations at a distance from that berg that bit us, so to speak, and by this sample, it's formed from super- cooled water of some thousands of years ago. If you look at its mother block and some of the others around what can you deduce from them?"

John looked at the massive floating island and the smaller ones around the ship but said he could only see different coloured ice.

"That's right. The almost translucent ones are super-cooled, therefore much harder than the other almost opaque ones are of slightly different construction, although it's pure ice never-the-less." Lovatt stated, giving John a small lesson on Icebergology. When they had finished, although John was almost non-the-wiser, he thanked them enthusiastically and hoped that they could come up with the formulae to make his basic theory possible.

"We would have to land on one to survey it to make sure we've got the right one. Preferably one strong enough to take the dead weight of the ship, because we've never had cause to find out such a phenomena."

After his rounds and back in the lounge for a warming cuppa, Chapman arrived to tell him that as the ship was still in great danger and appeared to be going nowhere, the captain would be holding another brain-storming session after lunch.

"I have other ideas to offer, but its someone else's turn, Frank." John said quietly, and getting up left Chapman to his refreshment.

"Afternoon gentlemen!" Freeman greeted civilly.

"We have a situation, whereby the ship has a large chunk of

ice sticking out of her side which is growing by the day. Our radar and radio are both u/s because of the massive amount of floating islands with ice cliffs a few miles away. The area is prone to severe storms and blizzards.

Although we're in a natural sea lagoon between all these ice mountains, we need to get out of here before we ultimately become crushed by the new ice field that is building up." he droned. Then went on to mention the worsening conditions on board and other such things, until he stopped and asked for suggestions.

Van Heyden suggested that whilst the weather was favourable at the moment, maybe he and his team should land on one of the bergs to survey it and possibly use it as a lookout post to see if they could find a way out of the maze of bergs. All they had to do was let loose an orange weather balloon if they did find one.

This was discussed with the decision that whilst the scouting idea was a fair one, it was far too dangerous to try and land with such a high sea swell.

Clarke whispered to John, egging him on to speak about his hobby, and although John was reluctant to do so and earn another round of scorn and derision, he gave in to his Aussie engineer companion, then stood up to speak.

"I used to make box kites when I was a lad, then fly them from the top of a little hill near my home. I suggest that a much bigger one could be made to take a man, who could fly above the ship to see if he could find a way out of the maze of icebergs." John volunteered.

He waited for the usual furore after the dead silence he created, and was not disappointed with its mixed reception.

On one side he found the usual doubters such as Freeman, Brown with a few others saying it would be too dangerous, what if the wind dropped and the man fell into the sea. He'd be dead in seconds if he fell into it. Or the line might snap and he'd be blown against one of the ice cliffs, or be blown so high to lose oxygen or be struck by a bolt of lightening, or, or.

On the other, he had the scientists who said they could make such a kite, they only needed a volunteer for such a mission, who was not scared of heights and had good eyesight.

The debate went on for a little while until Freeman stood up to make his decision known.

"It seems that Grey has offered us another gem. I will get the crew together in the now empty forward cargo deck to pick out our volunteer, although as it was Greys idea, it really should be him." he announced, then despatched the junior deck office to the bridge to relay this meeting over the ships tannoy system.

"But then as all of a sudden, you seem to have taken over the idea, it should be you captain!" a scientist retorted, which drew a withering glance from Freeman.

The meeting drew to a close with everybody satisfied with the outcome as Freeman made his way down to meet the crew.

"Listen up men!" Freeman shouted over the noises in the cavernous cargo hold.

"I need two good men as volunteers to fly a kite." he commenced, then waited for the round of flippant jokes and remarks to die down before he started again.

The men were silent and apprehensive at first, but soon the camaraderie and jokes began to flow again, and Freeman got two 'persuaded' volunteers standing up for the task.

"Leading seaman Kirk and Able seaman White, at your service captain!" Kirk said, stretching out his arms pretending to be an airplane.

"Yes, thank you Kirk. We'll get you fully kitted out. You have the cream of the scientific world to make your craft and instruct you on how to operate it." Freeman said with a brief smile, then left the men to file back into the warmth of the accommodation compartments again.

John was on deck with the two professors helping them make an identical copy of his toy one, but on a much larger scale.

Once the box kite was made and inspected they had it secured to a winch with several hundred feet of strong but lightweight rope. It was tested using weights to substitute a body, and even extra weights to compensate for the extra clothing and gear the 'pilot' had to take with him. All was set for the first manned flight with everybody gathered around to watch John and the scientists launch a man, not into space but high enough to see over the next lump of ice.

Kirk was strapped to the massive kite, and listened to last minute instructions before he was ready to be winched to the top of the for'ard derrick to be caught by the strong winds.

The words of encouragement and the banter of, 'Never mind Dick! You'll be safe enough. If the wind drops you can always fart yourself back up again.' followed by 'If you get lost you can always ask a penguin.' and even 'Bring us back an ice cream' helped make the tricky launch go without a hitch.

"Ready Kirk? On three I'll let the winch go." John said calmly.

"Let's hope this rope is strong enough 2nd." Kirk said nervously, as his bravado was now running away from him.

"It's strong enough to tow a battleship. Just keep speaking to us down your mouthpiece so that we know your line and phone cable is okay. Remember, we've got one of the stores landing craft in the water ready to pick you up." John said reassuringly, as Kirk nodded his head.

With a sudden gust of wind the red coloured box kite soared away above them, as everybody looked at the dangling feet of Kirk.

Freeman and the scientists were now on the bridge watching through their binoculars.

"Kirk is one of the best. He's pretty good with navigation and chart work, so we've no problem there." Freeman said softly, watching the kite pull at its tether.

The scientists had rigged some of their field telephones together so that every word that Kirk said, could be heard at the launch pad and in the bridge.

John heard a clatter and someone shouting,

"He's dropped his ice pick and other things!" which prompted John to reverse the winch and pull Kirk back down onto the deck again.

When he finally landed, most of the onlookers cheered, apart from one sceptic.

"The skipper will charge you for losing your equipment, mark my words. And you'll be grounded for good."

"Ah shut your mealy mouth. If you can do any better then hop up here and do it!" Kirk shouted back, as a bridge messenger arrived to tell him that the captain wanted to see him.

Kirk and John followed the messenger up to the bridge where Freeman and the two professors were standing.

"Leading seaman Kirk. Welcome aboard!" Freeman joked.

"Hope you got a good look up there, because that's all I've got for all my troubles, Kirk!"

Kirk was not to be put off.

"Aye captain! I could see for miles, and a fair distance too!"

"Well tell me man! Don't frig about, tell me how we are laying in these infernal icebergs?"

"Everything is like a broken jigsaw puzzle captain. I wasn't able to tell you to let me up higher as I accidentally dropped some of my equipment, before I got winched back down again. If I'd got higher I'd be able to see over that big berg in front of us because it is a massive one, and the one on to our starboard. But we've got about 5 miles of sea room around them, almost oval in shape. That's all I can tell you captain." Kirk said, drawing a pencil mark over the navigational chart.

"That's not good enough Kirk! Get yourself back up there and do your job properly. If you drop anything again, I'll personally come and cut your line and set you adrift!" Freeman snarled, causing the professors to gasp at the idea.

"But captain, it's freezing up there!" Kirk protested angrily.

"No buts Kirk! I thought you volunteered to go up there anyway. And I gave you special privileges because of it."

"Captain, may I make a suggestion" Lovatt interceded on Kirk's behalf.

"We can always send up the second man to get his first solo flight too, but with the telephone wire strapped to his body instead of the cable. That way the telephone wire won't be cut by the kites' wire as it was this time. Kirk reached his maximum height, so we'll have to extend the lead until the pilot can see over the berg. After all, it's got a peak of about 150 feet that is probably preventing him seeing beyond it. He won't be needing half of his equipment now as Kirk here has given us an initial appraisal of the immediate area."

"That sounds interesting, professor." Freeman said, stroking his thickening beard.

"Now why didn't you think of that one Grey!" he said sarcastically to John.

"First mate. Get Kirk below and see that the professors instructions are carried out."

"Aye aye captain!" Brown said woodenly, as they trooped off the bridge.

John went back with Kirk to his mess and found the sailors still in a jovial mood.

"What's up mate, out of wind or is it farts are we?"

"Hark at you load of smart-arsed gits! I didn't see any of you lining up to go up there" Kirk snapped, while John quietly helped him out of the precious harness.

"That's right! That's exactly why we are smart-arsed. Only a fool would go flying kites in the middle of the Antarctic. Now sit down, have some tea and shut up!" someone stated.

Kirk glowered at them and left with John to go back to the launch area again.

White was being strapped into the new kite harness and given brief instructions on how to operate it, but that was taken over by Kirk, who showed his friend exactly what was required. John just stood by and smoked a cigarette and waited until he operated the specially adapted winch.

"Pretty wild up there I guess?" John asked Kirk when he was finished with White.

"Aye 2nd! The wind pulls you so much that it takes most of your strength just to hold on. With the wind blasting in your face, its difficult to breathe properly and so cold that ice starts to form on the cross members we're supposed to hold onto."

John took in these details and went over to Lovatt.

"We can do that no problem, and give the pilot extra clothing to keep him warm. As long as the weight to cable strength is not infringed." Lovatt replied.

"The cable has a tension of 3,500lbs before it destroys itself. So our pilots should be safe enough!" John said slowly, finishing his mental calculations aloud.

"Yes, that's about right. Mind you, he has an emergency line of 1000lbs with the telephone cable too."

White and Kirk heard this conversation and thanked them for their assurance.

"Okay White? I'll count to three just like the last time." John asked, sticking his thumb up to him.

"Ready when you are 2nd!" White replied, sticking his thumb up in return, and was swiftly taken aloft into the strong winds.

Everything went to plan for a while, as White's voice gave a running commentary on all that he saw and what was happening to him. But his voice started to panic as the wind began to abate and he was dropping lower and lower.

John immediately switched the winch to reverse, and swiftly hauled White back onto the deck again, with a thump.

"Thanks 2nd! I thought for a moment I was going for a swim, and me without me cossie too!" White said, picking himself off the deck, with others around to unharness the kite from him.

"Much longer up there and I'd have frozen and fallen as a ruddy great snowball." He added, blowing on his hands and stamping his feet to get warm.

"Well at least you gave us a good commentary. One of the researchers wrote it all down in case the bridge wasn't able to understand you. Better we take it up to the bridge and see the captain in case." John advised, and was given the written narrative by the person.

The light was fading fast now, which made another launch impossible, so the 3rd mate instructed the sailors to get the equipment stowed away and the deck cleared for the night.

John and White arrived onto the bridge to see Freeman scowling menacingly at them.

"I couldn't understand a word you said White. I hope you've got something written down to give me." He shouted.

John threw the narrative in Freeman's face.

"Here captain. Here's what you want to know. Read it and learn." John growled angrily, which made Freeman look surprised at the treatment he was given by a junior officer.

White marched over to the chart table stabbing his finger at where the ships position was marked on it.

"Here captain, I'll show you exactly what is what. I'll even draw a sketch for you!" White snapped, prodding the chart with his gloved hand.

Freeman walked swiftly across to the chart and watched as White drew his sketch.

Lovatt came over to see, asking White how it went, and told him how brave he and his friend were.

While Freeman was looking at the sketch and reading the narrative, White related his experience of how he couldn't breathe properly. How the wire cable rubbed his leg, how the kite handled and how absolutely fantastic the view was from up there.

Van Heyden gave John and White a steaming hot cup of coffee into which he slyly poured some brandy from his hip flask.

"Here you both are. You deserve something to warm up with" he said soothingly.

Both of them gulped down the hot liquid as if it were cold, thanking the professor for his kindness.

"White, come here and explain some details." Freeman commanded.

The two scientists also moved over to the chart table and took some measurements along with Freeman, as White pointed out the details required from him.

Freeman turned to the two professors and said with a sigh.

"I have some serious calculations to make in order to get us out of this death trap, but need some of your expertise to help me!"

"We'll do what we can captain!" Lovatt said, nodding in agreement.

"Okay. First Mate, take over the bridge, and I'll be in my cabin with our professors here if you need me. Post extra lookouts and get White below. He is excused watches until 0800 tomorrow." Freeman ordered.

John decided to stay for a while and talking to Brown.

"White was very lucky today Dave. I discovered that the main crossbar of the kite had fractured its weld from the pilots resting plate. If that had gone, then the kite would have collapsed into itself." he said softly so the rest of the bridge team could not hear him.

"You mean that Kirk or even White would have plummeted into the sea, and drown before the landing craft could get to him?"

"Well yes. Mind you, either that or being blown onto a berg with no way of being rescued."

Brown whistled through his teeth and cursed.

"Flippin' heck! Almost another good man down the chute."

"That's why I stayed on the bridge to tell you. You'll be needing as many able-bodied men you can get hold of. And you can bet your bottom dollar, tomorrow is the start of some very fancy fun-and- games too." John said, nodding his head to emphasise his statement.

"Subject to weather conditions and the cursed drag on our starboard side, John."

"No. Subject to how soon the captain wants to start and for how long."

They talked for a while about the state of the upper deck, the problems of the weather conditions and the general state of things, but were interrupted by the bridge messenger.

"Excuse me, but engineer Grey is required to go and see the chief engineer in his cabin."

John thanked the messenger and looked at the ships clock above the chart table.

"My how time flies when you're not looking, Dave. See you at dinner." John said then left the bridge.

He went down to Chapman's cabin and stepped inside to find the chief almost buried under a pile of ship designs, drawings and other plans.

"Hello is that you under there Frank?" John asked cheerfully.

"Hello John. First, give me your deck rounds report and as briefly as possible if you would. Then help me sort out a particular problem given me by the captain." Chapman replied swiftly.

John described his rounds, keeping only to brief technical terms; stopping only to answer questions put to him.

"So unless we maintain the steam pressure to the de-icing hoses the ship's top weight would be too much. We'd either capsize and turn turtle at best, or sink under the weight!" Chapman observed, then added,

"Okay then John I'll get Clarke to stay on top of it overnight." The two engineers folded and stacked the mountain of books and drawings and sat down by Chapman's writing table.

"We've only got a few minutes before dinner and the captain wants yet another meeting to include the scientists afterwards. So best have a breather now and come back here after the meeting John. We're staying put in this space of the ocean by the looks of it, so the stokers can be off but standing by in case of a sudden move!"

"Hooray for that. At least we'll have a restful night without watch-keeping Frank!"

"Yes. That is the plan as it stands. Heaven help us at the meeting though!"

"I think we'd better be off and show willing. Are you coming?"

"Aye John. Lets go and meet the public." Chapman sighed, switching off the desk light and stepping out into the dimly lit passageway with John.

After their nondescript meal and with a large drink in their hands; the two engineers sat at their respective seats on one side of a long table, with the corresponding number of deck officers on the other. The professors with other scientists sat at the opposite end of the table near to where the captain was going to sit.

"We've almost got a full house here tonight Frank!" John whispered in Chapman's ear.

"Yes John. We're in for some serious orders tonight, mark my words!" Chapman whispered back, and nodded to Brown sitting opposite him.

"Now that we're all here!" Freeman boomed as he entered the lounge with his arms full of charts and ships plans.

"Maybe we can get a co-ordinated plan of attack to relieve ourselves from a very serious mischief. If not then we'd all better start swimming now!"

"What have you in mind captain?" Brown asked civilly.

"All in good time 1st mate! All in good time!" Freeman replied, then turned to the scientists.

"First off. I'd like to thank our professors and his team in assisting me with certain aspects of, shall we say, Icebergology. Somehow an ice cube in my whiskey won't be quite the same any more." Freeman said with a smile to the scientists. He lifted a prepared tumbler of whiskey then raised it to his lips saying.

"Here's a toast to Icebergology." then took a large swig from it before revealing his master plan of escape.

Various questions and answers ebbed and flowed across or up and down the table, lasting for several hours, until finally Freeman was satisfied.

"Enough gentlemen. I think you'd better get a good nights

sleep, or what's left of the night, as we have our allotted duties to tend to in the morning. This was the most productive meeting so far. 1st mate, Engines, and you 2nd engineer Grey, see me in my cabin at 0700 tomorrow. Thank you all and good night!" Freeman announced, and picking up his bundle of papers marched out of the lounge.

Everybody seemed to have the same idea, so they finished their drinks and left to do their own thing.

'I wonder what the skipper wants of me this time. Better get some kip as tomorrow looks to be yet more fun and games.' John muttered to himself then switched off his bunk light and settled down to sleep.

Chapter X
Rollercoaster

"**M**orning 2nd! Here's a cuppa and some toasted rolls."
Baggs said quietly when he entered John's darkened cabin.

"Morning steward. What's the time?" John asked sleepily, stretching and yawning himself awake.

"It's rounds time, 0530, and before you go for that meeting of yours with the skipper. As you can see, Dr Brandon is already up carrying out his experiments." Baggs volunteered.

John looked at the other empty bunk and then out of his cabin porthole.

He saw nothing but large ice mountains sitting majestically in a black sea, with rays of moonbeams darting down between equally black clouds, making the bergs glow and shimmer like giant crystals.

'All that raw natural beauty to behold, but man would perish in its coldness' he said softly to himself then ate his breakfast as if in a trance, whilst he continued to stare out of the window.

He climbed into his heavy, cold weather gear and made his way onto the freezing deck.

He started from for'ard this time working his way towards the stern, checking the steam hoses, winches and other machinery as he went. When he got to the ice plug in the ships side he met the 3rd mate with a small working party.

"Morning 2nd. Glad you've arrived. We've got a problem with our guest block of ice." the 3rd mate shouted over the howling wind, pointing overboard to the ice.

John looked over the side and saw that the block had grown like a giant blister and was peeling more of the side plates away from the ship.

"I see it 3rd mate. The ice will seal itself around the damaged section so we won't gain much more water in the hold. The only thing you can do is to chip away at some of the bulk to keep the weight down or it will get too big and make us keel over even further." John advised, then added.

"You'd better report this immediately to the 1st mate who's on the bridge, or even the captain. I have to put it into my report to the chief as well."

"Thanks 2nd. I'll do just that." the 3rd mate replied as John left them.

He finished his rounds and managed to get another light breakfast before making his way up to the captains cabin to find he was the last one to arrive.

"You can make your rounds report afterwards 2nd, now gather round." Freeman ordered when John entered the hallowed portals of the captain's domain.

Freeman had a sea chart spread out on his large table, with a little toy ship placed to mark their exact position. There was a dotted green line going around what was the iceberg-island on their port side: A blue line going around the ice island on their starboard side; with a large red blob to mark where the lines met on the iceberg.

"As you can see gentlemen, that monster on our starboard side is next to the very one that nearly capsized us, and thanks to the 2nd engineers inkling of my idea, is where we'll be heading to make our repairs." Freeman said quickly, with his eyes darting around the cabin to see if there were any challengers to his statement.

He spoke about landing most of the cargo and the men on it today in preparation for their attempt at beaching the day after tomorrow, then produced a large sketch of the iceberg.

"This is by courtesy of Able seaman White. He has captured as much detail as he could to produce this drawing. Good isn't it."

John and the others murmured their admiration and approval at such handiwork.

"The berg is growing daily, making it rise slowly out of the water. So we're going to have to work fast and hard to make this concept work. There is a nose sticking out of the berg that looks like a ramp and appears about 70 feet wide and 90 feet long. Beyond that there's what looks like a wide gully that turns to port and in an arc, which opens up into a shallow 'D' shaped depression. Our task is to prepare this landing site and ourselves for this." Freeman said calmly, with a slight of hand, producing some drawings.

"This is the work of one of the scientists, who has given us an artistic impression of how the ship would rest on the ramp, or in the shallow lake. Here is one with Grey's idea plus one with my development of it." He said, handing them over to be looked at.

"These lines on the chart. The idea is for the men to follow the blue route; board the berg to make a quick survey and, shall we say, improve the place for us.

We on the ship will follow the green line to build up our speed to the required 16 knots. That will give us sufficient momentum to mount that ramp like a toboggan, slide ourselves out of the water enough to fix that hole in our side. Mind you, there's a chance that we'll just ram the berg smashing ourselves to pieces, or rattle over the berg, then go straight through the gap on the other side." he added, then paused to let his statement sink into the surprised officers.

"At its thinner end, the ramp looks a good 45 degree angle from the berg. If we approach at that angle, and get turned to port, then we would have a good 900 feet before reaching that depression, at the widest part of the berg. If the ship can be turned to be broadside on to the berg's main peaks and especially in the depression, then we will stand a chance. Our professors tell us that in Icebergology terms, the berg's depression will provide us with a nice sheltered pocket. Well above the waterline, high and dry so to speak." John stated.

"So let's get this straight captain. We steam full speed into an iceberg hoping we will skate out of the water to use the berg as a dry dock, just like Grey suggested? The thing is, the Titanic was 46,000 tons and tried to do the same to an iceberg some 10 to 15 times its size and weight, so what chance have we got if it all goes wrong?" Brown asked in astonishment staring transfixed at the drawings.

"It's like a launch in reverse, so to speak." John enthused looking more closely at the artistic impressions of what was only an imaginative idea spoken about less than two days ago.

"You've got it in a nutshell 2nd. A good plan of mine don't you think?" Freeman crowed, stroking his beard again.

"We need about 10 miles of clear water and roughly 40 minutes to reach even three quarters of that speed captain. Am I to understand that the green arc behind the port berg is to give us more time and room to reach the 16 knots?" Chapman asked.

"As it happens, we just go round and round until we've got our speed then use the 3 mile straight piece of water to line ourselves up with the ramp before striking. If the ice is smoothed down like glass then the ships weight and momentum should do the rest, as the professors explained to me."

"So our bilge keels would act as skates, and we'd slide across the berg and hopefully land in that hollow!" John said excitedly, seeing that his idea was starting to take tangible signs of working.

"Exactly as I've calculated!" said a voice from behind them.

"Professor Lovatt. Glad you could make it. It appears that our 2nd engineer has a better grasp of Icebergology that the rest. Maybe an assurance from you as one of the leading scientists in this field, would convince all the others!" Freeman stated emphatically.

"It's not so much scepticism captain. It's more of a word to the wise. The nose as you call it, is our sea exit point. If that gave way then we'd definitely sink within seconds." Brown retorted in self-defence.

"As far as I'm concerned captain. The original idea from Grey is sound. But…!" Chapman started to say.

"But what chief?" Lovatt asked calmly.

"My mind is on the damage you'd do to the bow if you miscalculate our landing point." Chapman answered.

"I've only got an artists impression to go on, and only when we've done our site survey can we say for certainty that this plan can work. It's just a minor adjustment here or there we need to make." Lovatt stated in an assuring manner.

"Besides that, we've got another 2 options captain. Stay here and slowly sink under the growing weight of ice, or stay here and get icebound and finally get crushed." he added.

"That does it! That's just what we'll do gentlemen. Now lets get moving as we've only got a six hour day before it goes dark again." Freeman boomed and ushered his officers out of his cabin with a wave of his arm.

The engineers left Freeman's cabin and went down to the engine room to muster the stokers.

"Is every man here? Hands up who's missing?" Chapman asked aloud.

"Aye chief! The gang's all here!" Morris said as he nodded his confirmation.

"Right then men! We've got a quick run ashore lined up, and I mean literally a quick run ashore and for the very first time you'll take a lady with you. In fact a 450 foot long, 15,000 ton lady to be precise. But for the benefit for those that may have any fancy ideas, its this ship." Chapman said amongst the cheers and banter from the men. Then went on to explain exactly what was to happen.

The men stood open mouthed in astonishment with some who looked and sounded entirely sceptical to the plan.

"Yes! I thought I'd surprise you all. So here's what I need doing." Chapman continued.

"I shall split the officers and you men into two teams. I shall be in team A with the 3rd engineer. The Electrical engineer and a volunteer steaming crew to remain on board. The rest of you will form team B with the 2nd and 3rd engineers plus some of the other junior engineers. But for now, the watch will remain here until relieved by those volunteers. So hands up who wants a run ashore, and who wishes to remain on board?" Chapman asked, then went on to pick the men who volunteered to stay on board, leaving the rest to go with the B team.

"All officers report to my cabin in about 10 minutes. That's all men, and good luck to you all." he said loudly over the increasing voices of the men.

John arrived into Chapman's cabin first, before the inevitable squeeze of the others trying to pack into such a tiny cabin.

"Everybody playing sardines again!" the ever cheerful Aussie quipped.

"And any would be Sheila's keep their hands up in the air so I can see them!"

"Hello sailor, give us a kiss!" Morris said, reacting to Clarke's request.

"Quick Aussie! He's behind you!" said John, with a chuckle.

"Oh no he's not!" replied the other 4th engineer.

"Oh yes I am." Morris insisted.

"Oh yes he is" everybody said in unison.

"Okay gentlemen, that's enough!" Chapman said aloud.

"It's good to get rid of your tensions and your fears, but these next few days will definitely not be a pantomime. So settle down and listen up." Chapman said evenly and the officers sat quietly to hear what their chief had to say.

Chapman explained certain engineering problems, and answered questions from the officers as he went along. Their meeting was interrupted by Comerford's knock on the cabin door.

"Excuse me gentlemen, but the captain wishes to see the chief and 2nd engineer immediately on the bridge." he announced.

"Thank you 3rd mate. Tell the captain we're on our way." Chapman replied, then quickly ran over the main orders for his officers, before leaving with John for the bridge.

They arrived on the bridge to find Freeman in a full spiel of orders and despatching the dwindling band of deck officers and men.

"You wished to see us captain?" Chapman asked aloud during a rare moment of silence from Freeman.

"Yes chief! You've got about 1 hour to get your team of men and any equipment on the for'ard cargo deck. I'll be needing engine power enough to get me over to the target berg. There some of your men will embark on one of the stores landing craft, boarding the berg at the back end of it. They will make their way along the berg to the front with one of the professors and this team. But you two will accompany me to the other end to see our landing point. You, Grey, will board the berg with half of your men to prepare to receive us. You chief, will need a closer look to make your own calculations, so bring what you need. When we get alongside, I shall be off-loading as much of the scientists equipment as possible today to lighten the ship. Maybe it will lessen our draught somewhat, to help us, but we need to reduce our draught enough to chop that infernal iceberg stuck into our side." Freeman paused to give telegraph and steering orders to the bridge crew.

"Right then chief! We've begun phase 1 but you have your own schedule. So I'll see you later on. Grey, get on deck and co-ordinate your orders with the 1st mate."

Both engineers nodded in agreement then left to prepare themselves.

"Morning Dave. I have a stack of equipment being mustered here. 4th Engineer Clarke will divide it and the men, as I'm to board the target at the front end." John announced meeting up with Brown.

"Morning John!" Yes, I'm expecting two piles of your equipment plus two teams of men. Have you any idea what weight we're talking about?" Brown asked.

"My total weight without the men and their personal belongings is around the 80 tons. So we'll say 90 tons."

"Phew! 90 tons? My men and equipment are only 55 tons. That's including cooking equipment and two days rations. The launches can only carry 25 tons so will have to take part loads."

"The thing is, we need to off-load the donkey boilers and some fuel to provide power and steam. Couldn't we just off-load most of our gear along with the scientists stuff, using the derricks, Dave?"

"That should answer the problems. Once I've got the boarding party established ashore, I can then use both launches to take the men going around the back end. I've got five men and a 4th deck officer to accompany your lot."

"That will be Aussie Clarke's team, Dave. Speak to him." John said, leaving to go up onto the bridge, but decided that a swift breather would be in order.

The bleak sunlight was playing hide and seek behind the snow-laden clouds and the ship was riding the swell, shuddering, as the ice plug was tormenting her side.

'She can't take much more of this punishment. Wish we had a calm day for once' he muttered under his breath as he flicked the last of his cigarette over the ships side.

"Oy! Who the fuckin' hell is the bleedin' joker then?" came an angry voice seemingly from nowhere.

John was surprised to see a bearded face surrounded in fur, bob up from over the side.

"What the?" John gasped.

"What's the fuckin' bleedin' game mate? Flicking your dog end in my face! I nearly fell into the oggin, cause of it. I've got a good mind to come over and give you a bloody good thumping!" the angry person threatened.

"What are you doing over the side mate!" John asked in amazement, then added more assertively,

"And I'm no mate! I'm the 2nd engineer to you, but who the devil are you?"

"Oh sorry 2nd! I'm Able Seaman Paterson. I thought it was a certain idiot just trying to be funny again." The man said sulkily.

John looked over the side and saw him standing in one of the stores launches that was bobbing up and down in the deep swell.

"My apologies to you Paterson. You look as if you're on a

roller coaster in that. Who's that with you?" John apologised but totally intrigued

"The Bosun's mate Jones, Kirk, and a stoker. We're waiting for the 1st mate to load us up."

"Well he's gone to see the captain about a change of plan. So stand by." John explained and left to see his own men.

"2nd engineer! You're asked to report to the bridge!" spoke a muffled voice that came from a well wrapped body.

John looked at the body and realised that he must look the same to that person, who was equally wrapped up to protect a frail body from the brutal weather.

'So much for orders and plans' he thought waving to the man in acknowledgement, before going to the bridge.

"2nd engineer! Yet again you pop up with surprises and suggestions. Is suggestions your middle name?" came the tired voice of Freeman, finishing off his drink from a large mug.

John removed the sheepskin lined hood from his head and asked innocently.

"You wish to see me captain?"

"Yes. The 1st mate tells me you've got over 200 tons of men and equipment to lug around in this weather, apart from the several thousand tons of stores to be offloaded. Put all that in the launches and Mr Neptune will have an early Xmas present." Freeman remarked acidly.

"I have my orders issued, and I deem every item vital to the success of my phase of the operations."

"Aye aye! All right 2nd!" Freeman conceded reluctantly.

"But what's this stores transfer by hoist? It might be feasible providing we get close enough. We don't have much time in daylight hours to do everything I would like to do. If we're successful then you'll be able to transfer much of the scientists equipment needed ashore." Freeman said in a conciliatory tone of voice, and the more he spoke the more he stroked his pointed beard.

John stood by Brown for a while watching the captain pace

the bridge, muttering and arguing with himself, when suddenly he stopped his pacing and beard stroking.

"Right then men. Here's the amended plan for phase 1." Freeman said, revealing the basic points. The officers agreed on the actions and after the final solution was thrashed out, Freeman concluded the meeting with his final statement.

"Whilst the first landing party is being unloaded, we'll launch the motor whaler, and go round the other end to do a quick survey. We'll re-embark the ship when she comes to our end. So lets go for it men."

John arrived at the pile of gear and huddled men, to find Clarke writing onto a clipboard.

"What's the delay 2nd?" he asked, looking up from his board.

"Another change of plan. Get the men below for some grub. We won't be needed for another hour or so. I'll tell you the news later."

Clarke dismissed the men amid a muffled cheer, who left their gear exposed to the elements.

"Better get this gear under wraps before they get below." John ordered, then went back to his cabin.

He was making his final drawings and calculation when he felt the ship tremble and instead of a steady up and down motion, she started to lurch and roll badly from side to side.

'I'll bet its nice and warm down in the engine room now the boilers are flashed up' he whispered to himself, shuddering at the thought of going on the icy decks again so soon.

A hurried knock on the door interrupted his thoughts.

"Yes?" he asked angrily.

"It's me, Baggs!" came the reply.

"Come in steward. What's the problem?"

"Can't 2nd. I'm covered in snow, but everybody is waiting for you on the port ladder."

"Cripes! Where's the time gone?" John gasped, looking quickly at his watch.

"I'll follow you out steward!" John replied as he hurriedly climbed back into his heavy outer protective clothing. He put his heavy boots on, stepping out of his cabin door and shutting it quietly for fear of waking his sleeping cabin mate.

"Where've you been 2nd? Get over the side and join me and the others in the launch!" Freeman screamed.

John saw men and equipment being transferred onto the berg from an earlier trip clambering into the launch that was behaving like a yo-yo, in the sea swell.

He looked behind at the receding spectacle of the ship as the launch sped away, and saw that the acquired ice plug was like a baby whale close by its mother.

"We'll have to take that growth of ice into account Frank! " he said to Chapman pointing to the offending ice.

"Yes. It looks big, but most of it will be sheared off when we hit the berg and emerge from the water." Chapman replied, crossing his forehead.

"Hopefully it will drop off. But the way I see it, the real worries come threefold." he added.

"Stow it chief and come over this side to see our target." Freeman said crossly as he too was worried with what he saw.

The launch had come around to the weather side of the berg, with the sea making the flimsy fair weather launch bob up and down like a cork. The high sea-swell raised them almost high enough to see over the lower ridge of ice, then down enough to see the so-called nose.

"White did himself proud. Its just as he drew it." Lovatt observed gladly, noticing the difference in wave height.

"We're too low to attempt a landing this side, and will stand off until the ship arrives." Freeman said, instructing the launch cox'n to stand off the dangerous ice.

Freeman, Lovatt and Chapman were scanning through their binoculars, every which way over the berg, until the sound of the ships siren announced its arrival.

"Keep her off! Keep her off! Stand off, man!" Freeman shouted, waving his arms frantically as the ship was turned slowly towards them.

John saw that the wake was almost full length of the ship and that the bow started to move away from them.

"She's reversing and turning away captain!" he shouted.

"Thank god! I thought he was wanting a second bite of the cherry with my ship." Freeman said hoarsely, then ordered the launch to go back alongside the ship.

John clambered back on board the relative safety of the ship, breathing a sigh of relief.

'*Home sweet home!*' he muttered.

"Aye I'll second that, John!" Chapman said in total agreement, climbing up and over next to him.

"When you get yourself organised John, come and see me in my cabin." Chapman said quickly, following John up the Jacobs ladder.

John and his team had finally landed on the berg and stood on the powdery snow of the berg listening to his men cursing and swearing as they worked on their tasks. He watched the ship slowly disappear out of sight with only a smudge of smoke curling itself around the peaks of ice.

It was a tap on his shoulder that brought him back to reality.

"2nd. Is it all right if we have a breather now?" came a voice from behind him.

He looked around and found one of his stokers peering into his face.

"Yes. And get a blower on the go. We need to keep warm too." John replied.

"Engineer Grey! I've been working out some of the logics needed to solve our particular situation." a scientist announced, striding over to him.

"Let me see. You are Mr Langley. Yes?" John asked, trying to remember the man's name.

"Yes, but please call me Peter, it's easier." The man replied.

"Okay, Peter it is. We've got about two hours daylight left I shouldn't wonder. Lets have a quick brew up and get some heat, you can feel free to enlighten me on your findings."

"The conditions on these bergs are treacherous and mostly separate from the rest of the weather conditions, as it creates its own mini weather system. I agree that a hot drink would be most beneficial." Langley agreed with a smile.

John and the scientist joined the men and huddled around the fiery nozzle of a blower.

"Okay men, listen up!" John announced.

"I'm going to split you into two groups, so who's the senior deck hand?" he asked.

"Me 2nd. Leading seaman Kirk!" was the swift reply.

"No I am. Bosun's mate, Leading seaman Jones." came another.

"Leading seaman Kirk and Leading stoker Dawes will lead team Bravo. You Jones, and you Leading stoker Baker, will lead team Charlie. Mr Langley will be in charge of team Bravo, so listen to his instructions carefully. Team Charlie come over here to me."

After their break, John and his team hacked, scraped and shovelled the ice to make a giant groove into the berg. The men had their donkey boilers flashed up to provide the steam hoses and thermal lances which they played over the ice to melt it, whilst others were rubbing it smooth as glass. This went on for hours, before the scientists team met up with John's team at the middle of the man made groove. Everybody greeted each other boisterously, admiring their handiwork and bickering in good fun about who worked the hardest or did the best.

John and the scientist walked the entire length of the slipway, taking calculations and measurements of ramps, cambers and anything else they were concerned with.

"Your exped team have constructed some sort of camp, maybe we can use it to shelter in overnight, Peter?" John asked.

"Yes! We've set up our camp overlooking the targeted area

for the ship, as this berg provides more answers to our intended experiments than previously hoped for.   I mean that it's so massive, probably weighing more than a couple of million tons, that its producing its own mini weather conditions. Because of it, we've no need to land on the permanent ice shelf as originally intended.   Despite our unfortunate circumstances it was an extremely lucky find. But at least it is big and strong enough to take our ship, John!" Langley said in a matter of fact tone of voice.

It was getting dark when Clarke and his team arrived, much to the delight and cheers of John and his men.

"Engineer Grey I presume!" Clarke greeted and shook Johns hand.

"Hail fellow well met, 4th Engineer!" John replied joyfully, realising that the extra men arriving couldn't have come at a better time.

When the commotion receded, John stood on a ledge and motioned the men to gather round.

"As I'm the senior officer ashore, it is the duty of the deck officers to assist me." John commenced, looking around to see if somebody challenged his authority.

"What I propose to do is that as we still have several hundred of yards of ramp to prepare before we can signal the ship that we're ready, and now that we're all together, I'll split you into two teams again and work through the night to complete what we need to do." John explained, producing a large drawing of the ramp.

"It will be watch on watch off, but each watch will be kitted out in suitable attire and warm food in their belly to do this duty. Remember you are all volunteers, so I've no reason to suppose any of you will shirk your duties. If I thought that, then I would not be here amongst you." John said with conviction, which brought a muffled cheer from the men.

"The thing is men! It looks as if Mother hen has abandoned her chicks for the night, so we'll shelter in these buildings, kindly provided by our scientist friends, but we need to construct other shelters behind the ice wall just in case some of you get caught out in the open.

You will also build heads, shelters and other such items on the plans to accommodate the donkey boilers and the like. One of the exped team will assist you when it comes to ice block or igloo constructions, as necessary." John instructed, then went on to order watch and other duties to the other officers.

"4th mate. Make sure that the watch system has the ratio of 1 sailor to 1 stoker, on a two hour watch system. Commencing right now. Also make sure that everybody gets a good measure of rum and any hot food that's on offer, before and after they go on watch. That way nobody can be accused of branch favouritism. Mr Langley the scientist will have two of his men with each watch to help and advise on the technical requirements needed, but if there's any dispute come and see me immediately." John concluded, leaving the prefabricated building to have one last look around.

The last rays of sunlight were being extinguished by the black clouds gathering above them, as the men entered their hastily made shelters, and after a body warming bowl of hot stew, everybody settled down to get as much well earned sleep as their individual watch keeping allowed.

The four officers and the scientists talked quietly, discussing their day over a magically produced bottle of brandy.

"Gentlemen! I give you a toast! Here's to the successful conclusion to Phase 1, and God speed our luck holds for a successful phase 2." John announced wearily. The others agreed unanimously.

"We'll definitely drink to that Mr Grey! And for you to know, we've already named this new invention, to always be known as 'The John Grey Ice Docking Phenomena'." Langley stated, raising his glass for the second little toast.

Soon, fatigue set in and slowly, one by one, each man nestled into his sleeping bag and slipped into the oblivion of sleep, leaving the night to the howling winds and the sub zero temperatures.

Chapter X
Ice Skating

"**M**orning 2nd! Time to start phase 2." a voice came that sounded as if someone was speaking to him in a tunnel.

John woke up with a start, automatically unzipped his sleeping bag as if to rush off somewhere in a hurry, before realising where he was and who was talking to him. The warm glow of Helena's memory vanished with his dream as the freezing cold caught hold of him.

"Oh hello Peter! What time is it? Did you have a good night?"

"It's 0600. Slept like a log, must have been that fine brandy we had last night. Today's another day, so here's some breakfast soup for you. The rest of us have got the same!" Peter said apologetically.

"Never mind. As long as it's hot and nourishing!" John sympathised, swigged his meal down before it froze up on him.

The men were packing up the sleeping bags and generally clearing away, reluctant to leave this cosy haven

"Okay then men! Lets have some hush. We've about four hours to get ready for our expected guests." John announced loudly.

"For those just coming off watch, get some food and turn in. Muster in four hours. For the rest of you, assume working party as for yesterday. 4th mate, make sure all the men are in a safe place but especially where they're supposed to be. 4th Engineer, take your men back to the lake and start draining it as much as you can with the suction hoses. You've got all the pumps now to do so. Remember! Keep an eye for the signal to clear away to safety. Peter, I need your assistance right away." John commanded.

The men stepped out into the freezing snow and commenced working furiously in the half-light that was the dawn. Whilst everyone worked, they kept an eye on the lookout and an ear cocked for the siren signal, to tell them that the ship was in sight and on its way.

"See that metal plate on your right John?" Langley asked as the men stood at the top of the ramp.

"That looks like the missing part of our ship, maybe we can salvage it and weld it back on again. By the look of the ice, the berg has grown an extra 10 feet or more to seaward."

"Yes John! It's the sea-spray crystallising when it hits the berg. I'll warrant we've got an extra few feet of ramp in our favour too. Judging by the swell and the colour of the water, it'll make the nose a good 100 feet thicker. We estimate this vast piece of iceberg weighs approx. 2 million tons. Its average height above water, apart from the 125foot peak on the other end, is at around 40 feet; therefore the depth will be on average, about 700 feet deep below the water line.

So the only damage done would be superficial and probably only to that ice plume at the entrance to the gully." Langley said, pointing to the small pyramid of ice.

"If that breaks, then we won't have anything to secure the ship to stop her sliding back again, Peter." John pointed out.

"Think positive John! This ship will clear the bend then stop nicely in the lake by the time it rattles round the groove we made. Her bows may make a hole on the far side, but at least you'll be above water to patch her up without any further mishap." Langley replied cheerfully.

"Then there's the depression the ship will slot into, Peter. I can't help thinking about how deep it was."

"Tut tut! Oh ye of little faith! All the water we used to create our ramps flowed into the hollow and creating its own lake. As you already know, this size of ice creates its own climactic conditions, enough to make the lake to freeze from the underneath and I'll wager the water is less than 1fathom now." Langley said gently to calm John's fears

"You read too much into situations like these John. Just relax and let us scientists do the worrying. Besides, its good for our field studies. Nothing to touch it!"

"Aye. I try to reason everything out, maybe that's my problem, Peter."

"In my experience, that's just what we scientists do all the time. Relax and have one of my cigarettes." Langley replied, lighting up two cigarettes, offering one to John, who took it gratefully.

The two diminutive figures of the men stood by the towering peak of ice and watched as a distant smudge of colour suddenly gave its shape to the ship, as if a curtain had been drawn back to reveal its appearance.

The wail of the siren must have been a spur to the men, who were hastily gathering up their equipment starting to climb to a higher and safer part of the berg.

John looked down the gully through his binoculars and saw the 4th and his men in position, then turned to see the ship coming straight at him.

"I make it 1100 yards now! Time we shifted to our position." Langley said anxiously.

"Yes, I'll be glad to get shot of this orange lollipop stick Peter." he replied, sticking the marker into the middle of the ramp, but smiled when he saw someone had written on the abandoned plate. 'Under new management'

He also looked at the ship through a pair of binoculars watching her progress towards him.

"Let's hope they judge the swell to lift the bow up for them, Peter. The depth of water down to the start of the nose is only about 12 feet below sea water, but her forward draught is about 14 feet." John observed.

"They must have lightened the load because we've got most of our exped equipment on the berg, as the bow markings are showing 12 feet. The swell is running at about 20knots and rising approx 15 feet. The width of the waves are roughly 50 feet and about 150 feet apart, so she will be carried up onto the ice no

problem, providing of course, she catches the first wave, John."
Langley said calmly and confidently, handing over the binoculars
for John to see.

"Judging by all the black smoke from the funnel, I'd say she's
running almost full speed. If so then we've got about 15 seconds
before they hit the ramp."

"Aye, best hold on and brace yourself." Langley replied
swiftly, sitting down on a bank of snow.

John watched the men scampering around on the foc'sle with
large wicker baskets dangling along the ships side like a string of
fat sausages.

They watched with fascination as the ship looming much
larger by the second, raced towards them.

"It looks like it's shit or bust time Peter. Either she launches
herself out of the water, skating herself around the ice tunnel
we've provided, or a dirty great bang followed by an instant
sinking of one freighter!" John managed to say despite his total
awe at the spectacle before him.

The bow lifted out of the water to expose her 'spoiler cone'
then she ploughed her way up the icy ramp with a large whoosh
and screeching metal, whistling past John's observation platform.
He was totally mesmerised at what he was seeing. A 15,000 ton
ship pushing past him with only a few feet to spare. He looked
where the ship was to go and decided that the ice alley looked
frail compared to what was about to hit it.

"Nice piece of ice craft John. The ship should go through it
like a bob sleigh landing nicely into the lake just as we planned.
Her bilge keels will act as ice skates for her to perform as we
predicted." Langley whispered in John's ear with total relief in his
voice.

They watched and listened to the bows sliding along the wall
of ice, turning the ship in an arc to the left. It started to slow
considerably so that when the stern passed him, he saw that the
propellers were still spinning.

The stern swung along the groove where the bow had gone and

with a loud 'whump', the ship slid sideways into the lake of slush. It was the roaring splash that jolted John out of his trance-like stare.

He looked along the alleyway seeing deep grooves and scars along the walls with a neat pair of parallel lines along the floor of the berg.

"I wonder if the crew liked their ice skating lessons, Peter?" John asked in total amazement.

"I've just taken several photos of the sight John. People back home won't believe me when I tell them what you and I've just witnessed. Also to record your discovery I might add." Langley said breathlessly, running around taking snap shots at all and everything in his way.

"I could do with a large drink, Peter." John said, feeling himself shivering and shaking, but not with cold.

"And me. If the ship had hit the ramp just a few feet more to the left, you and me would be playing harps now, let alone having the port anchor drop into our laps. Once the ship came ashore, it was crucial for the port anchor to drop into its target hole to swing her round."

"That's one thought to be kept at bay Peter." John said softly, realising the implications of Langley's statement.

"Come on John. If we climb up to that ridge there, we'll get a bird's eye view of the ship around this wall." Langley suggested, so both men clambered up to the ridge to look over the precipice on the other side.

"It looks as if the bow shoved most of the slush like a giant snow plough plugging the exit point John."

"The bow is wedged in but it looks like the stern is free. The bridge is clear of that ridge below the large peak. Unless we prop her up the bow will be ripped off or bent with the weight of the rest of the ship." John observed then added.

"Can we get blocks of ice to use as shoring pillars, Peter?"
"Yes. We could use about four pillars and angle them so you could get around them."

John looked at the large pad of ice stuck to the ship like a large limpet.

"But in this weather, would the metal get welded to the ice? And how do we protect the keel, Peter?" John asked in rapid succession.

"If you use those orange wicker baskets as pads for the shoring struts, put canvas or tarpaulins under her to keep the ice from forming, she'll be okay."

"Hmm. I suppose that will have to suffice then, Peter." John said, leading the way down from their lofty perch following the tracks made by the ship.

They met the others standing in a group, who were pointing to various items of interest.

"Is everybody here, 4th mate?" John asked aloud.

"What a sight, isn't she just beaut? A 15,000 ton ship ice-skating! Look at this. Just look at that!" Clarke started.

"4th! I asked if there were any casualties?" John reiterated loudly.

"Only 1 man killed." Clarke replied casually.

"What happened 4th! I thought we had covered all the safety angles?" John shouted angrily at the man.

"We had 2nd. But we didn't take into account falling ice boulders when the ship landed. It was like an earthquake where we were positioned. But an able seaman got drowned when the ship swiped most of the oggin from the lake onto his position. We've a few men with minor injuries but otherwise, everything is okay." Clarke explained slowly.

"Thank you for that, 4th. I want the rest of you officers to give me your reports!" John ordered sharply.

He heard each officer give their reports, reminding them to give brief technical details only. Then gave orders for the men to shore up the ship.

"2nd Mate, 4th Engineer, accompany me to the other side of the ship closest to the ice cliff." John requested but was more of an order to them.

When they arrived John looked around to survey the area.

"We need an access on the port side. As the bridge deck is level with a large shelf we can make a gangway over it, and cut steps down the cliff to get to the bottom of the lake.

Get a landing stage constructed to take the Med ladder for'ard of the superstructure to come down the starboard side. Then get a donkey boiler on the go to create a steam hose, also the suction pumps to provide water for the ship's intake valve." John ordered to the wide-eyed officers who looked everywhere but to where John was pointing.

"What's the matter gentlemen? Haven't you seen the underside of a ship on a dock bottom before?" he asked sharply.

"Most certainly 2nd. But not one parked on a block of ice." The 2nd Mate replied.

"Strewth mate. I didn't think we'd pull it off. Now look at her. Like a Joey in its pouch!" Clarke drawled, starting to get to work on John's orders.

When the Med ladder was secured, John ascended the steps to the main deck of the ship, where he met Freeman, Lovatt and Chapman who greeted him as he stepped on board.

"Well done 2nd. We went down that alley like it happens all the time. I need your detailed report on what occurred. Have you any casualties?" Freeman asked with a smile.

"I've kept a log and all details captain. I've also provided an initial appraisal of the ship's state for the chief engineer. We have one man dead due to being drowned. I have had some shores made to prop the ship up, but you'll need to put some of the fenders between us and the ice." John replied quickly.

"What depth of lake water 2nd?" Lovatt asked.

"Practically none, as it got swept away by the ships sideways movement." John responded.

"Must have a dekko for myself." Freeman said swiftly,

"Are you coming Peter?" John asked as he disappeared down the Med ladder.

The working parties were streaming back on board to much cheer and banter from the ones who had remained on board.

The back-slapping and merriment was quickly put to an end by Brown, who told them to get off the deck and below for some food and rest.

John went to sit in the lounge with his fellow officers swapping their recent experiences, when Freeman came in followed by the two professors.

"Gentlemen." Freeman boomed.

"It looks like we've done a fair days work today. Our professors have informed me that our re-entry into the sea won't be as dramatic, but not for a while yet. So they have decided to set up camp here and be ready to re-embark when we sail again." Freeman announced, but paused for a moment and holding his hands out in front of him as a signal to stop the rapid string of questions being thrown at him.

"Let's put it this way gentlemen. The engineers have about 2 to 3 weeks to make good the hole in our side and other minor damages we suffered getting here. So as of now, and until such times we get re-supplied, everybody is on half rations.

Chief, you'll need to work out a system of heating without reducing our fuel supplies too much. I need enough fuel to get us to our next port of call and refuelling facility which is on the Falklands, calculated at some 2,000 miles from here as the crow flies." He announced

It wasn't the fact they were stranded on a large floating dry dock that silenced the officers and the scientists, but the prospects of weeks on half rations in this weather.

"Tomorrow we can start phase Three, but let's have a glass to celebrate the successful conclusion to my idea and of phase 2. Tomorrow we bury our dead." Freeman concluded.

Everybody on board had their party that night, then the men succumbing to the night. When the ships lights were switched off, it left the ship marooned in darkness, silent in her cradle of ice, being dusted by the ever-present wind stirred snow flurries.

Chapter XII
Coloured Scratches

Chapman, Langley and John walked along the ice inspecting the underside of the ship. Apart from where vast stretches of paint were stripped off by the ice when the ship had scraped along and round the ice tunnel, the side plates looked good in John's eyes.

There were minor damages such as a few rivets missing, but the joggles seemed watertight. The bilge keels were good and all holes that should be there were okay.

"The hull got a good scraping, but the only big problem we're left with is how to fix such a large hole with suitable metal. The spoiler nose cone will be easy to weld back on. But how to re-rivet the side plates, that's my big question Frank?"

"More to the point, where is the steel coming from? We'd have to remove an entire bulkhead to patch this up, and that's only the half of it."

"I suppose we could salvage the one we lost. Its stuck in the ice over at the ramp. It may be a little bent mind you."

"Fair enough, but that only accounts for 1 plate, we'll need at least 1 more. Especially if we damage one when removing this damn ice barnacle."

"We used steam lances to cut through the ice like butter, so that's no problem Frank."

"Steam lances?"

"Yes, I saw that earlier. Peter made a steam lance to bore holes for the men to put pegs into." John said, pointing to the ropes and stays coming from the ship that had been tied to the stakes in the ice.

"See Frank? The ship is all tied up just like Gulliver."

"Steam lances! Pretty clever stuff! What temperature and pressure Peter?"

"Apparently its salt water heated only to plus 40 degrees, as the ice is over minus 20. Then it gets blasted out at approx 6 bars."

"Cuts the ice like butter does it? Wonder if it'll work on cold steel. Let's talk about that later John, because I've got one of your ideas coming into my head." Chapman laughed and gently slapped John on his back.

They walked slowly over the ice ramp, slipping and sliding as they went, making their way to the place nicknamed 'Point Grey'. Chapman stood by the dugout where the port anchor and its chain was piled up and looking at their handiwork.

"Phew John! That alley is definitely a work of art. Look at all the paint smeared on the ice, no wonder there's hardly any paint left on the ships hull. How did you work out the camber to take us round that point over there? I see that the port anchor has dug an even deeper hole."

"Ask Peter, I'm just a marine engineer. Maybe something to do with the boffins grand scheme of things!"

Chapman looked at John and chuckled, turning to Langley for his answer.

"If you look at the different coloured scratches and score marks, it should tell you how. The ship took about 7 seconds to pass this point. Then the port anchor was dropped into this hole to swing the ship round in a tighter arc, to line it up for the right hand turn. We had to do this because the berg wasn't wide enough for her to park herself athwartships so to speak. So we used the length of the berg to send her down to the wider part. Therefore when she came down the bottom slope and was about to enter the lake, the starboard anchor was used in the same way to swing her back around again instead of ramming the facing ice cliff. That was my only problem, how to stop her from ramming that cliff. The 1 fathom deep lake of slush would eventually stop the ship as she swiped round to create the port broadside, hence no water or slush starboard side." Langley admitted.

"If I remember correctly, there was a 50 foot pyramid over there. The weight of the ship probably snapped it off as she passed. This extra ice must have formed this new wall across the ramp as it's keeping the water from coming over the crest of the ramp anyway." John observed pointing to the alterations.

"Where's the plate you're on about?" Chapman asked

"On the other side of that wall. But we must be careful in case it's only water there now." John warned.

They climbed up to the top of the new wall to see the open spaces of the ocean.

"Under new management!" Chapman laughed as he saw the sign. "Who was the joker who wrote that tease, John?"

"Don't know, but it was very prophetic in its own way, Frank, as we'll be leaving our dead crewmen behind."

"That's true, but we'll have to rescue it in case it goes diving. So lets go back and put a plan together." Chapman stated, for them to make their way back to the ship.

The biting wind, with the blinding snow was hampering John and his repair gang, who were trying to clear the repair site and get it ready for work.

John went and sought out Brown who was on the main deck.

"Don't we have several rolls of canvas in the hold we can use Dave?"

"We can't touch any other cargo, only load or unload it, John. Why?" Brown asked with his own question.

"If you cover the ship with awnings or some of the canvas just like you do in the Persian Gulf to keep the sand and sun off, we could form a tent around the ship to keep the snow or at least most of the weather off." John explained then added.

"It would cut down on the snow shovelling for the crew."

"Hmmm. I'll see the captain later, he's the only one who can give such authority."

"No Dave! I want an answer now if not sooner. The longer you leave it, the worse my job gets." John said crossly.

"Oh very well then. I'll send you word." Brown conceded with a sigh.

Seeing as it was pointless working in those conditions, John dismissed his men for the day. He went to speak to Chapman about his disruption, but was intercepted by the 4th mate.

"Captain's compliments 2nd! But you're requested to report to the bridge, the chief is there too."

"Lead on 4th." John replied as he followed behind the man.

John acknowledged each officer with a nod of his head and listened to Freeman rattle out a series of orders before he saw John arrive.

"2nd. The 1st mate tells me you want to plunder my cargo of canvas. So you and your men can do a spot of camping, is that true?"

John was surprised and his voice reflected it.

"Camping? Who said anything about camping? I don't know what you mean captain?" He began, but quickly regained his composure by stating.

"I have an exposed repair site with little chance of carrying out any work on it without some form of shield or shelter. The object of my request was to get tarpaulins or canvas draped over the side, and stapled to the ice to form a shelter to work under. I.e. keep the weather off the repair area until I've plugged up that big hole in the side of your ship. The rest of the ship could also be covered up the same. That way captain, the men would spend less time on deck just shovelling snow off it."

Freeman looked as if he would explode at the condescending voice of John.

"Now look here you pip-squeak! I'm the captain here, and don't you ever forget it. Now get your men back and get that hole fixed, by," Freeman paused and looked at the ships clock.

"By 0800 tomorrow morning. If you don't I'll see you stranded on this god forsaken chunk of ice when we leave."

The other officers gasped at the thought and started to protest.

"Enough! If you carry on I'll take it as mutiny and treat you all the same as Grey!" he shouted and shaking his fist at them.

Clarke walked slowly up to Freeman poking him in the chest.

"Now look here you over-stuffed Pommie bastard. We've all

been there, so forget the fighting Navy. You're a civilian just like the rest of us now. You're just as much stuck on this raft as the rest of us whether you like it or not. The way you're working us on this ship in these conditions and on an empty belly, there'll be nobody left to sail her, and your precious cargo of canvas will end up in Davey Jones's locker like the rest of us." he shouted, then paused to get his breath back then concluded.

"Now lay off captain and give us some breathing space, or else!" Clarke threatened ominously, drawing a finger like a knife across his throat.

Before he could say any more, Brown and Comerford grabbed hold of him to restrain him from actually hitting Freeman.

Freeman saw his aggressor was restrained, extricated himself from the corner he was backed into.

"Tie him up and put him in the after cargo hold. As of now he's finished. I'll see he won't work on any ship no matter what navy it belongs to. He wont even be able to hire a paddling boat in the park when I'm finished." Freeman said indignantly.

The two deck officers tied Clarke up, but he managed to wriggle free, saying.

"I'm not staying here to be tied up like a stuffed pommie pig. I'll leave your stinking ship, but here's something to think about captain. Just one foot outside this bridge, or one foot on the deck and you're dead. I'll be watching your every move!"

Clarke disappeared off the bridge in a blink of an eye, leaving the rest of the officers looking anywhere but at Freeman.

"Thank you very much 1st mate. Now see what you started. No wonder you got passed over as captain!" John shouted angrily.

"Why can't you just tell it straight and not put fancy words around to make things out different." he added, then moved quickly off the bridge to try and find Clarke.

"2nd Engineer! Just where do you think you are going?" Freeman screamed.

"I haven't dismissed you yet, so get back in here at once."

"So bloody well sue me!" John replied continuing down the bridge ladder

The rift between the engineers and the deck officers over the next week was as cold as the weather conditions outside, with neither side wanting to break the deadlock.

The crew sensed something was up but dared not ask, nor did they get any help from the team of scientists.

"I've tried all shapes to fix that hole Frank! I can't seem to get the rivets to hold, and the metal is becoming brittle in the freezing conditions. Not only that, I need more sheet steel." John stated.

"Yes John. I know your problem, but it's all down to the captain's refusal to give you cover. Can't you build a wall to shield you?"

"The wind will only funnel along between it and the ship, Frank. Besides, it doesn't solve the problem of the boundary heating to the metal, despite the help of the steam pipes."

"In that case it looks like we'll try, or be forced to try and weld the patches on. How's the welding equipment?"

"We've only a few bottles left, because of the bow spoiler cone."

"Mmm. There is a crate of welder gas in the cargo marked for the Falklands Ship Repair yard. But as you know, all cargo is off limits."

"Despite all our recent efforts, this ship is going to perish, all because the captain won't use a few bits of cargo to save her."

"Maybe. Because we're so far behind schedule the outside world thinks we have perished anyway John."

"Is that what the captain is wishing for? Just another line crossed off the Lloyds register of ships?"

"Not if I have anything to do with it!" a voice came from behind them.

"Hello sparks! How are you keeping? Got your spares okay?" Chapman asked.

"Yes thanks chief. But I need a favour." Wallace replied.

"What can we do for you Jock?" John asked politely.

"I need to borrow a few lengths of angle iron to be made into this." Wallace said, producing a sketch from his coat pocket.

The two engineers looked at the drawing but Chapman wanted to know what the contraption was for.

"I want to remove then remount the radar dish and a spare radio on the top of this heap of ice. The radio and radar beams just bounce around the ice, going nowhere. But if I mount them above the ice, then the radio's natural propagation waves, would get us heard as far away as Singapore, let alone Cape Town or the W/T station in the Falklands." Wallace explained as he pointed above the ship.

"Sparks! If you can do that, then we'll tote your stuff up there ourselves." Chapman declared enthusiastically.

"We'll have it ready for you in a jiffy Jock. Its worth a try anyway." John agreed as Wallace went back to the ship again.

The ship was in its 3rd week on the berg and just like the barometer, the morale of the crew plummeted to yet another low, with no prospect of escaping their icy prison.

Chapman was getting deeply concerned about the fuel always freezing up, which was taking more time to unfreeze it. The ship needed to burn it in order to keep the ship warm, the galley working and to run the fresh hot water system.

Because of the lack of warmth and food, some of the crew were getting openly hostile towards the officers, especially when the captain passed by.

First of all, it was signs and gestures behind his back, then the near miss of snowballs thrown at him, until an incident involving an overhead rigging failure.

Freeman was crossing over the for'ard cargo deck when there was a loud crack, like someone firing a rifle. He looked up and saw a length of rope with a heavy block and tackle swinging down towards him. It was sheer luck he slipped on the ice, for the heavy block swung through its arc and passed through the spot where his body was a split second before.

The block slammed into two deck ventilation cowlings knocking them over like skittles.

"Bastard! It's missed the bastard." someone shouted angrily. Freeman got up shakily and shouted to his unseen attacker.

"All right! I know it's you Clarke! Come out wherever you are, Clarke!" he screamed, but got no reply.

"Clarke? Is that you Clarke?" he asked again with uncertainty, but saw nobody and only heard the sniggers of the men and the rustling of the wind in the riggings.

The following day when Freeman was climbing up the peak to where the Sparkers had built an igloo as a temporary radio shack, a large ice boulder came rumbling its way down to meet him. He managed to step aside but it thumped his arm as it passed.

"Is that you Clarke? Come out wherever you are, you bastard." He shrieked.

Wallace came out of his igloo and looked down at Freeman clutching his arm.

"Did you want me Captain?"

"Is that Clarke with you sparks?" Freeman asked with clenched teeth and in a lot of pain.

"Only me here captain. Come up and see for yourself." Wallace offered.

"I'll make another visit later sparks." he replied and made his way back down the ledge that led to the bridge.

Brown came out to meet him.

"That makes it 9 incidents in 4 days 1st mate. I know its all Clarke's doing." he snarled and winced, showing Brown his injured arm.

"Are you hurt bad captain?"

"I'll survive, don't you fret. I want Clarke found and brought to me. Someone must be helping him, and I want him too."

"What would you like me to do captain?"

"Gather the men and search the ship, including the bloody iceberg. If you can find out who's been helping him he'll lead you to Clarke. Start with Grey!"

"Very well captain. I'll get on it right away."

"Do it now 1st mate!" Freeman screamed, with spittle foaming around his mouth.

Brown had the men mustered and began the search, but the crewmen were taking it as a lark.

"Here kitty kitty! Come to mama."

"Mr Bogey man where are you?" they taunted, lifting up snowballs to look under them.

"No, he's not under there either 1st mate."

"I know. He's dressed up as a snowman and we can't see him! Maybe we'll bump into him like this!" said another, pretending to bump into each other.

Brown scowled feeling exasperated at the total lack of respect the men showed for their captain.

The search lasted for several hours but drew a blank, which Brown reported back to Freeman.

"But he can't just disappear into thin air, then turn up as and when!" Freeman said, exploding into a fit of temper.

"Nobody has owned up either captain!" Brown said apprehensively.

"Nor will they man! He's been helped, but by who? Who're his friends? Find out who his close friends are. I've already said Brown, start with Grey. Have them watched, we'll soon see."

Freeman stayed in his cabin for a few days, resting and trying to figure out what had gone wrong since landing on the berg. He had Brown report to him every 8 hours to save him from leaving his cabin.

"There's been nothing! Nobody appears to be acting suspiciously, nobody has spoken out of turn either." Brown reported.

"Maybe if I put myself somewhere so he could get to me easily, and you look out to see where he comes out from. Well get him then."

"Lay a trap? You as the bait captain?"

"Yes Brown. That's what I said. Now you're getting the idea."

The officers concocted their plan that excluded everybody else, and agreed to start it in the morning.

Freeman summoned the steward for something to eat, and grunted his agreement for the steward to come in. He turned round to face the steward and found to his horror, Clarke was standing there with a loaded spear gun, pointing his way.

"Cl - Cl - Clarke!" Freeman stuttered hoarsely.

"It's like this see, you miserable excuse for a Pomm!" Clarke drawled

"I've been here all along, and know your every move."

"H - H - How? But where?" Freeman gasped.

"Now that would be snitching. So shut your snivelling furry face and listen very carefully if you know what's good for you!" Clarke said vehemently, swinging Freeman by his sore arm that landed him into a chair.

Freeman watched Clarke stand there for a moment, still trying to recover from his sudden face to face with Clarke.

"The way I see it captain. You've been way out of order, hoping to bully the rest of us officers like you've been doing to the men. Now I don't take too kindly to that. Do you realise you had a perfectly good crew until you started your performance in Cape Town.

Then you worked them all for nothing. The men don't mind half rations, providing everybody else is. You've been stuffing your face whilst we've all starved. That's stealing from your mates. Where I come from, any person caught stealing on board, gets his fingers chopped off." Clarke said as he waved the spear gun into Freeman's face again.

"Another thing. You've kept quiet about the government grant given you to take us down to the arse of the world, but that's only stealing from your country. Where do you go from there?"

"How! How did you find that out?" Freeman stammered.

"Our friendly boffins let it slip the other day when Sparks was rigging up his shack on this raft!"

"What do they know? You've no proof Clarke, and anyway, nobody will ever find out." Freeman threatened.

"Oh! How are you going to manage that captain. Just a squeeze of this trigger and your gizzards will be on the end of this harpoon."

Freeman backed away, cowering behind a pillow cushion.

"I'll have you done in before we leave here you just watch!" Freeman said with a slow nod of his head.

"Pretty brave of you, considering one itchy moment and my finger could somehow work this thing. You'd be eating cold steel for a long time, as it disappears down that cake hole of yours." Clarke said menacingly.

"You wouldn't dare. I'm the captain, and what I says goes, by the International seafarers law."

Clarke sighed shaking his head.

"From where I'm standing, you're bush tucker for the sharks that's surrounded this raft."

"What do you intend doing Clarke? Is there any way we can come up with a truce?"

"That's better captain! For a start, you'll inform the entire crew they've got full rations and that they've got equal shares in the salvage money from the cargo this crap tub is carrying!" Clarke said slowly.

"But that's blackmail Clarke!" Freeman started to protest.

"Blackmail captain? You accuse me of blackmail? A poor colonial 4th engineer of blackmail?" Clarke asked in mock surprise.

"You blackmailed us all just so that the 2nd could have a few days off to attend his funeral. Then tried to buy his idea with a couple bottles of duty free whiskey. This floating dock and where we are now, is all down to his idea. Even the boffins will tell the world about it. So how do you square the circle with that one?

135

Then of course, the sudden appearance with a 15,000 ton ship fully loaded up and ready to claim the salvage?"

"His ideas and anyone else's thought up on this ship, become the copyrights of the company. As I'm captain, they come to me as my right of command."

"What a load of roo dung. The scientists are from the international fraternity. Any creations of theirs belong to them. Lets see you lay claim to their experiments." Clarke countered angrily.

"Anyway let's stick to the point. You tell the men about their food and equal shares." he added.

"You must be off your head Clarke. Why let them have it. Besides, we've already buried quite a few of them in this ice cube we're on. We could always split it 50-50. Just you and me." Freeman said narrowing his eyes, sensing a small victory.

"50-50. you and me! So how much is that then captain? Millions or diddley squat?"

"Current ship prices and insurance, say in the region of 4 million pounds sterling. What could you use 2 million pounds on then Clarke?"

Freeman was playing his knowledge of human nature to good effect on Clarke, sensing that Clarke's greed would be his undoing.

"Jeez! 2 million smackeroos!" Clarke repeated.

"Yes Clarke!" Freeman said smoothly and quietly.

"Just think of all that lovely lolly. More money than you could shake a hairy stick at."

Clarke said, but saw the look on Freeman's face and guessing the captain's ploy, snapped out of his visions of wealth and good times.

"Okay then captain. If there's 4 million quid in the offing why can't everyone join in?"

"Don't be an Aussie fool all your life man! Think of all that money in your pockets."

Before Clarke had time to answer, the cabin door slammed open, as Brown, John, Chapman and Lovatt barged in unceremoniously.

"We've heard enough captain and we've had enough of you." Brown announced angrily.

"I'm not sure what you're saying No 1! Quick, grab Clarke. He's gone mad and needs locking up!" Freeman said quickly to grab the initiative and take charge of the situation.

"Aussie, Just give me your weapon. You won't be needing it now." John said softly and calmly, reaching out slowly, took the weapon gently from Clarke's hands.

"As senior representative of your passengers and the reason for your voyage, I intend submitting my log of experiments with the field trials obtained on this iceberg to the International Scientific Research Institute. You have no jurisdiction, nor your company any claim to them.

It is apparent you have been intent on placing this ship and all on board in deadly peril. 2nd engineer Grey's idea on using this berg as a makeshift floating dock is also recorded.

Please yourself what you do to the cargo, but I suspect it will end up like the cargo missing in the Gulf of Mexico" Lovatt said flatly.

Freeman's face went bright red as he started to pull at his beard.

"That's slander professor Lovatt. I'll get you all for this." He hissed.

"Now get out of my cabin. I'm still the captain whether you like it or not." he said petulantly

"Aye! You might still be captain, but everyone will be watching you very closely for any false move." Brown stated as the other officers stood around the cornered captain.

"Pah! You'll never command a rowing boat after this Brown. I'll see you all beached after this!" Freeman snapped venomously.

"Let's put it this way captain. When the engineers patch the ship up with all they can use at their disposal to get us re floated, and when we undock and sail from the Falklands, you'll be sailing it on your own. A modern Marie Celeste, if you like." Brown replied with matching venom.

"What do you mean by that you excuse for a 1st mate?"

"Every man jack of us will stay ashore to make other travel plans that wont include you. You get to off load any cargo you've managed to save. In fact you can have it all. The insurance money, cargo salvage, everything." Clarke said

"You lot wouldn't dare! That's more money any of you'll ever earn in your miserable life time."

"Just try us captain. Not all of us are motivated by money." Lovatt joined in.

"And by the way, we've only got about 4 days like this before the berg starts melting big time."

"4 days? 4 days? You promised me 4 to 6 weeks." Freeman shrieked.

"Even captains of ships must obey the rules of nature captain Freeman." Lovatt said with a sneer.

Freeman turned to Chapman.

"Why haven't you fixed that hole chief? I thought you said it was a straight forward rivet or welding job?"

"The facts are captain, I haven't the shelter to work under, as you've denied us the use of some canvas. Because of that, when we light the torches, they get blown out every time. The metal can't get heated for the rivets to hold and you won't let us use the welders gas from the hold." John said quietly.

"All right, all right! I get the picture. You're all incompetent fools." Freeman cut in.

The others looked at each other in total disbelief at the captain's latest outburst.

"Chief. I've had enough of this, I'm leaving to get some fresh air." Lovatt remonstrated.

"Me too!" Brown added, and both men marched out of the cabin.

"Wait for us!" John and Clarke shouted after them, leaving Freeman mouthing obscenities at the departing officers.

Chapter XIII
Spare Ribs

"The canvas makes all the difference, Frank. It has formed an ice shield for us to work under. The snag now is that we need another section of side plate." John informed Chapman, who arrived at the repair site.

Yes! We'll have to use the welding equipment, we're out of suitable rivet making material." Chapman agreed.

The only suitable sheet steel left to make such an extensive patch is probably the internal bulkhead separating the lounge from the dining room. It may be only half the thickness of the metal required for the hull, but at least it's better than nothing. That's if we're not to upset the captain any further. Any advances on that Frank?"

The captain has calmed down these last couple of days. He'll do anything now to get us afloat again. So, shall I give him the good news or would you like to, seeing as you're in charge of this repair project?"

"Let's say you pulled rank on me, and you're to tell him." John smiled and patted Chapman on his shoulder.

"Discretion the better part of valour is it John?" Chapman grinned back leaving to give Freeman the news.

"Take what you need chief. Half a ship is better than none." Freeman sighed.

"Very well captain. I'll need a dozen hands to clear away the furniture etc. I also request you organise a cargo sling to land a batch of welding equipment in the for'ard hold." Chapman said evenly.

"Welding equipment chief? To weld the side up? But we're all rivet!" Freeman asked with surprise.

"We're out of rivets and any suitable material to make more. But the 2nd will place strengthening bars to act as spare ribs. So the welds should hold out until we get to a repair yard."

"What is the plate thickness chief?"

"It's only about half an inch captain. But as long as the expansion joints perform correctly and you don't overload that hold or bump into anything, then we'll be okay." Chapman replied civilly.

"Do what you must, but just get me off this floating coffin." Freeman sighed then waved Chapman away.

Chapman nodded and went to get the much needed equipment.

"Have you checked the welds, Aussie?" John shouted over the noises of the ship.

"The microscope shows a powdery line John. I think the rods may be suspect. Come and have a look."

John went over to Clarke to look for himself, inspecting at random, marking areas on the steel.

"Get another torch flashed up and re-weld over the areas I've marked. Look at each rod before you use them. If you rub them across the palm of your hand and find crumbs, then the rod is no good." John instructed.

The men worked long and hard, creating an eerie spectre under the dimly lit canvass, as weld sparks flew like Fire-flies, around them.

The final stretch of weld had just been completed when Chapman arrived among the sweating men.

"All done John? Checked all welds?"

John looked at his watch, stood up, wiping his face with an oily rag.

"Just finished Frank. We've worked all night and the men are totally knackered" John said

"Strewth chief, we've been working like Goliahs. That's been one heck of a night shift." Clarke chirped.

"Aussie. Give the chief the scope to see how well you and Dawes have done." John asked.

Chapman looked at various places for a while, satisfying himself that the repair was perfect.

"You've done a good job men. Get some breakfast and get turned in for a few hours." Chapman announced among a loud cheer from the stokers.

"Well done!" he added, as the men picked up their gear and left the site.

"Make sure all is well in the cargo bay before you get some rest John. 4th, clear away the repair site before you get turned in as well." Chapman ordered.

"Do you require a report Frank?"

"No John. But report to my cabin some time this afternoon." John arrived in his cabin feeling totally drained of energy. But found enough to take a short shower and some coffee Dovey had brought him.

"Get me up for lunch if you please, steward. Please see that I'm not disturbed."

"Did you complete the repairs 2nd? Only the lounge is now open plan because of it."

"Repaired and inspected." John replied sleepily, and on laying his weary body gently onto his bunk, he fell fast asleep.

John was on deck later, making a detailed inspection with Clarke, but their new task was to re-ship the radar dish for the Sparkers.

"Did your temporary office work out on that ice mountain Bruce, Jock?" John asked as the two engineers stepped into the warmth of the ship's wireless office.

"Aye John, worked a treat! We had Cape Town wireless almost first shout!" Larter replied jovially.

"Jeez mate! You must've a good pair of lungs on you. Cape Town is a good 3,000 miles away." Clarke quipped.

"We're going to re-locate your gear. Come and show us where you want it placed." John asked.

"Jock. Show them what we need. I've got a radio schedule in 5 minutes." Larter ordered.

The radar dish was turning slowly now like a little key in a clockwork toy.

"That's our eyes John. We'll be able to get through the bergs' rush hour now." Clarke joked.

"You're incorrigible Aussie!" John laughed at the thought.

"Apart from checking those spare ribs again, will we have an early night for a change, John?"

"I could do with a few Barbie spare-ribs right now instead of that crap we've been served lately."

"Couldn't we all! " Larter agreed, licking his lips at the mere thought of it.

"We've a meeting in the lounge at 2000, Aussie. Our illustrious captain's giving us another pep talk." John reminded them.

"He's just like bleedin' Fagan. Always reviewing the situation. Probably trying to see what else he can screw us for." Clarke sneered.

"Now now Aussie. Control your Antipodean urges. Leave his throat alone." John chuckled.

"Let's get from here John. The thought of being near him is making my trigger finger itch." Aussie replied and leaving the top deck they went below.

With their labour done, John settled in a comfy chair in the lounge nursing a large whiskey, talking to Clarke about the day's work.

The other officers and the professors and their team were also present, talking among themselves, until Freeman marched in.

"First mate. Take this chart and spread it out." he ordered abruptly.

This order would normally be issued to the 4th deck officer, but Freeman picked on Brown in an attempt to belittle him.

Without a word spoken, Brown got slowly to his feet, unfolding the chart onto the large table.

"Now gather round everybody." Freeman ordered condescendingly.

As he leaned over to point at the chart, it rolled up quickly trapping his hand in the process, much to the delight of the various officers present.

"First mate! You've done that deliberately! Are you a total idiot? Freeman exploded.

John dug Clarke in the ribs with his elbow to stop him from laughing.

"Shhh! For God sake contain yourself Aussie, or we'll be back to square one again." John whispered.

Brown sighed, walking around gathering up several ashtrays to weigh the charts corners down.

"Thank you. That should have been done first off." Freeman said sarcastically.

"Here we go again, John. My finger's itching!" Clarke groaned.

Freeman looked with a belligerent stare at the officers gathered around the long table, then started a lengthy monologue of what had happened since arriving on the berg, winding up his speech by asking if anybody had a suggestion on how to get off.

Van Heyden stood up, unfolded a large drawing and laid it on top of Freeman's chart.

"We scientists have managed to get our ice measuring box working effectively and have built up a statistical picture of our temporary home." he began but was interrupted by Lovatt.

"It is a remnant of a huge glacier as opposed to sea ice. That gentlemen, makes a different story." He announced, then went into details about the thickness and exact composition of the berg, and, how just like solid ground, there are natural faults and fissures in the ice.

"So instead of waiting for the ice to melt as was the original plan professor, can we force an exit if we wish? And just how would you propose we do that?" Freeman responded with his own question.

"If your latest midday sun sight and calculations are correct captain, we've drifted some 500 miles north west. If that is so, then we're drifting towards an area of Sub aquatic volcanic activity of the Scotia Basin." Lovatt stated

"So? What's that got to do with the price of eggs?"

"Simple captain. The volcanic activity heats the water around it, sufficient to melt any size of iceberg long before it gets to the latitude of the Falklands. Because of that, this berg's been slowly eaten away in chunks to almost a third of its size now, which still leaves us perched on the solid lump in the middle. The waters around that area I've just mentioned will melt the lump from underneath us. Once that happens, the weight of the ship will put pressure on one of those faults and crack the ring of ice caps around us wide open, possibly fall right on top of us." Van Heyden said, joining in the discussions.

"But if that happens, we'll end up in the middle, not daring to go near any of it in case we get holed again." Freeman said with annoyance.

"Hold on captain! What say...!" John started, only to get a loud moan from Freeman.

"Not you again. Its you that got us into this trap in the first place."

John waited until Freeman finished his tirade before talking clearly and slowly.

"Judging by the scuff marks on the side of the ship where our ice cradle is holding us up, the ship is settling lower and lower down into the berg, therefore proves that our nest is getting deeper." he started.

"Well get on with it." Freeman said impatiently.

"So if we pump water into the hole and re-float us again, we could break that ice barrier and move out under our own steam." John finished explaining.

"Just like a barge in a canal lock." Lovatt added to John's explanation.

"Yes. We'd be able to test our repairs for leaks, before we did that, and see the spare ribs can take the strain of a full load too captain. If we did find a leak, we could do something about it before leaving here again." John ended.

"Checkmate captain! And he can't be fairer than that!" Clarke said laughingly, clapping his hands in approval.

"Stow it 4th!" Brown hissed, giving Clarke a withering look.

Freeman looked at Chapman for a moment, then looked down at the scientists' diagrams.

A deathly silence fell over the meeting as everybody was thinking in weighing up those possibilities. The silence was broken by Freeman's series of barked orders.

"First mate. Commence phase 3. Chief, I want main engines on one hour readiness for full steam by 0900 tomorrow morning. Professors, I want you to show me these faults as soon as it gets light again in the morning."

"Frank! The captain doesn't realise that we've got to create a dam wall on our starboard side to keep the water in." John whispered, as Freeman terminated the meeting.

"What do you mean John?"

"If we start pumping water in, it will only run off, unless we can contain it. The side-walls would have to be at least 15 foot thick and about 10 foot high to re-float us, just to hold our weight. That will take some doing and take a fair time in the process." John explained.

"Maybe so, but that's already been worked out John. My main concern is your leak test, and whether the props have been welded solid due to the cold and ice." Chapman replied.

"I've steam hosed the props, rudder and lower hull, greased all the stern glands, checked all the inlets, discharge holes, and we're in good shape considering, Frank."

"Well done John, that saves us a lot of time. I've got some fuel figures to work out, so I'll see you in the cargo bay later." Chapman stated, leaving John hurriedly.

John and some of the other officers decided to have a last drink before finding things to do, which left the now cavernous lounge-cum-dining room empty save for a few stewards.

But John went on deck for a while, watching the crew and the exped team building the required barrier John had his mind on earlier.

* * *

The bleak dawn was heralded by the noise of men and equipment moving across the now very slippery iceberg, where every footstep taken was perilous.

John was back on deck again with his repair crew, watching the new plates very closely as the level of water crept up the ships side before she started to float freely from the ice.

"Morning John!" Everything okay so far?" Chapman greeted when he arrived on the scene.

"Yes Frank. We need to totally immerse the plates to see if the upper section of it is dry. The only way to do that is to tell the captain either to start shifting the cargo or have the ship pulled over to make a 10 degree starboard list. Once it's proved dry, then the scientists can re-load their stuff on board then the stores launches re-shipped and stowed away ready for sea again."

"On my way John! Chapman replied then left.

John and his team felt every inch of weld and rivet they made, giving a cheer when they could not find a single drop seeping into the hold. He sent one of the stokers up to the bridge to tell the captain the news, which was received with equal cheer.

Chapter XIV
Logs

The explosive charge smashed the dam head away, allowing the water to flow onto the berg whilst Brown worked his men hard to get the ship into an even trim again.

The ship floated off the iceberg gently to take her first bite into the heavy swell since her icy piggy -back ride some weeks ago. With a thrum of her propellers, a puff of smoke, she set out into the wide open spaces of her natural element once more.

John stood on the poop deck looking at the rapidly disappearing pile of ice that marked the watery grave of the dead crewmen they left behind.

The ship's siren blast off a few times amid the cheers of the crew, bringing him back to reality as his thoughts of the events that took place over the last several weeks started to fade away.

"Port Stanley, look out!" he said ominously to Clarke who somehow appeared by his side.

"Little does the skipper realise it, but there's another company vessel arriving there soon. He thinks he'll have it all his own way with the Island's governor." Clarke chuckled.

"What's all this Aussie?"

"Wallace sent a mayday the day you and I went up to his little perch. He also sent a signal for the scientists, and got a message to the company agent about Freeman." Clarke revealed.

"That will put the cat amongst the pigeons. Unless you're sharp you'll get beached in Port Stanley. Up the proverbial creek Aussie!"

"No worries John! I know quite a few whaler skippers operating this part of the world." Clarke said bravely, trying to convince John of his gung-ho attitude.

"I'll be tanning myself on Bondi beach with some lovely Sheila's before you get home that's for sure!"

John looked at the thinly disguised worry on Clarke's face, but smiled.

"I like your style Aussie. Is everybody in Aussieland the same as you?"

"Apart from a few whinging Poms and the odd Abbo, we've all got the same idea. Stuff 'em and run!"

"Run Aussie? Won't your ball and chain stop you? You lot are bunch of ex-cons, I gather."

"Nah mate! That's all bunkum and rumour. We're like the Manxman, no tails but got three legs you see!" Clarke said with a smile

"Excuse me 2nd. But the 4th engineer is required on the foc'sle by the 1st mate. I'm to wait for a reply, a sailor announced as he butted into their light-hearted banter.

"It must be that ruddy port capstan John! I've a good mind to heave the ruddy thing overboard, and have done with it." Clarke snorted.

John smiled at him as he remembered just such an incident seemingly a life time a way.

"Let's both go and have done with it Aussie." he said and turned to the waiting sailor.

"Thank you White. Tell the 1st mate that we'll be along shortly."

The two engineers finished their repairs to the rogue capstan to see that Brown was satisfied with it. It was getting dark, so they returned to their cabins to prepare for supper in the new lounge diner.

"I could eat a scabby Roo between two slices of mouldy bread, with several bottles of Stubbies to finish off, John! How about you mate?"

"A nice piece of beef, preferably a T bone steak covered in buttered mushrooms with a quart of double X to wash it down, will do me perfectly."

"Sorry 2nd! It's powdered egg and pom with spam on the menu." Dovey informed, meeting them in the passageway.

"Never mind the powdered stuff. What wouldn't I give for a nice juicy fried egg, sunny side up. In fact make that several of those beauts steward."

"Sorry 4th. The skipper scoffed the last half dozen way back. So its powdered this and instant that until we get into port."

"Any chance of a juicy whale steak then steward? Got to have something to weigh my stomach down with."

"Sorry again 4th!" Dovey said as he shook his head.

"And just guess who had that stuffed down his great gob! The bearded wonder no doubt!" Clarke inferred with an exaggerated nod.

"Now, now 4th! Lets enjoy the night before we both turn to more serious things." John said, and stepping into his cabin, left Clarke to go onto his.

'Home sweet home, and all to myself!' John breathed, divesting himself from his bulky foul-weather gear, and busied himself before leaving for the lounge.

John stepped into the lounge to take his first good look around at what alterations he had made to the ship, and decided that if the ship was big enough why not make a two in one with sliding panels to separate the room again, if required.

'A little space suddenly becomes a big one, now that's worth remembering.' he said to himself, startling a steward who was just passing him.

"I, I beg your pardon 2nd?" the steward stuttered.

"Here we have a large room, not unlike the cargo hold. I had to take the dividing bulkheads to use them for our ships outer skin. Just think steward. A few, ahem, tiddly screens, as you call then, placed across the middle, you'd have the two rooms back again. But if anyone cared for a dance, just fold the screens back like a concertina again." John said with relish at his newest thought.

"Blimey 2nd! Take it easy will you. Your ideas'll be the ruin of us all before we know it!" the steward gasped in amazement, following John's gaze around the room.

"My brother-in-law runs a posh place in Worthing. He's always looking for something extra. Do you mind if I write and tell him what you've just said 2nd?"

"Be my guest steward! Maybe he'll return the favour one day."

"Thanks 2nd!" the steward replied gratefully and left John to continue his duties.

John got himself a drink from the small bar, making his way towards his allocated seat at the dining table.

'Acting 2nd Engineer J. Grey the little place card displayed. He sat down with his drink and looked round at those already at the table, each person nodding to him in recognition.

How life repeats itself. Not so long ago it was Acting 5th Engineer' he observed wryly, then felt a heavy hand on his shoulder.

He looked up to see the large build of Morris sitting down beside him.

"Good evening 3rd. I haven't had much time to see how you are. Your watch keeping in good order I hope?" John enquired politely.

"Thank you for those kind words 2nd. Yes! I should be getting my ticket endorsed again, after this trip, and its no small thanks to you."

Morris' rancid breath and his still oily face, jutting close to John made him feel uncomfortable, forcing him to move his chair away slightly.

"Thanks Morris. When I've got time, I'll go through your work along with Clarke's." John replied as Larter arrived and spoke to him.

"Hello John. You got the news from Jock then!" he said amiably but was jostled by Morris who tried to move closer to them.

"3rd engineer, if you need extra space at the table I'm sure I can arrange that for you." interceded a steward who was watching them.

"Shut your mouth steward and get our grub on the table. Some of us have watch keeping duties to perform." Morris snapped.

"Oooh, get her!" the steward replied, hanging his wrist limply.

"Does ducky wants a full plate of the crab tonight or will a few in his pants be enough!" the steward intoned with a lisp.

"Just give me my dinner!" Morris snarled.

"Take your bleedin' time and your turn in the trough!" the 3rd deck officer opposite sneered.

"Kindly serve me before him if you would steward." he added.

"And me! And me!" other voices piped up.

Morris looked round at the others with loathing.

"You don't know what its like to starve. I was in a Jap P.o.W. camp, lucky to survive I was." Morris commented.

"Swing those lamps somebody and put a sock in his mouth!" a voice shouted.

"Never mind Ken. If what's on the menu is what I suspect it is, then you can have mine." John whispered in his ear to pacify him.

"Thanks 2nd. In return you can have one of my special smokes in the bar after I come off watch!" Morris said gratefully but with a hurt look on his face.

Their first meal at sea since the berg was eventful if not a little sad, as the officers began to realise that what had happened over the past few weeks would either make or break them. Even the scientists were showing less enthusiasm to join in the camaraderie that had existed prior to their detour in the Weddel Sea.

John was puffing merrily on one of Morris's fine cigars, trying hard with the help of Clarke to keep everyone's spirits up, but it seemed like a damp squib.

Nobody appeared in the mood for a party befitting an illustrious escape, and nobody dared speak of the pending aftermath from the incident with Freeman in his cabin. Everybody on board had heard it all due to the ships tannoy system being switched on throughout Freeman and Clarkes supposed little deal. Clarke knew about the tannoy, but Freeman didn't. In the end, everybody retired early to their cabins for a fresh start on a new day.

* * *

This mood persisted for a few days more as the ship was nearing the Falklands, but instead of getting land happy again, the crew still sensed trouble.

The foghorn blasted its long low soulful warning signal as the ship crept slowly over the freezing waste of open waters, with only a half moon to offer the mariners a safe course through the rolling fog

'*I remember another night like this, better get on the bridge.*' John said quietly when he was conducting his upper deck rounds, deciding to make his way up to the bridge.

"Keep a look out port side. You should see a series of port hand buoys with flashes of white light, then two with constant red flashing lights. They're special navigation buoys." Freeman said.

"We have a steaming light appearing from starboard side!" Fields shouted.

"Very good signalman! It's probably the harbour tug. Make to him!" Freeman started

"Light on the port bow captain, and its not a navigation beacon." the lookout shouted.

"Bloody hell! What can it be?" Freeman cursed as he walked out onto the open port wing.

"First mate. Come here and help me identify this." he ordered.

"It looks like an ocean going tug captain!" Brown stated, looking through his binoculars.

"What makes you say that 1st mate?"

"The steaming lights indicate it's a tug, captain! They're the same as the ones on the starboard side."

"Very well. Get the signalman to flash him up. See what he says."

"The signalman reports two ocean going tugs each side of us captain. They are the Royal Navy tugs *Sampson* and *Delilah*." Brown revealed.

"What? Two ocean going tugs?" Freeman shouted angrily.

"Go and find out what they want."

Brown came back after a while with his report.

"It seems they were alerted ten days ago, then were despatched on a search and rescue mission to bring us back."

"Rescue us? Who asked them for me?" Freeman asked angrily.

Freeman and Brown were becoming agitated due to Fields failed attempt at speaking to the tugs by aldis and in thick fog.

"Messenger, get me the Chief Sparker!" Freeman snapped, just as Wallace arrived onto the bridge and stood by John

"What's the commotion John?" he whispered as Freeman saw him arriving.

"Ah Sparks! I have two tugs out there, see if you can get hold of them by radio, and let me speak to them, if its possible."

"Will do captain! But I need the signalman to tell them what frequency to listen out on, for me to do so." Wallace said, moving over to the signalman, before going back to his office behind the bridge.

"I've got the *Sampson* on a voice channel patched into your receiver!" Wallace shouted from the wireless office.

"Hello Sampson! This is captain Freeman of the SS *Inverary*. State your business and your intentions. Over!"

"Good evening Captain. This is Captain Gregory of the *Sampson*." announced the whistling, crackling voice of reply.

"We are in company of the naval tug *Delilah*, who you should see on your starboard side. We were despatched from Port Stanley about 10 days ago for your search and rescue. But where have you suddenly appeared from? We were given a position but could find nothing. Over!"

"Thank you for your concern Captain, but as you can see we're all right. Very sorry to trouble you! I hope to meet you for a wee dram when we dock in Port Stanley. Over!"

"Glad you're alright. We'll make your acquaintance ashore. No doubt the harbourmaster and the Islands' Governor will want a report from you when you arrive. Look forward to seeing you, over."

"Thanks for the info. Just one thing captain, how did you manage to find us? I've had no radio or radio contact for weeks, over."

"The whole world knows about you and your exploits. Your Mayday caused quite a stir, because everybody thought you were sunk in the storm or caught in the ice. Congratulations captain. See you later, Over!"

"Thank you again captain, over"

"That's a pleasure from both of us captain, over and out!" Gregory finished and the radio went silent.

"Mayday? Bloody Mayday?" Freeman shouted above the noise of the foghorn.

"Chief Sparker. Come to the bridge right now!" he shouted.
Wallace ambled through the bridge doorway into the dimly lit bridge.

"How was your patch through Captain?" Wallace asked calmly unaware of the drama unfolding before him.

"Never mind a patch through. What's this about a Mayday Wallace? I did not authorise any such signal."

"Oh that! Yes captain. That was a minor miracle and the completion of some damn hard work. We managed to get an S.O.S. through some time ago, around the time we moved the radio off the ship and up to the top of that ice cream cone. It's all in my log and it's got your signature on it to authenticate ship of origin captain."

"What? Show me your log right now!" Freeman shouted, struggling to contain himself.

Wallace shrugged his shoulders and went to get his radio log.

"And any other evidence that you've got asking for assistance." Freeman added vehemently.

Wallace came back with his operator's log, and the other logbook then opened it to the relevant pages.

"See captain! You're the only originator on this ship. Every time we send a signal you sign each one before we've sent them. That also applies to each incoming signal that we give you.

154

Including any SOS signals, which were still on your orders at the time." Wallace said, showing Freeman his operator's logbook.

"It's the law for acknowledgement of transmissions or receipts of any SOS. You always sign our logbooks at the end of every day, as a matter of course. That way you, as captain, have total control over the radio and any signal coming from us. The only occasion when that can be broken is if for any reason you are incapacitated or cannot perform your duties as captain, then the 1st mate has the honour. Or we are instructed by any of the ship owners that may be on board at the time." Wallace explained.

Freeman's eyes scanned the logs and found nothing that he could find fault with.

"You must be keeping other logs in there Wallace! These are not the ones I see every day. I did not authorise any mayday signal." Freeman insisted.

"I don't know what you mean captain. Your signatures are on these logs for all to see." Wallace said guardedly, and saw John standing a little way off.

John just shook his head and tapped his head pretending to scratch the side of his temple.

"Oh come off it Wallace! You've heard of the double entry expression used by a bent accountant, yes? You've got a double entry log somewhere. Now fetch them to me. They belong to the company, and as I'm the company round here, they belong to me."

"That's where you're wrong captain! Wallace started to shout as his temper began to rise.

"The log belongs to Marconi and the Admiralty in Whitehall."

"You what? Admiralty? Nonsense man. Everything on board this vessel belongs to the company." Freeman bluffed.

"Except for the scientists and their equipment, captain!" John interceded.

"So think again."

Freeman spun on his heel and glared at John.

"Grey, just who the hell asked you to poke your nose in. And what are you doing on my bridge. Get off it at once and don't come back." He screamed.

"Can't do that captain! Company rules and all that." John replied in a small voice, and just stood there.

Freeman turned round to Wallace again.

"What are you standing there for? Go fetch me those logs right now." Freeman screamed and stamped his foot to emphasise the word 'now'.

"I can't captain. They're in the office safe and it's only the Senior Radio Officer who keeps the combination." Wallace replied simply, standing his ground.

Freeman was beside himself with rage now, ranting and raving about this and that.

"Just wait until we dock! I'll have your job and guts for garters mark my words. If I don't, then the gentlemen at Lloyds certainly will." he promised with an exaggerated nod of his head.

"Do you realise that it costs the company several thousands a day, just for 1 tug to stand by or come and look for us. But what's money to you Wallace? You've got two and god knows how many more cowboys riding over the horizon to try and put a line on us!" Freeman continued in his rage, as Brown, John and Wallace stood in silence listening to him slowly running out of steam.

"Pilot waiting to board now." Fields announced when he arrived onto the bridge.

"Tell him to come aboard. But we're not quite ready for entering harbour." Freeman said with a sigh and went over to the chart.

"Good evening captain! Welcome to Port Stanley. I'll take the conn. But I need you to observe each order and take a plot as when we enter the harbour."

"Hello pilot! Do as you must!" Freeman acquiesced then ordered Brown and John down onto the foc'sle to take charge.

"He's gone right off his rocker now 2nd! I shan't be surprised if the Doc forces him to take a few weeks off ashore to let someone else sail the ship back to Cape Town." Brown muttered to John as they went swiftly onto the for'ard deck.

"I can't understand why he needed a pilot, when the Boson's been in and out of here before. And I have, come to think of it." John replied.

"It's his and my first time in these waters. Anyway it's the protocol that has to be followed."

"Let's get on with it then 1st mate." John said as he left to stand on his usual spot at the back of the foc'sle, yet out of the sailor's way.

The ship passed the outer breakwater walls that stretched out from the land, like a giant crab's claw, as she entered the sheltered waters of the harbour.

John was looking everywhere trying to remember various objects from the first and last time he entered the place.

He saw the Super Floating Docks, the Harbourmasters block, the warehouses, with the cranes standing like statues on the dockside. He was not unduly surprised about the almost doubled increase in size of the dockyard and the amount of ships tied up alongside. His biggest surprise was to see that one of the harbour breakwater walls was part of a runway that stretched right back behind the enclosed dockyard. When the ship had cleared the end of runway, he watched as an aircraft arrived to land neatly onto it. *'I wonder who the Ship Repair Manager and the Harbourmaster are these days'* John said quietly, reflecting on his last visit.

When the ship passed the SFD'S and turned round to tie up, port side, he noticed that there were now 4 of them, with two welded together forming one big one, and a bit of a tanker sticking out on the ends of them.

The ship tied up and the gangway was lowered onto its deck to the strains of a military band, with several people on the jetty anxious to come on board.

John decided that he'd stay on deck for a little while and have a smoke before going back into the lounge to join the circus of the welcome party and media. This was not his scene, so he took the long route via the bridge to his cabin in the hope he would not be noticed.

"There you are 2nd!" Dovey said delightedly.

"Everybody's waiting for you to come and meet their lordships and the Islands Governor. Come on and I'll help you get your glad rags on. Mustn't keep your public waiting!"

"Thank you steward, but no thanks. I'm not available. I'll have some supper here and maybe get some sleep. I'll probably go ashore tomorrow when its light!"

"Suit yourself! But don't say I didn't warn you! I'll have some supper brought up just as soon as we get the fresh supplies on board. In the meantime, its ships biscuits and the dinner time coffee grounds!"

"Whatever Steward. Have a good time ashore, there's a nice pub down in the town, or in the Harbourmasters accommodation block!" John informed.

"You've been here before have you 2nd?"

"Yes steward, many years ago now." John sighed. looking out of his darkened cabin porthole towards the bright lights of the surrounding dockyard and the SFD's.

He stood there for quite a while, whilst his memory conjured up faces, places and events of what seemed a lifetime ago.

It was a gentle knock on the door that brought John back to the present, when he turned around he saw Sinclair, Larter and Wallace come through the door.

"Hello John! We've decided to come to hide in here with you. We've got some fresh food and the appropriate supplies for our own little party, what do you say?" Larter said quietly, as Sinclair stacked fresh sandwiches and booze onto the table. Wallace slid the little sign over that said 'OUT' and bolted the door behind him.

"Shh! Keep quiet for a moment. Everybody from the lounge is on the move ashore. Wait until they've gone." Wallace whispered, and hushed the men to be quiet.

The ship was now safe and secure in harbour, with its engines off and its crew ashore, and was settling down for a short but peaceful rest from its icy ordeal. Not even the little party in John's cabin woke her slumber through the night.

The friends ate and drank until the early hours of the morning before they too decided to sleep a sleep of the dead. Or until some fool came and disturbed them.

Chapter XV
Big Surprise

An insistent knocking on his cabin door woke John to the rigours of the day, stumbling across his cabin to open the door.

"There you are John!" Chapman said cheerfully.

"Not only were you missed, but you also missed a good bash back at the Governors place last night. Pity you never came, as you would have been feted all night. But still, there's always another time when the shipping bosses get here soon."

"Not my scene Frank! I had a quiet drink here with Larter and Sinclair. Old pals and all that, you understand. But come in and tell me what's up."

Chapman came in, switching the light on.

"I need you to help me in the engine room office in about an hour from now. After." Chapman looked at his wristwatch.

"Breakfast. It's now 0700 John." He added.

"What no rounds Frank?"

"No! The ship's to be unloaded and ready for a 1100 hours cold move into that massive floating dock behind us."

"So we'll be living in the Harbour Masters' accommodation block then."

"Yes, but only for a couple of days." Chapman said, then stopped in surprise.

"How do you know that John? Unless you've been here before."

John looked out his porthole at the now empty floating dock.

"Yes Frank, something like that." he said softly with a smile, deciding to change the subject.

"What news about Morris and Clarke. Do we get to keep them or what?"

"Don't know. But lets hope we get replacement stokers for the ones we lost back there. Brown's getting a couple of sailors for his replacements. Anyway, we'll know soon enough when Belverley and Company gets here."

"The only person to be sorted around here should be Freeman." John stated, and commenced getting dressed.

"Amen to that. The only thing there is that we'd have to wait until his relief arrived. Now that means money lost, especially if the ship has to wait any longer here instead of Cape Town." Chapman concluded, as John completed his transformation from a sleeping man to a smart ever-efficient 2nd engineer.

Both men stepped out of the cabin and made their way to the still cavernous lounge / diner.

"Morning Chief, 2nd!" Dovey greeted.

"Thought you went ashore so I didn't bother with the food you asked for. I went ashore and found that pub you told me about." Dovey said, escorting the officers to the table.

"Hope you had a good night, steward. What's for breakfast?" John asked, sitting at his usual place.

"You 2nd, will be having a full English breakfast." Dovey said, placing a plate full of hot food before him.

"Get that down you. Bon appetit!" Dovey said then left.

He looked at this feast and took little time to devour it hungrily. He swigged the last of his tea and lit his after breakfast smoke.

"Morning John!" Larter said with a smile, when he came in for his breakfast.

"Hello Bruce. Fresh food for breakfast this morning!" John greeted, licking his lips.

"What's on the menu steward?" Larter asked, peering at John's stained breakfast plate.

"You've got porridge, then kipper." Dovey replied, laying Larter's plate in front of him.

John smiled at the complete change of menu.

"Bon appetit! Bruce." John said jovially, at Larter's look of disappointment.

Chapman had already had his breakfast earlier but remained seated, drinking a cup of coffee, relaxing and reading a paper, when John joined him.

"Newspapers. Now there's a novelty." John quipped, for Chapman to look up.

"Yes John. It appears there's a big storm looming, and I don't mean the weather. Look at what the papers are saying and look who's causing it." Chapman said, showing John the front page and the headlines.

'*Captain to face corruption charges! Eminent Scientists to prove allegations!*'

John just stubbed out the last of his cigarette then sat down with a fresh cup of coffee the steward brought over for him.

"Oh well. Better get things sorted before we go." John said simply.

Morris, Clarke and the other junior engineer officers filed in for their breakfast, greeting Chapman and John as they passed.

"Don't get too comfortable gentlemen, I'll expect you lot down in the engine room in about 15 minutes." Chapman announced, picking up his cap.

"Coming on deck for a bit of fresh air John?" he asked, whilst buttoning up his white overalls.

John nodded his head and followed Chapman out onto the deck for a quick breather before going down into the stuffy boiler room.

"This place has changed quite considerably since I first came here Frank. But I'll tell you more about it later once we've got a little more time."

"Fair enough John, lets go." Chapman said, leading the way.

"Gather round men!" Chapman called, as he arrived in the boiler room.

He announced the docking and the work to be done for it. Then went briefly through the work facing them during the time the ship was in dock, with the eventual prospects of preparing for sea again. His news about getting extra men on board was greeted with a cheer, for the men to finally disperse to their allocated tasks.

John helped Chapman with the drawings and the amendments affecting the work done on the berg. Then produced a polished handwritten report.

"This is for the Dockyard Engineer, if you care to read it first Frank! Its all there warts and all." John said evenly.

"Oh right! Thanks John. I've got mine buttoned up and ready too." Chapman said appreciatively.

"But how did you know he was due to visit us so soon John!" "Your cousin Happy Day should have clued you up on that score Frank. Let's put it this way. Ship repairs at sea, always gets inspected thoroughly in case they contravene shipping laws or whatever. As this place is tailor-made for such an inspection, it seems to fit." John replied succinctly.

Chapman looked at John.

"Ain't that the truth!" he agreed with a nod.

"He's meeting us in my cabin very shortly before the ship is moved."

Both men moved quickly, making themselves comfortable in Chapman's cabin, making small talk when a loud knock n the cabin door suggested that their guest had arrived.

"Hello Frank." the man greeted and shook Chapman's hand, then turned around to look at John.

"Hello John! How the devil are you, as if I haven't heard!"

"Jack Cunningham! Why you old dog!" John said with surprise and a big smile, and stood up to shake Cunningham's hand vigorously.

"Congratulations on your promotions Jack! Must have a drink to celebrate those, some time." John nodded at Cunningham's gold rings on his jacket cuffs, and the silver oak leaves on his cap.

"That's a promise John." Cunningham said enthusiastically.

"I take it you two know each other then?" Chapman asked with equal surprise.

"We go way back. Barbados wasn't it John?" Cunningham said, smiling at his old friend.

"Yes! That was some voyage! But how have you come to get

this post Jack?"

"I've been here for a couple of years now. Remember Chief Gregson?"

"What Jim Gregson? Yes of course I do. Why?"

"He had a very nasty accident on one of the SFD's. As the local hospital wasn't able to help him much, he was flown to Cape Town, but died shortly afterwards. I had just been confirmed as Chief on the *Tobermory Bay* when Belverley and Co decided that I would take over." Cunningham said at length.

"How sad! He was a good chief too!" John said glumly.

"Did you know Jim, Frank?" John asked.

"No! But I met his brother on the *Inverlochy*. He's now 1st mate on it." Chapman replied.

"How long is the duty here Jack, if you've been here two years?"

"As long as you want. I like it here, so I've brought all my family down and have now settled here. There's my house over on that hill." Cunningham said, pointing to a brightly painted crofter's cottage, sitting on top of a hillock.

John and Chapman looked out over the dockyard to the distant cottage and nodded their approval.

"Nice and snug in these cold places Jack?" Chapman asked

"Yes and lovely and cool in the summer. At least the Falklands idea of a summer!" Cunningham added. Their conversation progressed on a personal level until Chapman suggested that they get on with the task in hand in view of the docking down.

Cunningham smiled at Chapman then commenced his meeting. He went through the plans, the altered drawings and John's report.

"It appears that everything is in order Frank. John's reports are comprehensive enough for me to recommend any future repairs." Cunningham stated with satisfaction.

"Just two items though. Your re-inforced bows will have to be replaced. Any stores required by will be ready before you leave the dock again. If we get ashore now before the gangway is taken off, we can re-convene in my office. Bring some personal effects with you as it's a long trek from ship to your temporary cabins ashore." Cunningham advised.

The 3 men walked over the gangway to where Cunningham had his jeep waiting for them.

"Here you are, my personal transport! Its jeep country around here and only the Governor gets to use a proper car." he explained.

"It's better than walking anyway, Jack!" John enthused, for he knew just how far it really was from the berth to the office.

While the jeep sped along, Cunningham pointed to several changes to the place, for John's benefit, until they arrived at the large floating dock that was sunk and ready to take their ship.

John stepped out of the jeep and went over to look at the SFD.

"She's much bigger than I thought, but still the same design Jack?"

"Yes John. Jim Gregson tried to make it a permanent dock with the end blocked off and a caisson on the other one, just like a real dry dock. He altered the pump system but one blew up right in front of him and made a big hole in the side of the dock wall, hence that big patch you see." Cunningham said, pointing out the area for John to look at.

"Jim was standing over it at the time and caught most of the blast." Cunningham said in a matter-of- fact way.
John looked at Cunningham and then at the side of the dock.

"I'll have to remember this Jack. Maybe I'll get a few things altered and dedicate them to Jim's memory." he said sombrely.

"You know of these SFD's, John!" Chapman asked, listening intently to the conversation.

"Know of them? He practically invented them. Ask Happy Day and Superintendent McPhee in Gib!" Cunningham replied on John's behalf.

Chapman looked at the SFD's, scratching his head.

"He did say something about that, but I wasn't quite clear of what it was, until now." Chapman revealed, looking down again at John.

"You did all this?"

John just shrugged his shoulders, tipped his hat back onto his head and smiled.

"Only helped to get them down here Frank, that's all!"

"He has a habit of understating certain things, Frank". Cunningham laughed, patting John's shoulder.

"But then, how do you know Happy Day, Frank?" It was Cunningham's turn for surprises.

"Why, didn't you know Jack? Happy is only Franks first cousin!" John stated, answering for Chapman.

"Well blow me down! It's a small world all of a sudden. Here's you and me, meeting up after all these years. Frank knowing Jim Gregson's family and is belonging to Happy Day. It's like a reunion of sorts." Cunningham said with an infectious smile at the other two.

For the rest of the afternoon, the three men went back through detailed drawings and the store requirements until they were satisfied.

"Right then gentlemen. That's all the business done. Unless you have any other major repairs to be done, we can adjourn until you sail again. Incidentally, your stokers will only be doing a minimal amount of work, mostly fire-watching and the like. So have a nice rest when you can. John you know where the officers cabins are, so I'll get one of my men to bring some of your personal gear ashore for you." Cunningham concluded, standing up shaking the departing friends hands farewell.

"We'll have a drink, probably tomorrow, once I've got your ship docked and the tanker replenished and away."

"So long Jack. See you soon!" the two officers vowed, walking slowly towards their accommodation block.

* * *

They eventually arrived into the block, deciding to go into the NAAFI for a quiet drink before evening dinner, when a tall, immaculately dressed officer came over to them looking into John's face.

"Sorry to intrude, but aren't you John Grey?" the officer asked politely.

"I am, who are you and state your business. " John said gruffly as he didn't like being stared at.

"I'm Commander Richardson, off that destroyer over there, the *Challenger*." Richardson said, nodding to the powerful looking warship tied up opposite them.

John looked at the man for a moment then out to the ship, but shook his head.

"My apologies Commander, I cannot place you as readily as you can me." John admitted.

"You were the Engineer on one of the SFD's I sailed down here from Gib, quite a few years ago now. The Captain was Tomlinson, Joe I think his name was. Yes that's it, Joe Tomlinson."

John looked up at the man and finally recognising him.

"Of course, now I remember. How are you Commander! How's your diving pal." John asked, clicking his fingers to help him recollect the person.

"Officer Morris wasn't it?" John asked in triumph.

"Yes that's him. Haven't seen him since though. Anyway how are you Grey? Care for a pink gin or something? Who's your friend, would he like one?"

"Commander Richardson, this is my chief engineer, Frank Chapman. That's our ship in the SFD that you and I sailed on " John stated, introducing the two men.

"I'll have a large whiskey and soda if you please." John requested and for Chapman to make his.

Richardson went over to the bar and told the steward to bring over some drinks to their table.

"It seems that today was a 'Big surprise' day for us all Commander, with you making it the latest. Here's to you and your ship!" John said, raising his glass in a toast to this impromptu meeting.

Two other Naval officers, and another Merchant officer came over and joined the table, and before long the social intercourse between the two maritime services were enjoying a good chin-wag and exchanging notes or ideas on various maritime themes.

The party lasted all evening until it was time for everybody to return to their respective ships or cabins. Tomorrow would be another day in each Mariners life.

Chapter XVI
Evidence

The following morning, John was ready with his borrowed fishing tackle, making his way through the reception area of the block.

"John, you can forget that. We've been ordered to attend a hearing up at the Governors place. It seems that Belverley and Co, have taken umbrage on what our scientists have said in the local and world press." Larter said tensely.

"Whatever for Bruce?" John asked in puzzlement.

"Freeman has certain allegations to answer to, that the press demand to know, presumably. I was hoping to romance a certain stewardess off the tanker that's unloading behind us." Larter informed him.

"But I was asked to arrange this Officers meeting instead." He added.

"Shades of Bermuda, here we go again Bruce. And here's me thinking this particular voyage, you know, a quick trip across the pond and back, was easy as pie. Silly me!" John said sarcastically, nodding his head in agreement.

"I've spoken to everybody now, but I haven't seen Aussie Clarke since we arrived. Any idea where he is John?"

"He did mention something some time ago about knowing a lot of Japanese and Norwegian fishing boats and whalers. I noticed a few of them further down the harbour, just below the dockyard. I'll send Dawes down to see if he's there. But can't you phone through the dockyard exchange system to save time?" John ventured.

Larter nodded then went swiftly over to the phone booth, whilst John went to look for Dawes. They met up again with Larter stating that Clarke had been on board one of them and was now on his way."

Clarke sauntered into the reception hall looking as if he didn't have a care in the world, still making his jokes and wisecracks.

"Jeez, you Pomms have a nasty way of putting a man off his stroke! I was on a winning streak with a Sheila on one of those whalers who I had met in Japan years ago! An old flame if you like!" Clarke moaned.

"Ever heard of a whinging Goliah Bruce? Well we've certainly got one here." John chuckled.

They left the building and caught the dockyard ferry that would take them by sea, directly to the Governors special landing jetty that was next to his offices.

They arrived amidst a throng of cameramen and TV reporters who followed their every footstep, demanding answers to their questions. Neither of the officers spoke, shoving their way past them.

"They think they own the place. Ignorant bastards!" Clarke growled, shoving a reporter out of the way who landed in a ditch.

"Easy Aussie! Keep your powder dry and stick with us." John whispered, when they arrived into the calm and sedate Governors building.

As the senior officer, John led the way into a large hall where they recognised several familiar faces, with quite a few they didn't. Sinclair came over quickly and ushering them into a side room.

"In here John, and you others. Be quick!" he whispered.

They stepped into a large room that was almost akin to a courthouse, with the Governor, lord's Belverley and Invergarron and others they did not recognise.

"Thank you for joining us gentlemen. Sit over there. Now we can begin." Belverley said crossly, pointing to a row of seats that had the rest of the officers sitting there.

"See, I did tell you Bruce. Barbados all over again." John whispered.

"Yes, except that it's not Trewarthy this time." Larter whispered back from the side of his mouth.

The inquest took several hours, with so many twists and turns in the proceedings, that even a professional sleuth would be hard pressed to guess the outcome.

A procession of bodies, statements, and evidence, was produced before the Governor stood up to give his pronouncement.

"My lords, Gentlemen of the court, officers of the shipping line, eminent Scientists and those who bear witness to this inquiry." the governor started pompously.

"It is the opinion of this special inquiry that whilst there has been a certain amount of a temporary lack of judgement, or a temporary loss of faculty by captain Freeman, it never-the-less does not excuse him of his misconduct.

Also in view of the overall facts, in that several officers and crew of his ship mentioned cases of incompetence or lack of command by captain Freeman, we also recognise the need of the shipping company.

Captain Freeman will remain in command of his vessel. The company will also retain the copyrights to anything derived from the vessel, but not to the extent of the work carried out by the International Scientific group."

"In other words John. A total whitewash!" Larter whispered.

"Tell me about it!" John nodded slowly.

"In regard to the two engineering officers. The Shipping Board of Governors do acknowledge a certain amount of undue stress was imposed on them by their captain. And as these officers were instrumental in returning the ship back safely, those officers will remain in the service of the company to carry out their duties as normal, as befitting their rank.

Unless there is anything else to discuss, I now conclude this inquiry." the Governor said before gathering up his sheaf of papers and leaving the room.

Clarke looked round to John.

"Who let the bulls in here? The dung is everywhere!" he shouted.

"Shh! Aussie, for god sake shut it!" Chapman whispered.

"You've still got your job, so be thankful." Wallace growled, looking ominously at Clarke, but it was too late.

"Bullshit! What a cop out! Freeman tried to stitch us all and you bunch of idiots fell for his truck load of shit!" Clarke shouted angrily, standing up to wave his fist at them.

John and Chapman stood up to grab him by the shoulders to calm him down, but he managed to get free.

"Freeman offered me £2million to keep quiet about the insurance money he was going to collect." Clarke shouted, which had a lot of angry and embarrassed faces looking back at him.

"Officer of the court. Get this man removed!" Belverley shouted angrily.

"Never mind me! What about Freeman! He's done this before and thanks to you stupid bastards; he's gotten away with it again. I smell rats all over this rotten corrupt place." Clarke remonstrated before he was frog-marched from the room.

"Lock him up until he cools down!" Invergarron snapped angrily

"Then put him back onto his ship where he will remain until the ship sails."

"C'est le vie!" Larter muttered, as the scrum of reporters gathered round Clarke being taken away.

"Out of the frying pan and into the fire!" Wallace said ruefully.

"Don't worry Jock! He's got the press on his side now they sense something. Providing they print something near the truth." Larter said knowingly.

"They've usurped your ideas John, just as Freeman said. But I fancy it will cost the company dearly because the scientists have launched a formal complaint to the Nobel Prize people and the Universal Scientists Institute. Belverley and Co will have to fork out millions to contest those people." Chapman said stoically as the commotion out in the foyer started to get louder.

Freeman came over to John and his friends, with a wicked smile on his face.

"See Grey! I told you everything belongs to the company, and me. Thanks for making me rich!" Freeman gloated, rubbing his hands before he left John, who was prevented by Larter's intervention, from thumping Freeman there and then.

"Come on John! For god sake, calm down, he's not worth it. Let that idiot think he's won, we've got plans to prove otherwise!" Larter said, forcibly taking John away from the room, followed closely by Sinclair.

The islands were rife with rumour and counter rumour. The officers and crewmen were harassed everywhere they went, and hounded from pillar to post by the media. Nowhere was sacred or safe for them to hide or get some privacy, not even taking a shower or a meal.

These pig-ignorant, self-important people, who laugh at any crumb of decency, are prowling around preying on the men at will. Clarke and John got particular attention, whereas Freeman and the scientists were left in comparative peace.

John decided to go back to his cabin on board, as did some of the other officers. Sinclair was given special instructions that nobody was to come on board unless they had business to conduct. He and his men were kept busy repelling the media hordes, even from trying to board the ship from its outer side. The culmination of this came when the UK Parliament sent the Foreign Minister down to sort it out. That meant even more unwelcome pressmen who came in their droves from the nearest country of Argentina.

Whilst the world press was having a ball, everybody else felt used and totally emasculated by not being able to get rid of them. Such is the their power, or their 'Freedom of the Press', nobody can or dare legislate against them. They know it full well, that's why they act the way they do.

After a day of discussions and a brief news bulletin, the Foreign Minister declared the incident was over and everybody should get back to normal, including Clarke.

This meant that the ship was to sail out of port ready or not, adding the extra burden on the engineers to get the ship seaworthy.

This was done in double quick time, to save further embarrassment to Belverley and his Board of Governors.

Chapter XVII
Leaks

"Single up! Let go for'ard. Starboard 20. Half astern!"
Freeman ordered, as he watched his ship move away from its berth.

"Get those fenders port side aft! I don't want to paint the jetty with my ship!" Freeman shouted into his megaphone, as he pointed animatedly towards the deck crew.

John looked around him, observing the features of the harbour diminish into the distance as the ship passed out of the outer breakwater and into the massive Atlantic swells. He thought of the demise of Gregson, and was sorry he had, because his recent memory of Helena started to filter through his defences, making him feel sad and morose. But his thoughts were rudely interrupted by a loud voice from behind him.

"All finished for'ard 2nd!" Comerford said, as the sailors trooped past him on their way back to other duties.

"Thank you 2nd mate! I'm satisfied with your machinery on deck. See you later in the lounge probably." John replied civilly, as Comerford nodded and left John to his duties.

"Hello sparkers!" John called, arriving onto the lifeboat deck where the wireless office was situated.

"Come in John!" Wallace invited as he was changing crystals on his transmitters.

"What can I do you for John?"

"Hello Jock. Bruce asked me to look at your vent system!"

"Oh yes. It's not keeping our equipment cool enough despite being on top of the ship, if you like!" Wallace informed John, looking at the vent control box.

"No wonder nothing is working Jock! What are all these?" John asked, dumping brown canvas bags onto the deck.

Wallace looked at them and starting to cut open one of them when Larter arrived.

"Jock! For god's sake don't open those bags." Larter said

anxiously, grabbing the bag off the surprised Wallace and equally startled John.

"That is our evidence. These are the entrusted documentation that Lovatt and Van Heyden gave me. I'm to crate it up and put it with the other Scientists cargo. They'll come to pick it up when we arrive back in Cape Town. In the meantime Freeman has ordered a special watch to ensure this type of cargo doesn't arrive there." Larter said anxiously, with deep concern on his face.

"Okay Bruce! Let me check your vent system before you put things back again. Otherwise I'll have to log it in my rounds report." John replied softly.

"In fact I know a better place to stow this. Somewhere the captain will never suspect, or find in a million years." John added, and grabbing hold of a sack asked the other two to bring the rest. He took them to the deck on top of the bridge and pointed to a small compartment under where the radar machinery was kept.

"Here you are!" John said, opening the compartment to reveal a dry space big enough for their needs.

"Freeman will never know that the evidence against him was above his head all along." John chuckled at his subterfuge.

"You crafty devil! Not even we knew about that little space, despite all our maintenance checks and such like." Larter said, suppressing his laughter.

"Just keep quiet and walk softly, as we're right above Freeman's bridge cabin." John whispered.

When they retraced their steps back into the office, they had a good laugh at what they'd done.

"Must be getting back now for my engine room duties. See you later perhaps!" John said, then went below.

"Morris!" John shouted over the noise in the engine room, then whistled and waved his arms to him.

"Hello 2nd! What's the problem! Everything here is all gas-and-gaiters!" Morris said in John's ear.

"Ken! You and Aussie will come and see me in my cabin after your watch and before evening dinner. I need to give you both an ongoing assessment before my report to the chief!" he informed.

"Right ho 2nd! Will do. I've got my task book as you told me!" Morris said cheerfully.

"Make sure Aussie has his completed as well before you come. The chief has a purge on and I'm the last one to upset him, if you get my drift."

"I've been around long enough to understand leapfrog 2nd! So don't fret about us two!" Morris replied angrily.

"Ken! I'm on your side so don't get on my back! I've been there myself and know exactly where you're coming from. The thing is, judging from what I've seen as your instructor, you both should be due for promotion before long. So it's up to you both to come up trumps for all our sakes."

"Fair enough 2nd! No doubt Aussie will agree." Morris said with a grin and mock salute then left to attend his duties.

'From where I stand, it seems there's no change in the system despite modern thinking.' John said aloud as the noise of the compartment swallowed up his voice.

The ship was almost half -ay across her 3,800-mile voyage to Cape Town when she met a vicious tempest that severely tested both her and her crew.

Everything had to be lashed down with the upper deck put out of bounds unless in an emergency, and even then the men had to be securely tied to safety lines in case they were washed overboard as the heavy waves swept over the decks.

John completed his between deck machinery rounds with great difficulty, being tossed around the various compartments like a rag doll. Going up onto the bridge to make his report, he was amazed at the large pendulum swinging motion of the inclinometer, every time the ship lurched in a corkscrew motion through the mountainous waters. He looked out through the spray lashed window, at the bow burying itself deep into another monster wave as the ship first went over it then plunged down

the trough at the other side. The derricks were lashed down onto
the deck for fear of snapping like twigs, as the winds howled and
whistled around the funnel and wireless aerials.

He could hardly distinguish where the dividing line was
between the ocean water and the driving rainwater, while the ship
struggled to prevent herself from drowning from either end.

John watched Freeman working at his chart table and Sinclair
wrestle with the ships wheel, calm as you like, but holding onto
something to prevent themselves being thrown around as he was
below.

"Here to report Grey?" Freeman asked off handedly.

"Outside, between decks rounds completed. No defects to
report!" John stated, then waited for any reply. As he got none,
he left the bridge very gingerly in case he was thrown down it
instead of stepping down it.

'Hello bunk! Am I glad to see you for a little while.' John said, and
shutting his cabin door behind him stripped off his wet overalls.
He dried himself then slipped onto his bunk to get a few hours
kip before supper.

'Could do with a hammock in weather like this though!' He sighed,
holding onto his anti-roll bar to prevent him from being dumped
unceremoniously onto the cabin floor.

His sleep was eventually interrupted not by the tumbling motion
of the ship, but by a loud knock on his cabin door as a person
barged in.

"John wake up! Its hands on deck, and I need your
assistance!" Chapman insisted anxiously.

"Hello Frank! What's the matter?" John asked, rubbing the
sleep from his eyes.

"We've sprung several leaks from our much publicised friend,
including a few from where the old re-inforced bow was taken
off!"

"There are leaks of the watery variety, then there are leeks of
the Welsh variety, Frank! One is a flood; the other is a drop.

Which is which?" John asked with a yawn.

"The drops are from our friend, but the others are from the bow section. And there's a flood due in both compartments!" Chapman said quickly.

"In that case Frank! I do not need to tell you your job, but I suggest you start employing the secondary pumps in both compartments."

"Fair comment John. Unfortunately all the pumps were taken off during our docking period but not replaced, and we were forced to sail back to Cape Town without them. Jack Cunningham has given me a chit of say-so as this was part of his undertaking whilst the ship was in dock."

"Sail without pumps Frank! That makes our seaworthiness a bit suspect. It means that we have no flood protection, therefore the ship is no longer in compliance with Lloyds insurance policy." John pointed out.

"Yes yes, I know all that, however we've got Jack's chit of paper on that. It's the captain who declared us seaworthy for our hasty departure from Port Stanley. But does that matter in the middle of the ocean? I'm duty-bound to tell him of this problem, so let's get this sorted before I do."

"A fat lot of good a bloody chit of paper is when we're manning the ruddy lifeboats." John growled, then climbed into a dry pair of overalls, grabbing his torch and notepad then led the way out of his cabin and down to see these problems for himself. "Our friend is okay. Jack has given us an extra skin, what you see is probably condensation forming between that and the outer one." John said, looking at then feeling all over the welded patch.

"How do you explain the buckets of water that the sailors have mopped up from this area then John?" Chapman asked, still not convinced with John's diagnosis.

John looked up to the deck-head, shining his torch over the cargo deck covers.

There were several drippers coming from it, looking like a mini shower in the light of the torch.

"That's your problem Frank. The cargo hatch covers are leaking. A good tarpaulin should do the trick. See that corner of the hatchway? That's where most of the water is coming in." John said, pointing to the offending rivulet with the beam of his torch.

"Now lets see about this bow. That would be our biggest problem, given that the waves are coming straight at us on this course." John said grimly, swiftly recalling a couple of incidents like it in the past.

"How do you know the waves are directly onto us John?" Chapman said with surprise.

"Simple. The motion of the ship." John smiled, not telling Chapman that he was on the bridge earlier to see with his own eyes.

Both men arrived up into the bow section where the chain and rope lockers were.

They had to hold onto something every time they took a step, as each time the ship rose out of the waves to go down into the trough on the other side, it was as if they were in a free fall lift.

There was nothing under the bow to stop the ship from falling. But when the bow crashed down into the water again it was with a heavy juddering motion and a loud whooshing noise.

There was a lot of water in those compartments, coming into the ship in jets every time the ship buried herself down into the troughs.

"See Frank! If the bows are up and out of the water, we're okay. These jets are only when we go back down again. The jets are made by water forcing itself through the remaining rivet holes. By the look of it, they were probably not sufficiently resealed again when the outer skin was taken off. The bow itself is sound enough, but all we can do is try to pump grease onto each rivet to seal it, much the same way as the stern glands are done." John pronounced.

"I'm not too sure John. I came across this a few years ago, and I'd recommend we shore it up and create an air bubble in the compartments to prevent any more water coming in." Chapman replied, flashing his torch over the weeping metal.

"If that's the case Frank. We'll have to shore up the next two bulkheads behind us and stack as much cargo as possible against them to help give weight to the shores. We can give the whole section an air chamber and hope the internal bulkheads will hold up in this pounding. The watertight doors to the bulkheads should keep us dry, once sealed shut. The skipper will have to slow down considerably or turn about otherwise." John said at length.

Chapman nodded his head, pointing to the safety of the cargo hold. They shut off the watertight doors and all other orifices that went through the bulkhead, before making their way to see Freeman.

"Hello chief! What can I do for you?" Freeman asked politely when the two engineers came onto the bridge.

"I, that is we have something we wish to discuss in your cabin captain, that we feel you should know about." Chapman replied, making his way towards Freeman's bridge cabin.

"Very well chief if you must. Nothing serious I hope?" Freeman conceded, leading the way.

"We have discovered some serious hull problems that you need to know of. The 2nd and I have just come from inspecting these problems." Chapman started but was cut short by Freeman's outburst.

"Not again chief! We've just come out of a dry dock. What sort of problems have you got for me now, as if I haven't enough on my plate already."

John looked at Freeman's worried face and asked what they were, saying that maybe an officers meeting could discuss what was to be done.

"Pah! That's all you think we do all day. Sit around talking like old grannies." he said, sneering at John then turned round to Chapman.

"Come on chief! Out with it. What's wrong this time?" He demanded.

Chapman was of equal rank to Freeman and stood for no nonsense from him.

"Now look here captain! Climb down off your high horse and start listening to some sense for a change. What 2nd Engineer Grey and I have to tell you can wait until you show us some courtesy. If your lousy ship sinks under you then don't come screaming for us." Chapman shouted angrily, indicating to John that they should leave.

Freeman looked daggers at the two engineers before he drew his breath and yielded to their wishes.

"Okay then chief! Just this once you get to tell your captain what to do on his ship!" Freeman said slyly, making John look in astonishment at him.

The crafty bastard. He's turned it right around to suit his own ends. I'll have to remember that if there's a next time'. John thought as Chapman went on to explain what the problems were.

"We're only about 50 miles south from Gough Island. We are already off track and it will take us slightly north but we can shelter there to finish our repairs at the same time. It will take us longer to reach the island if I drop down to 10 knots. But with that altered course you should be able to do a first aid job. In the meantime I'll get the 1st mate onto that cargo hatch straight away. No sense courting disaster a second time during this round trip." Freeman said pleasantly, then turned around to John telling him that the steering gears did not seem to function properly for the helmsman.

"It's probably low telemotor pressure captain, but I'll get onto that right away." John replied, then the two Engineers left Freeman's cabin.

When they got below to sort out the details of the work, Chapman turned to John and told him that he had spoken to Freeman in the only way he understood. But not for John to try and copy him until such times as he too was a chief engineer.

Chapman worked out the main details then told John to get himself some help to fix the steering gear, whilst he would sort out the bow problem. As they were in the engineer's office, Chapman called the other officers together to speak to them.

"Clarke, you assist the 2nd in fixing the steering gear. Morris, detail off one junior officer plus four stokers to assist me. But you are to remain in the engine room to take charge until I come back. The rest of you junior officers will assist Morris to the very best of your ability. Lets go!" Chapman ordered.

Chapman had the stokers shore up the bow section whilst Brown had his sailors stop the leaking cargo hatches, shifting the cargo forward to prop up the vital bulkheads.

Meanwhile John and Clarke were assessing their work.

"The Telemotor pump has packed in, John!" Clarke declared, pointing for John to see.

"Looks like it's popped its clogs. Lucky we didn't have a fire as well." He quipped.

John looked closely at the offending machinery for a moment before making his decision.

"Okay then Aussie. What we've got here is that the pressure pipe from the pump has blown its spring-loaded connector to the control valve. This diverts the pump delivery to move the rudder. In turn that operates the hunting gear, which brings the control valve back to the original cut off position. All we've got to do is isolate the system and repair the pipe." John stated, indicating to the various pipes and valves.

"It's bleeding itself, Aussie! Quick, grab that bucket and hold it under the discharge! Before we do the repair, we've got to put it into 'Hand Steering' simply by shoving this ' change over' cock. We'll put it back again when we've finished"

John unbolted the pipe onto the deck then opened up a locker behind him.

"Here's one I prepared earlier. I always keep a spare one handy." John said with a grin.

"Good on ya mate! What a player. Here's me thinking about having to operate the emergency tiller." Clarke said gleefully, helping John to renew the pipe.

"Right then Aussie, get that drum of oil from under the deck plate, then prime the suction pump up again!"

The pump was primed and engaged into the worm screw system, before John announced the repair was completed to watch it working correctly.

"You've got the privilege of reporting the completed repairs to your captain. How about it Aussie?" John teased.

"I'd rip his scrawny head from his shoulders if I went up there, but no worries mate!" Clarke avowed aggressively.

"Just joking Aussie! I'll spare you the bother. Get yourself back down to the engine room now. I'll finish off here and thanks for your help." John said with a grin, wiping his hands on a clean rag that he always kept with him.

"Steering gear and equipment tested and correct, but how is it your end Bosun?" John asked, when he arrived onto the bridge.

"I'm able to control my counter steering now 2nd! That means that we can keep a decent course."

"Keep a good eye on the pointer in case the rudder alignment has altered, but you should be alright now."

"About time too 2nd. And I thought you had checked it before you gave me your last report." Freeman butted in.

"The heavy, or over-use of the system due to the stormy conditions was the creator of the fault and the damage, not me, captain! Now it's fixed you can steer the ship to Timbuktu if you like." John replied sarcastically, then went off the bridge.

The ship managed to swim her way into the relative shelter on the leeward side of Gough Islands, which are slap bang in the middle of the Falklands and the continent of Africa.

This gave the crew a few brief hours to recover, with vital time to repair and restore the ship virtually back to normal, before Freeman turned the ship back into the maelstrom again.

"Only 1,600-miles to go 2nd!" Sinclair said miserably, wrestling with his wheel again.

"Never mind Bosun! At least you'll be able to work up a thirst and beat your ale drinking record." John replied in sympathy.

"The way I'm thirsting now, I'd quaff a gallon in the same time, let alone a couple of pints." Sinclair snorted, nodding when he saw John leave the bridge.

The lounge had been restored back to its former glory, but was still cavernous due to no passengers on board, with only a couple of officers occupying it.

"2nd! How's my write up going?" Morris asked, sitting down next to John.

"All done and signed. Now it's up to the chief and the promotion panel now. And before you ask me, no I'm not telling you." John teased, keeping a straight face, seeing the look of disappointment on Morris face.

"But to give you a clue! You've got a piece of work to prepare by the time we dock again. It's something to do with a worm screw." He added

Morris gave him a blank look for a moment, then with a large grin, stated that he'd just guessed what it was.

"Keep that under your size six and several acres hat, Ken" John whispered

"Keep what Bluey?" Clarke asked as he too arrived alongside Morris

"Let's say you've got to show me a certain piece of machinery you last worked on, Aussie!" Morris replied, putting a finger across his lips.

"Fair dinkum mate. But if I do that, then you can show me about another thing." Clarke bargained, as both men started to discuss their exam revisions and project piece to be done.

John smiled at his two junior officers, remembering the times when he'd gone through the same uncertainties and worries. That was why it was now by tradition, his turn to help them in their rights of passage.

* * *

After the sixth day of riding through the terrible Atlantic storm, it blew itself away leaving the ship in calm, almost tropical waters. This in turn, was conducive to the morale of the crew who were finally able to come up on deck again and enjoy some sunshine instead of the cold, damp conditions that existed below.

John's sea routine finally came together, dividing his time between his role as tutor to his two charges and his role as outside engineer.

The last night as sea arrived bringing the traditional end of voyage party. Especially when a ship earned her speed money, with her cargo safely offloaded at the proper destination.

On this occasion, John, Larter and Wallace kept a low profile, preparing for their prospective meeting with Lovatt and Van Heyden when they arrived back in Cape Town.

The fly in their ointment since sailing from the Falklands, was the nosey 4th mate, who always seemed to be around when the officers met or spoke.

John was in the lounge, sitting in his favourite armchair having a leisurely smoke when he saw Clarke coming in and approaching him.

"Hello 2nd! Care for a drink?" Clarke offered.

"I don't mind if I do, thank you Aussie! But I've got a favour to ask of you!"

"No need to ask 2nd! Fire away."

John gave him a piece of paper, asking him to read the drawings then to comply with his request.

Clarke looked at the drawing for a moment.

"No worries mate! Will do, just as soon as I wet my warbler!" Clarke replied with an exaggerated nod, but went over to the 4th mate.

"4th mate. As 4th Engineer, would you be so kind as to assist me in a certain project about the effects of ship lag. As you are of equal rank to me, it suits the requirements of the project.

There's a few beers in it for you." Clarke asked with the tempting bribe.

"Since you put it that way 4th. Certainly as long as it doesn't take too long." The 4th mate replied.

"Nah mate, only two shakes of a dingo's' tail. But I need you to come with me." Clarke urged, so the 4th mate stood up and followed Clarke out of the lounge.

John looked around the lounge and saw that he and Dovey were the only two left.

I'm going to my cabin for a while, if anybody wants me steward." he announced, leaving towards the access stairs to the accommodation decks.

This cleared his way to double back and up to the wireless office. But on his way he heard smacks, thumps, groans and shuffling coming from behind the stores launch. He crept over to the area to see Clarke thumping the much bigger 4th deck officer around.

'Not too hard Aussie! Not too hard!' he whispered and left to see Larter.

"Phase 1 completed John! I've sent an 'SLT' to Lovatt, and asked him to bring his special diplomatic bag with him when he meets us. Phase 2 is when our spy has been, shall we say, waylaid for a day or so." Larter stated.

"Aussie's already seen to that. Painful to the spy it was too." John grinned

"Must be getting back now!" he added and left to go back to the lounge, where he met Clarke again.

"It appears that our friend met with an accident! Possibly from a large dose of ship-lag if anybody asked me. I had to carry him to the sick bay and the Doc said he'll keep the 4th under observations for a day or so." Clarke said, rubbing his bruised knuckles.

"In that case sit down, let me get you a drink or three." John replied, pointing to a nearby chair. He came back with a tray of drinks.

"This is for your dry warbler! Cheers Aussie!" he said, placing the tray in front of Clarke.

Both men drank slowly and steadily, exchanging notes on different places they had visited and generally making small talk before Clarke announced he'd an engine room watch do to.

"Last one on this miserable voyage too John! No offence, but this ship stinks, and I just can't wait until tomorrow. " Clarke stated, then left John on his own again.

Chapter XVIII
Quarantine

The morning was bright and the sea like a millpond as the ship glided into the harbour. John looked as the impressive Table Mountain grew taller as he came nearer, but he was not taking in the beauty of the area. His mind was on his dead loved one and all who perished on that bridge. There was something about the bridge that didn't seem right to him, but couldn't put his finger on what it might be. He was brought back to the present by Comerford's customary remark as the ship tied up alongside its berth in Cape Town again.

"All finished John. The gangway is now being lowered."

"Yes, thanks. Just checking that capstan you seemed to be having trouble with. I'll be along as soon as I've finished here." John said automatically.

With his rounds finished, John was getting ready to go ashore when Wallace called into his cabin.

"The professors are due in about 10 minutes John. Better come and help us in the lounge."

"On my way Jock! I've got Morris and Clarke waiting there to assist you." John replied, following Wallace out of his cabin.

When they arrived he gave Morris and Clarke a pre-arranged signal that sent them away, before he went over to speak to Larter.

"Freeman's gone ashore to meet up with Invergarron. Now is our chance to get our evidence to Lovatt." Larter whispered.

Sinclair came striding into the lounge saying quietly that Lovatt and his retinue were approaching with a large black bag.

When Lovatt and the other scientists arrived, John went over to greet them.

"Hello gentlemen, welcome back on board again. Have a good flight from Port Stanley? Your cargo has arrived safely and will be offloaded by the dock crane in about 30 minutes." John announced with a booming voice, for the benefit of others he guessed were still keeping tabs on him.

"Yes thank you 2nd. Heard that you had a spot of bother coming over. More-or-less what happened to our own ship." Lovatt responded, shaking John's outstretched hand.

This was the signal for Larter to go with one of the scientists, down to the for'ard cargo hold.

Brandon gave Wallace the large black bag, who took it away. He came back shortly, with Morris and Clarke, carrying a much less bulkier looking bag.

Larter and John were the decoys, so that Wallace was able to complete his transfer of evidence by switching the black bags.

"Captain Freeman is presently ashore. Perhaps if you care to partake in some refreshments until he returns, then you're more than welcome." John invited diplomatically.

"Thank you for your hospitality Grey, I'll stay. But Professor Lovatt must arrange the berth for our own supply ship that's due in shortly." Van Heyden replied cordially.

The large group of scientists gathered around Lovatt and Larter as they left the ship, in view of John and the other officers.

"Phase 3 completed Jock!" John whispered.

"Here comes phase 4, look!" Wallace whispered back, nodding his head towards the gangway.

Freeman came storming up the gangway and made directly to the lounge.

"Professor Van Heyden! Where's Professor Lovatt and Doctor Brandon, I need to speak to them." Freeman announced pompously.

"Hello captain Freeman!" Van Heyden said calmly, unperturbed by Freeman's abrupt manner.

"Professor Lovatt, and the rest of the team could not stay, as we've got our supply ship docking within the hour. Can I be of assistance?"

"I need you to sign a declaration of intent concerning our business in the Antarctic.

And you do realise that none of your cargo can be offloaded until we're cleared via customs and quarantine controls?" Freeman asked belligerently.

"But of course captain! I know all about quarantine control. I happen to be on its International Board of Enquiry. Mind you, your ship will be impounded for 30 days, and nobody, not even yourself will be allowed ashore. I must warn you, if you have already been ashore, then you personally will be placed under arrest, then put into quarantine for 60 days. And that will include any person you have come into contact with ashore, as all will have to be inoculated." Van Heyden stated calmly, pretending to inspect his fingernails for some imaginary dirt.

"You wouldn't dare! Lord Belverley and Invergarron are here to stop you. I've just been to see them and...!" Freeman commenced but was cut short by the icy, still voice of Van Heyden.

"In that case captain! I'm putting you under arrest and under quarantine along with your lordships!" he said, signalling four customs policemen over to him pointing to Freeman.

"Take him away in the ambulance, and give him 100ml of Benzyactolide. Then arrest his two victims Lords Belverley and Invergarron. They may be lords but they are not outside the World Health and Safety Organisation. Give them the same dose." He ordered.

"But you can't do that! It's against company policy!" Freeman whined, protesting vehemently as he was frog-marched off the ship.

"That Mr Grey is International Power! It should keep him quiet until we get our equipment and scientific samples away safely. Our ship will come alongside yours to take a direct transfer, saving time and port facilities." Van Heyden said calmly, smiling at John and the other officers who had taken a back seat in all this.

"What's really going to happen to the captain?" Wallace asked with a grin.

"Don't worry about him. We'll keep them a day or two after we've sailed for Amsterdam. In the meantime, you and your friends are more than welcome to visit our ship, it's our turn for hospitality." Van Heyden said, nodding his head

"You mentioned coming alongside. Is that your vessel coming into harbour now professor?" Comerford asked, pointing to a brightly coloured ship coming slowly towards them.

"Yes! She is one of five such ships we have dotted around the world. This one is the..." Van Heyden began but John mentioned the name first.

"The *Mao Iti Princess.*"

"Oh you know her then 2nd?" Van Heyden asked with mild surprise.

"Yes, but how different she is looking now. Last time I saw her she was very nearly wrecked at the place of her name." John said in fascination, watching the graceful ship come closer to them*.

Van Heyden asked if Comerford could get some of his men to assist the berthing, who agreed and left shouting orders to seamen that were lounging on the deck.

Brown came rushing in, asking about what had happened to the captain, but was swiftly informed that he had to go onto the bridge to receive a ship that was about to come alongside.

This left Brown to take charge of almost nobody, because Comerford had already dealt with the berthing needs of the incoming ship.

Lovatt arrived with Van Heyden as the guest ship nudged the bigger one and got firmly secured alongside, with fenders to protect their hulls in case of sudden tidal bumps or whatever. Brown came down off the bridge joining John, Clarke, Wallace and other officers to form an impromptu welcoming party.

"Captain Neilson welcome back to Cape Town." Lovatt and Van Heyden greeted a very tall blond haired man striding across the gangway between the two ships.

"Greetings dear gentlemen!" the captain said, then was introduced to Brown and the other Deck Officers of the *Inverary.*

"It is good to have a welcoming party. Maybe we should be welcoming you back." Neilson said in all sincerity, looking at the

---

* See *The Beach Party.*

Inverary officers then over the side to the large patch on the side of the ship.

"Who is this engineer you spoke about, Grey is it?" he asked, looking around to meet John.

This was not John's scene, who had already disappeared back into the lounge for a cup of tea and a cigarette with Larter and Sinclair. But it wasn't long before the captain found him and greeted him.

"You know my ship 2nd? Where have you met her before?" Neilson asked with genuine interest.

"It's a long story captain. Sufficient to say it was at a beach party some time ago." John said demurely, as he still preferred to remain understated with his light under a bush.

Neilson did not pursue the matter, but invited all the officers on board for lunch, whilst his crew transferred the cargo over.

The *Mao 'Iti' Princess* was a trim and neatly kept research vessel, that enjoyed the cream of the International Scientific world that sailed on board her, which meant that some of her equipment was far more advanced than on the much bigger ships of the *Inver* line. But John did not let on, just made little notes on the changes and ideas that might come in handy in some future era.

He also managed to elicit certain facts and figures from the chief engineer, as did Larter with their Radio Officer. All in all, it was a sociable afternoon spent swapping notes and ideas, until the announcement was made for the ship to sail.

"Well 2nd engineer Grey! This is goodbye for a while. We will be submitting our findings and your part in us getting such fine samples, as soon as we arrive in Amsterdam. I have some friends in the International Ship Design Moratorium who will be interested in you, sooner rather than later. So keep a watch out for the ISDM logo, and good luck!" Lovatt stated as the other scientists nodded in agreement, clapping their hands in appreciation.

John stood on the foc'sle and waved to the crowded bridge of the departing ship as it sailed away into nothingness.

"Coming for that run ashore with me and Andy, John?" Larter asked, when he met John coming down the main deck towards the gangway.

"Why not, I'm dressed for it. Besides Clarke and Morris will be too busy swotting for their promotion exam tomorrow. But where have you put Mick Fields and Jock Wallace all of a sudden?"

"Mick Fields went over to the Naval base in Simonstown, and Jock has gone ashore with his motor-bike to some motor-bike rally or something." Larter explained.

"It seems that everybody has something to do except us!" John said ruefully, briefly remembering the last time he stepped ashore here.

Larter sensing this, told John not to be such a softie, after all, there were loads of rich young widows ashore just waiting to meet the cream of the Triple Crown Line.

Chapter XIX
Kidnapped

The taxi stopped by the Customs house where two policemen ordered the friends out telling them to go through the mandatory Immigration controls.

"You are British Officers, what ship?" the customs officer asked curtly.

"SS *Inverary!*" Larter responded.

"Your passports please! I need to see your passports!"

"We are British Merchant Navy officers in a British Colonial Port. We do not need to carry them. So why do you need them?" Larter asked.

"I need to see some form of identification. You must have something on you to state as to who you are yes? Then give it to me, now!" the officer demanded abruptly.

"No we won't. You have no right to detain us. C'mon lads, we're getting out of here." Larter said boldly and started to leave the building.

There was a loud piercing whistle and several burly men came swiftly through a door and surrounded the three friends.

"You are under arrest. Your ship has been put under a quarantine notice, with all of your crew to be kept on board for that duration. As for you three, you will be taken to the local quarantine holding area until such times as you co-operate with me!" the officer said smugly. He clicked his fingers, which gave the command for the squad of men to grab hold of the friends hustling them out through the back of the building.

"Get in that truck and sit down." a man shouted in a thick Afrikaan accent.

As they climbed into the truck other men who handcuffed them to a railing, as they sat down on a long wooden bench, met them.

When those men got out, the canvas flap of the lorry was pulled down and tied so that the friends could not see out. The lorry lurched and swayed as it sped noisily away from the dockyard.

"In quarantine now taken away like criminals! I thought Lovatt said that it would only be a couple of days and only for Freeman." John commented for them to start discussing the merits of this sudden event.

"Pass the tea and biscuits. Anyone for a smoke for afters?" Sinclair quipped but got no response as the three of them were tossed around the back of the lorry like rag dolls. After several hours the truck stopped, for a man to come and open the back of the truck.

"Get out here. You have five minutes to have a shit before we feed you and move on." the man demanded in a gutteral voice.

They looked around but could not see anything but a totally black void around them. John stooped down and scooping up some grit from under his feet, stuffed it into his pocket, before a paper package and a bottle of liquid were thrust into his hands.

"Now get back into the truck, its time we were off!" came the same guttural voice.

They sat on their wooden bench examining their packages, not trusting what it was they were given.

"I think we've been kidnapped lads! I heard something about a spate of kidnapping, the last time we were here. Some terrorist organisation or other trying to buck the system or something." Sinclair said.

"Oh is that all! And here's me thinking we're on a mystery tour, free bag meals and all." John said sarcastically.

"In that case we can eat this stuff with safety, because if they wanted to poison us why go to all this trouble of racing around the country in the back of a bleeding lorry."

"You just might be right there Bruce!" Sinclair said, opening his package.

"Oh look! A ploughman's lunch, and a bottle of beer!"

"No wonder the poor ploughman was hungry if you've got it Andy." John chuckled.

They ate their meal and had a cigarette each as the truck

bounced its way to some unknown destination. The swaying, bouncing of the truck didn't bother them and pretty soon all three dropped off to sleep.

It was the rattling and knocking of the truck's tailgate that woke them up.

"Get out! Get a move on. Get out of the truck!" a persistent voice greeted them, as they shielded their eyes from the glare of the morning light.

"You have another five minutes. But stay here!" came the order.

The three looked at their surroundings to find that they were stopped on a deeply rutted track, flanked by open grounds, that was thinly vegetated on one side with high hills in the background, and a thick expanse of jungle on the other.

John looked down at the dark brown earth, and emptied the contents of his pocket onto it.

"Look! This red soil is what I picked up last night, and this is black soil. To me it means that the red soil is from the south and this soil is much further to the Northwest. We must be up-country somewhere but where?" John said, pointing to the different coloured soil.

"Shh! Listen!" Sinclair whispered.

All three listened for a moment, before Larter asked what they were supposed to be listening to.

"Do you hear that?" Sinclair whispered.

"I don't hear a thing Andy!" John whispered.

"Exactly! Not even a cricket chirping." Sinclair said quickly, running round to the front of the vehicle, then came back just as quick.

"They've scarpered. It appears that not only have we been kidnapped, but we've also been left in the lurch, abandoned, even ruddy well marooned like the *Inverlaggan*." Sinclair said loudly

"I smell a rat! Nobody gets kidnapped then abandoned. We must be in big Ju-Ju country for the cowards to abscond like they did. But where the bleeding hell did they vanish to?" Larter asked, looking around the area of the truck.

"Well at least we're not stranded on the shores of a flippin' desert, with a crowd of women and children to worry about." John said softly as they looked at their surroundings, remembering the nightmarish journey they went through to get rescued.

"It looks as if we've got to rescue ourselves this time." Sinclair said simply, ending the few moments of group memory.

John went to the front of the truck and began to look it over, starting with the engine.

"The engine seems okay. Everything seems in order except it appears that we're almost out of petrol." He said after his swift inspection.

"There's a broken radio in the cab, but hopefully if I can find some tools I can make a new one from it." Larter said.

"There's a small clearing in the jungle over there where we can camp. If we can get the truck in there we can use it as shelter. I've noticed that there's plenty of game around, judging by the spoor I've seen." Sinclair added to the list.

They managed to drive the truck off the track and into the jungle before they started to camouflage it from the track.

"There's no sense us staying here, we will erase any signs in case someone is after us, otherwise why did those men disappear if they didn't want to be caught too. Judging by the other two dumped trucks in this neck of the jungle, they've done this before." Larter stated as the friends found a suitable campsite, and started to prepare it.

"Right then, I'll go and rustle up some 'bush tucker' as our Aussie friend would say!" Sinclair volunteered.

"I'll go and find some water!" John said

"That leaves me to start a fire and make the beds!" Larter said jokingly, and all three went off to their opted tasks.

By the time John came back, Sinclair had managed to trap and kill a wild pig, and was preparing it over Larters roaring fire.

The tall trees and thick jungle vegetation was a perfect screen to hide the smoke from their campfire.

"It appears that the track is hardly used, but there is a small river about 200 yards beyond that and almost running parallel with it for quite a distance. There's jungle on the other side of the bank, so if anybody comes it will either be along the track or by river." John stated, handing the beer bottles over to Larter.

"Let's go and look at it. The lorry won't be able to take us far, so the river might be our only way of getting back." Sinclair suggested.

"But be careful not to make any signs on the track or the soil."

They picked their way over the track, arriving at the river's edge. Sinclair started throwing little bits of stick into it, whilst John looked at its features and Larter waded out to see how deep it was.

"Bruce, you could be seen for miles, and there could be crocodiles along this bank. For God's sake come back!" John whispered. Which prompted Larter to hasten his exit from the water.

"It's running at about 3 knots. Judging by those hills they're facing south, with the sun tracking from left to right as you face them. Therefore I'd say this river is following a north westerly course." Sinclair said when he finished his mental arithmetic.

"That's a good start. I'll take the dashboard readings from the truck to work out how far we've travelled since arriving here." John offered, as they trooped back to the camp.

"Here we are. The truck has two 10-gallon tanks, but there's only about quarter of a gallon left. If it can do an average of 25 mile per gallon and we've been travelling constantly for almost 24 hours, that would put us a good 500 miles away from Cape Town." John stated as he showed them the dial readings from the truck.

"Not only that, when we came up-country for the funeral John, the predominant colour of the earth was dark brown just as it is now. Must be full of copper or other such minerals." Larter chipped in.

"Let's have dinner and think of our strategy after another fag, I'm ruddy starving." Sinclair suggested.

* * *

They munched their feast of roast pig until there was almost nothing left, then after their customary cigarette they set about their survival strategy again.

"We've only 3 choices: 1. To stay here and get waylaid by whoever chased our captors away; 2. To drive the truck as far as we can along the track hoping to bump into civilisation; or 3, we follow the river downstream until we do meet civilisation again." John started.

"Sod the first option. We'd only get a few miles on the truck on the second, so I'd choose the river." Larter opined.

"Yes! We could make a raft and float our way down. I'm in favour of that one." Sinclair agreed.

"Yes, we can strip the lorry down, and the others if necessary, then use them as parts for our raft. All agreed?" John asked

The other two agreed with a nod of their head.

"We'll have to devise something that will keep us afloat and out of lurking danger, such as those crocodiles I happen to see down river." Sinclair suggested.

John got hold of an old newspaper he found in the cab of the truck, using a piece of charcoal he began drawing a craft, listing materials and how to construct it. When he finished his drawings he showed it to the others.

"Here you are. Look at this and see what you think! You can be the captain Andy." John said, nudging Sinclair.

The other two looked over the drawing asking a few questions about things that concerned them. In the end, John had to describe it.

"Simple my dear friends. The truck floorboards will be our deck. Gather all the canvas up, with some of it to be used to lag them. The rest of the canvas will be made into a tube and lashed around the decking. This tube will have the inner tubes from the 6 tyres from our lorry and anything we can salvage from the other abandoned trucks. But the main canvas tube will be inflated with the exhaust from the lorry. A tiller can be made from the wooden bench; with all the petrol tanks sealed and put each end of the craft for extra buoyancy. The foam seats from the cab will be used as fenders and part of the truck's bonnet used as a shield for the bow to protect it from being punctured. We can have some of the stanchions holding the canvas up as strengthening bars across the deck to give it some rigidity. All the rubber tyres can be melted down and used as a coating over the canvas to waterproof the canvas. We can make paddles from the mudguards, and spears from some bamboo to catch our food as we sail down stream. We'll need a few stout poles to help push us along, or fend ourselves off some danger. It will have about a foot draught, but as the tube is inflated, it will give us about a two-foot freeboard. In short, we'll end up with an inflatable raft. Pity about an outboard motor though!" John said triumphantly, as the other two listened eagerly to him.

"I would like to take the headlamps and battery with us for signalling with John, but what about our weight distribution." Larter asked.

"I've calculated the deck space of 4 foot wide by 8 foot long, to sustain a weight of 600 pounds. Given our average weight of 12 stone, it means that we take some useful items, but we'll have to guess what the extra weight would be. If we have more than that weight, then we'll have to choose what we take or leave behind."

"We can always make a small raft to tow behind us if we want to take the truck as well, Bruce!" Sinclair teased, which drew a laugh from the others.

"Well that's fair enough, what are we waiting for, lets get cracking." Larter said, jumping up onto his feet.

They were old friends and had been in similar difficult situations, so worked as a team, but with nobody taking overall charge. They worked methodically and swiftly until they had completed it and it was getting nightfall again. The thick pungent smell from the melting rubber, mixed with the smoke from the engine exhaust turned the place into a stinking area that all the wildlife seemed to avoid. All except the humans who caused it.

"The truck is a total write off now, remind me not to hire one of them again, John!" Sinclair quipped, dabbing the last drop of rubber onto the canvas tubing that was now looking like a big horseshoe shaped ring of black pudding.

"Fortunately we had the sense to build it near the water Bruce. She looks sturdy but heavy." John chuckled, as they lifted the craft up to carry it into the water.

"No. She's lighter than I thought. But as long as she floats that'll do me fine." Larter said hopefully.

They let it down gently into the river, watching it float slowly away to the end of its tether.

"Oh ye of little faith!" John said with delight, when the other two dragged it back again.

"What did you name her John?" You must have named her for us to launch her?"

"We'll do that in the morning before we leave. I think its time we got ourselves organised for the night. Have some grub and secure our campsite." John replied.

"I'll go and set our campsite security." Sinclair said, slipping away out of sight.

"And I'll sit here and catch us some fish for supper." John stated.

"Well it looks as if I'm the duty cook again." Larter chuckled, as they tackled their opted tasks.

Darkness came swiftly as they sat around their new campsite, enjoying their well-earned meal, and their customary cigarette. The sky was becoming clear to reveal the stars, which started a navigational discussion between Sinclair and Larter.

The noises of the night soon took over the conversation, as the prowlers of the night went hunting.

"How good is the security this time Andy? Only I don't want to be the next snack to some passing lion or something." John whispered.

Sinclair chuckled and told him all was well from the animal kingdom, but he couldn't guarantee against the human ones.

The fire was just a faint glow of embers when they heard heavy rustling noises coming from behind them. Sinclair signalled them to be quiet, and to hide behind a tree, as he grabbed a sharpened bamboo stick. They saw two men dressed in paramilitary uniforms and carrying rifles emerging into the camp area.

Sinclair signalled Larter to grab the one nearest to him as he prepared to tackle the second one. Both intruders were grabbed and knocked out cold, without a sound. They were bound, gagged and hidden under some bushes when they saw a third intruder coming, who was quietly calling out to the other two. He swiftly met the same fate.

Sinclair signalled that more were coming but from a different angle, and pointed to the fallen rifles. They grabbed one each then hid to face the next danger.

As they heard voices, Sinclair indicated that there were four of them coming down the path.

Sinclair crept along the path to see the four heavily armed men walking slowly but carelessly, as two of them got strung up when they stepped into his animal snares. Another one fell into the bear trap he had made, leaving the leader still approaching, unaware of being alone.

Sinclair stepped up behind him striking him down with a vicious blow that knocked the man out. He then dragged him back to the others telling them that here was the last of them.

"The rest are otherwise engaged, even hung up for a while!" he chuckled.

The friends stacked all the intruders' weapons and equipment in a pile, with the men propped up against a fallen tree.

"Search them for clues. We have to find out who they are. These must be the ones our captors left us for, and were looking for us. They must have smelled the rubber burning." Larter deduced, searching the trussed up men.

"What about the others back there, Andy?" John asked with concern.

"Come and see, I'll need you to retrieve them and get them buried."

John followed down the trail with his gun at the ready, coming upon the ripped body of the man impaled on the sharp bamboos that Sinclair had placed at the bottom of the shallow pit.

"I can't remember this happening out in the desert, but is this what your brother showed you from his jungle training that you keep telling us Andy?" John asked, plucking the soggy body out of the pit.

"Yes, that and much more. Our two friends up there got hung. Give me a hand to drop them." Sinclair said in a matter-of-fact voice.

"We can either bury them or use them to good effect in case they have more friends trying to find us." Sinclair said, cutting down one of the bodies.

"Andy! Look what this one is wearing!" John gasped.

"Bloody hell John. We need to interrogate these bastards. And I'll bet they don't speak English, much!"

John dragged one body as Sinclair dragged another.

"What about the one from the pit Andy?"

"He's okay. He's our new sentry for the night. Nobody will get past him."

"Better bring him back Andy!" John replied, and went to go back for it.

"John! You just don't want to go back there, believe you me." Sinclair said gravely.

John looked at his friend and smiled.

"No contest Andy. I'll not argue with that!" and shrugging his shoulders carried on dragging the bodies.

They arrived back to the camp to find Larter in the process of interrogating one of the prisoners.

"I'll bet he can't speak English!" Sinclair said, and saw Larter hit the man with a heavy wooden cudgel.

"Oh yes he can! Watch!" Larter said, opening the man's trousers, exposing his genitals and waving the prisoners own machete at them.

"All right. I tell!" Came the terrified reply.

"That's better. Now where were we?" Larter asked, and began questioning him all over again. Every time the man didn't answer he got a flick with the machete.

Sinclair whispered into Larter's ear, pointing to the body John had.

"These men have mementoes from the train crash Bruce. I'm beginning to get a picture as to why we were singled out. But we'll interrogate them all, any problem just call me."

John and Sinclair looked through the men's possessions and found that each one of them had items that clearly did not belong to them. They even found two large metal spanners that John identified as engineers spanners.

"We were the only ones from the ship to come up to the crash site and the funeral. I think that because our pictures were in the paper, is the reason why we were kidnapped. The two men driving the truck must have been scared of these men, as these are the ones who were looking for us. It would have taken them all day to search for us when there was no lorry for them to find. They must have found it eventually and that is why they came crashing through the jungle, confident that we would be namby-pambys and succumb to their demands."

"Then we'll try to get them back to the authorities, especially with the evidence they're carrying." John said quietly, listening to the men being interrogated.

"Bruce is certainly not using standard court procedure this time John! But he's still taking too long about it." Sinclair stated, and rose up to take over from Larter.

"Still having a tough time? Too much bedside manner old boy!" Sinclair asked, turning and slapping the prisoner so hard that he was knocked out.

"Oh what a shame! Bring on the next prisoner!" Sinclair said, signalling to John.

John went over to the other prisoners and pulling one up onto his feet, marched him over to Sinclair.

"This one was carrying a wallet from some Minister, and a lock of hair from some blonde girl. Also a few hand grenades, obviously borrowed from our local customs officer." John said grimly, shoving the prisoner roughly to the ground.

"Speakie de English, No?" Sinclair asked him roughly, for the prisoner to shake his head.

Sinclair kicked him hard in his genitals, calling him a liar.

"Speakie de English Yes?" Sinclair asked again, and got the desired response.

"Good! Now we are getting somewhere!" Sinclair stated then asked the prisoner where he got all his loot and mementoes from, listening carefully to each answer.

He interrogated the next two prisoners, handing out the same treatment until he was satisfied. The men were staked out, face down and with a large tree trunk across their backs to prevent them from moving.

Sinclair disappeared for a moment then returning, placed an object in front of their faces. This produced muffled shouts and moans and they became agitated trying to get away from the object.

"That should keep them occupied for a while. In the meantime, we can now get some rest. We have another raft to build to take these bastards back with us." Sinclair said quietly, offering a cigarette to the other two.

The prisoners wailing got weaker and weaker as the night wore on, and the friends were not disturbed again until the dawn of yet another sunny day.

John woke up and stretching himself, found that Sinclair was already about and tending to the prisoners. He got up to see what the object was but found it had gone, so asked Sinclair what it was.

"Same as our other guard, John. But if you must know I'll show you. Bruce has already seen it, and was okay with it."

Sinclair said as he brought a hessian sack over and opened it. Out rolled two severed heads, each with their mouths sewn up, but instead of a tongue sticking out, it was a penis.

"That puts the fear of the devil in them, just as my brother said the Borneo tribesmen did to their prisoners. If you remember, it is the same ruse I used on those Arabs when they tried to bushwhack us when we were stranded out in the desert." Sinclair said woodenly, looking at John's face.•

"It appears that you have the same attitude as Bruce. So it's a good thing John, because we'll be making a few more of these as we go along."

"Good enough for them. I have reason to believe that these men were part of an outfit who sabotaged the bridge. Those spanners they were carrying are for track laying and no other engineering job. I cannot see any railwaymen running around in paramilitary style uniforms doing that can you Andy?"

"That confirms it then John. We must try and get them back. When we've done so, we have a score to settle with our customs man back in Cape Town."

"Yes, and I know just what it is too!" Larter butted in.

All three nodded their heads in mutual agreement then set about making something to eat.

As they ate, the prisoners were moaning and looking at each mouthful that was eaten, but got none. Instead Sinclair came over and kicked each of them and told them to be quiet, which they did.

They broke camp and made a crude raft to take the prisoners on, making sure that the raft wouldn't sink on them.

"I name this ship after the Truck Company who made her, but in female terms. She will be known as *Denise* and may god bless all who sail in her." John said when they re-floated their dinghy.

They marvelled at their own workmanship as they floated gently down the river, with the raft in tow behind. It was nearly

---

• See *The Lost Legion.*

noon before they decided to land and have some food. John was in his element fishing, and soon had enough for all of them.

Larter cooked the fish, and Sinclair organised the prisoners for their own food.

He sat with his rifle pointing directly at them as they noisily devoured their food and drank their water, before he tied them up again to eat his. Whilst he ate, John and Larter kept watch in case of more intruders or perils from the water.

Chapter XX
Big Ju-Ju

The river was still benign and there were no signs of any other humans to be seen on either side of it, as it got slowly wider and slightly faster.

The raft was still being towed, and the prisoners still quiet, when they started to approach a large sweeping bend in the river.

"We'd better pull in here Andy, the river is getting faster and I can hear something in the distance." John said, alerting his friends.

They rowed the dinghy to the bank and hauled the raft out of the water. They had the prisoners off their rafts and settled down, then decided to make camp for the night.

"I'll go and look at what I heard. It sounded like rushing water of some kind." John offered, and slipped away through the vegetation.

He came back shortly to tell his friends that there was a stretch of white water ahead of them as the river dropped down a slope some 100 yards long before becoming calm again.

He told them that they would have to carry the craft down the obstacle because the water wasn't deep enough.

"I'll get the prisoners sorted, as they will be doing the carrying. We'll do it in one lift as opposed to two. I'll be keeping them in check. John you keep them guarded with your weapon. Bruce, you go on ahead with yours, and shoot anything that moves, including these prisoners." Sinclair advised.

Sinclair had the prisoners docile enough now to be able to get them to do anything he wanted. It was also the staring eyes and offending penises from the severed heads that kept them quiet.

"How have you managed to tame these bastards Andy. I've never seen such a scared look. Big Ju-Ju as you would say perhaps?" John asked, standing almost mesmerised at these spectres.

"It's quite simple really John. I placed a few grubs into the heads so that the eyes move from time to time as the grubs craw around the heads. Thus creating the image of the heads still being alive and watching them." Sinclair whispered so the prisoners didn't hear.

"Besides, severed heads and dicks for tongues is a recognised Ju-Ju no matter what part of the world you are in. Our boys did this to the Japs, which scared the shit out of them, especially if it was one of their heads that was used. And if you remember we did the same with those bloody Arabs." Sinclair added.

John just smiled at the memory and carried out his part of the move.

They arrived at the bottom of the slope and found a nice secluded spot to rest up for the night.

"We must have covered the best part of 30 miles today. The river is looking wider, deeper and faster, so we could do more tomorrow providing we don't meet up with more of these friends of ours, or disappear over some waterfall." Larter remarked, as John handed him another fish to eat.

"Maybe we'll have some meat tomorrow if we land somewhere decent. Mind you, coming across a friendly village would be even better, I'm going off this brand of tea." Sinclair said, drinking the last of his 'tea'.

The prisoners were fed and settled down for the night and Sinclair set the security traps again.

Happily the were empty when the friends got up the following morning, but when Sinclair went to the prisoners he found one had tried to escape, only to drown. His head joined the others that they were looking at.

The procession drifted down the river all that morning until John heard yet another strange sound from around yet another bend in the river.

They stopped, and hiding their craft in the dense undergrowth, found a vantage point to look at what it was.

All three looked through the bushes and saw a metal bridge crossing way above the river.

John felt a very cold shiver run down his spine.

"That's the bridge. I can feel it." John whispered.

Larter grabbed John as he went to stand up.

"Get down John, somebody might be down there."

"Bruce, Andy. That's the bridge the train went off. I'm telling you that's the one, believe me." John whispered agitatedly.

"The train didn't just fall off the bridge, it must have been blown up. It has been bothering me ever since I saw it last time. Now I can see and realise what I have felt all these weeks. These prisoners we've got must have been on their way to sabotage it again." John persisted.

"Helena kept telling and warning me about the bridge, even afterwards. You really must believe me!"

"It's all right, we believe you John." Larter said gently as Sinclair looked at his small friend and nodded in agreement.

"It looks as if we've got a steep embankment on our side of the bridge, so we must approach it from the other side. But we've got to wait until dark to cross the river." Sinclair said, looking at the terrain in front of them with a pair of confiscated binoculars.

"We need to make a plan on how to go about this." Larter whispered but was hushed by Sinclair.

"I can see someone under the right-hand span and somebody propping up long bamboo poles against the other span. I can't make out who they are, but you can bet your last penny its pals of our prisoners." Sinclair whispered.

The friends returned to their craft and set up another camp. This time, Sinclair had the prisoners gagged and trussed up against a termites nest. He poked the termite hill with a big stick so that a swarm of them would come out to look for the culprit, before blindfolding the men. He trailed strands of fibre over their exposed skins and saw how they tried to get away, thinking that the termites were about to attack them.

"We won't have any trouble with them now. Once it gets dark, we can row diagonally across with the raft behind us, and make for that part of the bank that can't be seen from the bridge." Sinclair whispered.

"We still have these weapons, and the grenades at our disposal. We could sneak up and give them a nasty surprise. But that would be too noisy. I'm still pretty nifty with a bow and arrow." John offered.

"I'm good at throwing knives and a pretty good shot too." Larter offered.

"Yes I know that. But we need total quiet and the time to sneak up on them. God knows what would happen if a train came and spoiled it all. We'd get killed along with the train." Sinclair advised.

For the next half-hour they discussed their tactics, drawing little diagrams on the sand, and making any alterations to their plan as a snag or problem cropped up.

John and Larter checked the weapons whilst Sinclair made a few of his own and giving them to the other two, showed them how they worked.

"This is your garrotte. It's only the electrical wire from the trucks, but all you do is simply slip the noose around their neck, and put tightly towards yourself, but each hand must cross over each other. It's just like cutting cheese. Their neck will simply roll off, you watch. Next, here's your bow and some arrows. They will kill at 50 feet, so get some practice in now until you can hit something in the dark." Sinclair explained.

They practiced with their home-made weapons, and wrapping up the firearms in their shirts, started to rub mud all over their body to hide their white skins.

"In the meantime, what about our prisoners Andy?" Larter asked.

"I have a special job for them. Something that John will appreciate later."

"Appreciate what Andy?" John asked absentmindedly.

"Oh nothing. Just you wait and see. Oh! And by the way! We will carry a machete, as well as two grenades each and don't forget a full water bottle. It's going to be a long night on that bridge." Sinclair added, handing the weapons out.

The dark period between the sun going down and the moon rising was the time when the three friends made their move across the river. They arrived at their target point and prepared themselves for some nocturnal visiting.

"Here's me, a budding engineer traipsing around the bloody jungle playing Tarzan." John whispered into Andy's ear, who shushed him up.

"No more talking. You know the signals and signs, so lets go." Sinclair whispered to the other two. They shook hands and left for their own little derring-do.

John crept along the side of the railway track and found that the prisoners were tied in such a way that their heads were across the lines.

'Now I know what he meant. The train simply lops off their heads as it passes over them.' John thought to himself and smiled at the simple justice of it. He crept along the side of the railway embankment so as not to be profiled in the moonlight, and arrived at the iron reinforced wooden bridge. He looked at it admiring its craftsmanship, and continued to make his way to the start of the span that was actually right above the river. He saw flashes of white along the lines and realised that these were the fingers of the saboteurs.

He counted seven pairs of hands, and saw four men further along under the bridge holding onto some ropes and trying to climb up onto the bridge.

He was to wait and keep hidden until he saw signals from both Larter, who had gone ahead to take care of these four, and Sinclair, who had gone to the cliff end of the bridge.

He saw Larter's signal to say that he was ready, and it seemed ages before he saw Sinclair's signal.

John tiptoed along the sleepers making sure that he didn't kick any stones, and reached the middle of the hands that were fumbling and feeling their way around the rails on the track.

His machete chopped off several fingers before the screams of pain and the noise of bodies splashing into the crocodile infested river, was heard.

As he turned, he tripped over one of the rails and in doing so, felt a man fall over him as he tried to stab John in the back with a large spear.

John slipped the garrotte around his attackers neck and was amazed how easily the man's head rolled off just like Sinclair had said.

He picked up the bloody head and putting it onto an arch at the side of the track, waited until one of the attackers came into view. Moments later he saw a head poking through the metal struts, shoving the head into the man's face and said aloud 'BOO'!

The instant and natural reaction from the attacker was to scream in terror and let go of the bridge, only to fall away down into the crocodile infested river below him.

'Serves him right for not knowing who his friends are.' John chuckled, crouching back down again and making his way back to his end of the bridge again.

He had a momentary feeling again as he did when he felt Helena's presence on the ship and decided to lie flat for a moment. As he did so, several bullets whizzed past where his body had been a second ago. He rolled over into the safety of a bridge span, picked up his silent weapon and waited until his next attacker could be seen.

He saw a dull flash coming from where he had crept along to come onto the bridge, and took aim with his bow. His arrow hit the surprised man right between his eyes, who fell off the embankment and down into the river to join his other friends. Before he could turn around, morel bullets were zipping past him and he guessed they were for Larter who was slashing and slicing his opponents in close combat.

John picked up his rifle and blasted away at the area where the bullets came from.

He heard several screams and saw a few bodies falling, and ran towards them throwing away his now empty rifle.

He grabbed a weapon from one of the dead men and discovering it was a machine gun that he was familiar with, took cover behind some very re-assuring riveted steel girders. There was total silence from his side but he heard explosions and bullets flying from across the other side. It occurred to him that he had not seen Larter, and decided to go back and help him. He arrived to where Larter was hiding and found him covered in blood and sitting among a load of dead men.

"Yours or theirs Bruce!" John asked softly as he bent down to see to his friend.

"Theirs actually John. I'm just having a quiet crap on one of them for fear of giving my place away." Larter smiled, pulling up his trousers.

They heard someone running towards them and waited until the person had passed. It was Sinclair trailing a bunch of bloody heads tied together with some rope. They stopped and looked at Sinclair arranging the heads on the bridge spans, realising that those were not tongues sticking out of them.

"Now when do you suppose he had the time to do all that John!" Larter asked in surprise.

"Search me but here comes their bodies." John said, and popped out in front of the chasing men to mow them down with his machine gun.

Larter poked his head around to the dead men, saying

"Surprise Surprise!" then to John

"Tut tut, you're getting a right litter lout."

John smiled back and said.

"You should see what litter Andy is going to leave when that train arrives.

"What train John?"

"The one coming round the bend behind me."

"Bloody hell. Heads will roll if that train gets onto this bridge.

"They certainly will Bruce." John chuckled, thinking of the

prisoners tied up along the rails.

"Come on lads. We've got to stop the train from getting onto the bridge. There's dynamite in great wads all over the underneath of the thing.

They ran towards the train waving and shouting trying to attract the attention of the engine- driver, but to no avail, until Larter threw a grenade at the train and blew a hole in the track. There was a loud screech of metal on metal as the train ground to a halt, panting heavily as the steam was still puffing out of its funnel.

John ran up to the driver, introduced himself then told him of the danger ahead.

Soon there were several men from the train running towards them, all carrying guns.

"Bloody hell Andy, here comes the cavalry." John quipped when a tall uniformed man arrived with his gun pointing at them.

"Don't point that at us, we're the good guys!" Sinclair shouted, then introduced the friends to the soldier.

"I'm Major Borzman, and these are my men. This train is a 20 carriage passenger train, and I have a company of men on board, but there's a mineral ore train only 20 minutes behind us." Borzman said hurriedly.

"The bridge is double tracked yet the train approached on a single line. Where is the nearest point switching lever driver?" John asked

"There's one about half a mile each side of the bridge. But if there's dynamite on the bridge nobody can cross it in case it blows up." the engine-driver said with panic in his voice.

Borzman summoned one of his men and spoke to him briefly, sending him running off in the direction of the lever down the track behind them.

He then got several of his soldiers to go along the bridge and search for the explosives and others to keep guard on them.

"How many saboteurs did you find? Only they usually just set their charges then melt into the jungle." Borzman asked, looking over the bridge with a pair of binoculars.

"We met some making their way here, but they're dead now. I despatched about a dozen." Sinclair said.

"I dealt with about another dozen." Larter said nonchalantly

"And I helped about the same to go swimming." John added.

"I've spotted several more waiting on the other side of the river. Presumably they're to help rob the next trainload of victims. We had already captured some of them wearing their trophies from a previous attack." Sinclair said, and went on to describe what they had found.

"Yes! There's a black tribe insurgency movement backed by a few misguided white people operating in this area, but the passengers are only a side-line as they're after the arsenal trains and the gold shipments coming down the track. The last incident involving this particular bridge was a few months ago when several hundred passengers were killed. Some of the survivors got kidnapped, robbed then murdered later. Their bodies were found about 60 miles north east of here." Borzman stated.

John looked at the major, then at the bridge and then at his two friends, before he spoke.

"It seems that we may have an idea who some of these white people behind this are. Or at least someone whom we can call upon soon, to get his ideas about it all." John told the major, who looked surprised by this revelation.

"You know who is behind this? If that's the case then we can clear this murderous bunch up much quicker. They are only shadows in the jungle at the moment." Borzman replied.

"But in the meantime, it appears that you three have stumbled on a whole battalion of insurgents out to murder, rape and loot innocent people."

"We are only Merchant Navy personnel so don't ask us to start another war, Major." John said, standing next to his friends who were covered in blood.

"More like Mercenary Officers, judging by your appearances." Borzman smiled.

"But surely you can complete your mission by helping us get this bridge secured and the train out of danger?" he asked

"It's like this see major. We're supposed to be on our way back to our ship in Cape Town!" Sinclair started to say.

"Cape Town? What on this river?" Borzman gasped, then began to laugh.

"Gentlemen, Cape Town is nearly 600 miles away south west of here. This is the River Orange with about another 800 miles to go before it flows out into the Atlantic just south of the Namib Desert. In other words gentlemen, you're going 700 miles the wrong way."

The three friends looked at each other and smiled.

"We guessed more or less where we were major, but we thought it was one of the feeder rivers into the Zambesi. But we'd have to get to a road or in this case a railway to hitch a lift back." John said with a grin.

"But how the devil did you get onto this river and up so far?"

"It's a long story major. But as sailors we naturally sailed along it for a couple of days." Sinclair added.

"You've got a ship?" Borzman asked in disbelief.

"Why yes! It's the '*Denise*', she's moored just behind that point on the river." Larter boasted and chuckled along with his two friends.

"Well good! Maybe we can use it to ferry my men across the river and after those insurgents you have mentioned." Borzman said quickly, which left the friends looking incredulously at each other.

Their discussion was interrupted by the return of the runner, who after taking several moments to gather his breath again, reported that the lever had been broken off and that he could see the smoke of the other train only about five miles away.

"C'mon Andy, Bruce you too, lets get this thing fixed!" John said quickly and dashed off towards the end of the train.

John ran along the side of the track flanked by his two friends and reached the damaged lever.

He examined it and told Andy to get a couple of thick sticks to use as crowbars, and for Bruce to help him with the mechanism.

They worked furiously and managed to get the switching mechanism working just before they heard the long sad whistle of the monster rumbling swiftly towards them.

Sinclair looked around then followed the other two moving down the track to try and stop this train too. They were only a few hundred yards down the track when they heard a shout and a terrified scream behind them. They looked round and saw a man screaming and waving his arms about, before Sinclair raised his rifle and shot him dead.

"Just as I thought! He'd waited until we left before he tried his stunt again. That had him." Sinclair laughed, and told them about the skull.

"It means that there might be others making their way up behind the passenger train. Any suggestions?" Larter asked.

"We'll stop this train and use it to take us back to warn the others." Sinclair said, and started to wave a white piece of cloth at the oncoming train.

"Quick Bruce. Stand in the middle of the track and wave like mad!" John prompted.

The large engine slowed and finally stopped a few feet away from them, when the engine-driver came down from his loft platform and spoke to them.

"What is the problem Kaffir?" he asked in a thick Dutch accent.

"We've got several problems and need your help." John said and quickly reeled off the main ones.

"Get on board then and we'll do just that." the driver ordered and clambered up into the massive steam engine. He got out a box and undid the clasp.

The friends were amazed to see it contained an ancient machine gun, and several belts of ammunition.

"This is a present from my friends at Upslinger. This will take care of the bastards. I lost my brother on this bridge only a few months ago. He was the engineer on that new train we had." he said sombrely.

"Tell us about it sometime!" John said softly, and got his machine gun at the ready.

Sinclair and Larter positioned themselves either side of the engine platform as the heavy juggernaut rolled slowly along the track.

They passed the dead man and the skull still perched on the lever, as the train took the junction and rolled towards the passenger train on the other track.

The engine driver blew his steam whistle to warn the others, just as bullets started to whizz past them.

"You just keep driving, we'll see to this!" Sinclair shouted, and grabbing the machine gun squirted bullets into the bushes when the train passed them.

John had joined in the shooting as Larter lobbed their remaining hand grenades at the unseen attackers, until the train arrived alongside the other one.

John jumped down and ran towards Borzman and his troops who had been alerted by all the shooting, and were preparing their own weapons and positions to protect the screaming passengers still on the train.

"We've got several of them, but the rest are over the other side. How's the search on the bridge major?" John asked, breathing hard.

"Found several parcels of dynamite, but the other end of the bridge has been destroyed. In my opinion it might not take the weight of the train." Borzman replied.

"I'm a Marine engineer, not a civil one, but I'll take a look at it for you. In the meantime keep those passengers quiet, more importantly, safe." John said hastily and signalled to Sinclair and Larter to join him.

"The bridge has been damaged on the other side and I need to examine it. If it can take some load then we can get the carriages over one at a time. But whatever the outcome, we've got to stop the trains coming from that end too." John whispered.

"I did notice that a lot of the bolts were removed, and the rails loosened, but that was before I started throwing grenades around." Sinclair said.

Borzman came over to them and stated that he would take some of his men over to secure the other side of the bridgehead and that the three of them could come over at the same time.

"We need to stop the other trains coming over too major. But I need to inspect the bridge before anyone can cross it." John replied.

"Fair enough. Lets go then." Borzman ordered, and sent his troops filtering across the bridge carefully in case of some sudden ambush from the other side.

Sinclair had his hessian sack with him, which prompted Borzman to ask what was in it.

"You really don't want to know major. But this bridge is safe for us all to walk over because of what's in this sack, just take my word for it." Sinclair said softly and nodded his head.

Borzman never replied, but was shocked and surprised when his head came level with one of Sinclair's secret weapons.

"So that's why we can cross. A good old Ju-Ju present for them! Funny how the old tricks always comes up trumps!" Borzman chuckled and started to walk faster and of straighter back.

"Major, they're good but not that good. You could still get a bullet from those bastards waiting for us on the other bank!" Sinclair shouted, as several bullets whipped past them, causing the major to dive for cover.

The progress over the bridge was slow and laborious for John, who looked at vital load bearing joints and metal fasteners on it. He came across some loose fishplates from the rails and marked them by putting the scattered nuts around them to indicate where they came from.

It took them almost an hour before they reached the other end.

By then the noise of the battle and the bullets pinging off the bridge metal was at its' loudest.

Sinclair crawled over to John and pointed down through a gap in the bridge to a group of men trying to climb up behind them.

"Watch this John!" Sinclair whispered, and got one of his skulls out, placing a grenade into its mouth. He pulled out the pin from the grenade and lobbed the head down in among the men.

There was sheer terror in their screams when the head rolled among them, followed by a large bang then nothing.

"See I told you they don't like it. This punch-up has been a far better one than with those wogs we sorted out in the desert" Sinclair chuckled, preparing yet another one.

"You're right there. Those bastards didn't know what hit them!" John replied, and smiled at seeing yet another bunch of attackers get much the same.

"Have you finished yet John? Only I'm running out of ammo!" Larter whispered, appearing suddenly alongside him.

"Nearly done, but must get onto the bank and look at the track too."

Sinclair joined in telling them that the major and his men had rounded up the remainder of the attackers and that they could finish off the inspection without any further interruption.

The friends walked off the bridge and down the track towards the second lever and its mechanism, with Sinclair placing skulls in strategic places to prevent any re-enforcements arriving.

"Right then. Just as I thought! We get some of the soldiers to stop the trains approaching, and for us to get the carriages over. But the rails need to be strengthened again by replacing all the loose nuts and bolts." John said at length.

Returning to the two waiting trains, John spoke to the engine-drivers about what was needed to be done.

"The bridge can take the heavy engine on its own, and maybe the lightest engine with two carriages at once, but that would depend on the weight of the carriages. The important thing is that the weight must not be more than about 5 tons per 2 yards of bridge.

You will have to sort out some shunting routine to be able to get the engine back over again though." John informed them.

"Leave that to us. We'll have both trains over in no time." they said, rolling up their sleeves, starting their work.

Borzman arrived with the prisoners who were strung together like sausages.

As they were crossing the bridge and saw the skulls, the prisoners screamed with terror and tried to run away, but were knocked to the ground then forced to march again.

Sinclair grinned and wiped his machete on the back of a passing prisoner.

Maybe we can get a lift back on the next train John. We've still got a score to settle in Cape Town.

"Train to Cape Town, gentlemen?" Borzman asked with surprise.

"Heavens no. There's a small town due north from here. I'll get you a plane to take you back. But what about your ship?"

Larter laughed and said that if some of his men were to carry it up the embankment, they could take it back to Cape Town with them, as it was too valuable a ship to leave around without its crew.

Borzman was amazed at their 'ship' and started to laugh at the notion of a company of men trying to cross the river in it. But he also marvelled at its neat construction as he'd never seen an inflatable before. He said he wanted to own several of his own, but with outboard motors on them so that he could move up river quicker.

"You'd have to ask the engineer who built her, and not Mr Brunel either." Sinclair laughed, pointing to John.

John smiled and said he'd send him a drawing of it some day, but his thoughts were already in that little town the major spoke of. He didn't want to visit the place so soon.

"Bruce, Andy, we've been away from the ship over a week now. If we've still some quarantine days left, can't we take a train back? Even Phineas Fogg took time off," John said slowly and started to walk down the track.

"We know what's up John, and we agree with you. But look at this old newspaper one of the soldiers gave me. It's got our faces on it! Larter said, as he showed him the crumpled paper.

'3 Officers from the SS Inverary, made famous for their part in the rescue of the survivors off the sunken ships, the Chantral and Inverlaggan, have been reported missing, believed to be kidnapped by the Xmgongo terrorists. A ransom demand has been sent in for the payment of 1million Rand and the release of their men held as political prisoners.'

John and Sinclair read the article through and handed it back to Larter.

"All the more reason to speed up our return, John."

"Yet according to this paper, we're dead!" Sinclair stated, holding up a second paper.

'The Inverary 3 are feared dead. Believed to be executed by the terrorists as the deadline for their demands were not met. Shipping tycoon Lord Belverley stated that he regrets this incident, but believed his officers are still alive. However, his ships will not be held to ransom and will sail on time.'

"My case rests then. We go back by rail, and besides we can't get our ship onto those tiny airplanes." John concluded.

Borzman came back to speak to them for a while, and told them that there was a passenger train waiting on the far side to come over. He had arranged transport for them and their dinghy, first class.

It would take them about two days, but their travel bill would be picked up by his Garrison Commander in Cape Town, and if they needed anything be it ever so small, or how tall the bed warmer was, just ask the Pullman Inspector on board.

"Thanks major. The first thing we need is a cigarette, then a bath, a decent meal with a nice cold beer and a nice juicy cigar to enjoy the evening with, in that order." Sinclair stated, which had Borzman laughing.

"In that case, you can start with these." Borzman said and gave them his silver cigarette case and lighter.

"It looks like the one you lost Bruce." John said as he took a cigarette from it and examined the case.

"Same initials too, except other way round." Larter nodded, looking it over, then handed it back to Borzman.

"Well its goodbye from me. Must catch my train. Remember to get in contact with my commander before you go back to your ship. He will be more than interested in that customs officer you mentioned. Cheerio!" Borzman said and saluting the friends, marched back over the bridge.

The friends sat on their dinghy, smoking their cigarettes leisurely, when a gleaming black and chrome steam engine came puffing slowly towards them. It stopped noisily in a big cloud of steam alongside them.

"Afternoon! 4 passengers for Cape Town?" a skinny white man in a brown and yellow uniform asked, stepping down from the first railway carriage.

"Yes, that's us.!" Larter smiled as the man counted only 3.

"Where's the other one?"

John laughed, explaining the fourth one was the dinghy.

"Oh you mean Denise! Yes, she's here. But she only drinks water, so better put her in one of your goods wagons." He said.

"No! I've got four, and that's that. Here are your boarding passes, meal tickets and bar tokens. You will find all you need in your cabins." the man stated, handing the bits of paper over to John.

"I'll get the porters to lift that dinghy into the carriage for you. But follow me if you please."

"We're right behind you sir. " Sinclair chuckled and the friends followed right behind him onto the train.

They had a good bath and managed to scrounge some suitable clothing from admiring and enthusiastic male travellers.

The rest of the passengers started to question these strangers, guessing that they were in some way responsible for getting their train over the damaged bridge. For that they were feted, and treated with respect during the entire journey.

The next morning when the train stopped for fuel and water,

the passengers were allowed off the train to stretch their legs, buy some trinkets or fresh fruit.

When the train started off again, the passengers settled down for yet another marathon wait to arrive, the three friends ensconced themselves in the buffet bar enjoying their aperitif before their meal. A passenger, unknowingly dropped his local newspaper which Sinclair retrieved and read aloud what the headline banners were saying.

'Mercenary forces help foil ambush on immigrant train as government forces arrived to crush an Xmgongo terrorist army. The commander of the government forces, Major Borzman is reported to have the area in control and has either killed or captured most of the terrorists. When questioned about the size or number of the mercenary forces, Major Borzman stated that it was an unknown amount. And they disappeared just as quickly as they had appeared on the scene. This means that the Xmgongo terrorists have an unseen foe watching their every move.

An Xmgongo intermediary has denied any such claims and reports that the organisation is growing stronger by the week, and that no government forces will be able to stop their activities against the settlers encroaching into their homelands.'

"It appears that our major is taking all the credit. Still, maybe it's for the best, because we've got a score to settle." Sinclair said, handing over the paper for the other two to read, but was thrown into the nearest rubbish bin.

During their time on the train, enjoying a life of high jollity and living in comparative luxury, they had told and conditioned the people not to say a word for at least a day after they arrived, because of a special surprise they wanted to spring on their ships captain.

Everyone agreed, but little did they know the ruse that was played upon them.

The train hissed and breathed its steam and smoke as it rested against the buffers of the station platform. The place was almost deserted and the night was dark when the three friends gave the Pullman Inspector their instructions concerning the dinghy, then slipped away before anybody noticed them.

Chapter XXI
Pay Day

"Is that the Garrison commander?" Larter asked over the telephone, and got the right reply.

Telling the commander who he was and giving the secret message from Borzman, he went on to tell him what was wanted. After a few minutes he put the phone down and told the other two what to expect and when.

Sinclair had his now infamous sack over his shoulder as they walked down the deserted street towards the docks. They stopped in an alleyway to have a cigarette and a last check on their proposed actions before arriving at the main gate to the docks.

They went silently through a side entrance and crept up to the customs office to check that their target was there.

Sinclair came back and whispered that there were 4 men in the billet at the back, and that the customs officer was sitting with his feet up reading some girly magazine, and listening to the wireless that they could hear.

"Remember. Stick one head on the windowsills and hang one over the door before you knock the window. The door opens outwards, so as it opens, the skull will fall into them. They will slam the door shut and all you've got to do is slide something in the handle to prevent it from opening again. When you've done that, come around the front and do the same for the office. I shall be at the back ready to grab him. You will follow me into the office and wait until the army gets here." Sinclair explained, and gave them the sack, but took out a skull and wrapped it in some paper before signalling them to start.

John gave Bruce the nod as they tapped the windows gently at first, then a little louder.

The voices from the billet stopped for a moment, then an enormous terrified shriek, and the sound of footsteps coming towards the door, told the friends to stand by to lock the door as planned.

There were more shrieks as the skulls landed on the men, who in their terror slammed and locked the door again and started to wail and moan.

"Phase 1 complete Bruce!" John whispered, then sneaked around the front of the office and did the same there.

The customs officer reacted in the same way as his men and ran straight into the skull Sinclair was holding. He ran back into the office trying tried to shut the door, as Sinclair barged his way in and knocked him out with a vicious blow to his chin. The friends had the man tied and trussed up before he was brought round by a bucket of water.

He spluttered and coughed first as he regained his breath, then demanded to be released, shouting that they couldn't do this to a government officer of the Customs and Excise. He went totally white and started to gibber and rant incoherently when he saw the terrifying dangling skulls close to his face.

They took the skulls away and waited for him to calm down a bit before walking slowly around to show themselves to him.

"But, but!" he stammered. "You're dead! You have to be!" he whimpered, urinating in his trousers with terror.

"And why should we be dead, officer? Unless of course you wanted us to be." Larter asked, then started to question the now slobbering shivering mass.

John was rifling through the filing cabinets and other lockers and discovered hundreds of passports and effects from many people, mostly immigrants or well to do tourists, and seamen, including theirs that the customs office took from them. He found a bunch of keys and going into the billet, began to open the various lockers and drawers there. He came back with his arms full of confiscated belongings.

"Smuggling contraband is pretty rife around here officer?" John asked, dumping jewellery, passports, trinkets and other personal belongings.

Larter found some files that contained details on the people who appeared to belong to the terrorist organisation, and started to read aloud from them.

Sinclair searched the man only to discover that he had Bruce's cigarette case and lighter and showed them to Larter.

"How he got this I'll never know, but you always seem to leave it around." Sinclair said angrily.

Larter picked his belongings up and looked at them.

"I remember. He asked us to show some identity, and I must have pulled it out to get to my wallet." he said, pocketing his belongings again, then went over and kicked the man in the groin.

"That's for nicking my things, you thieving bastard." Larter shouted vehemently, just as two army officers and a platoon of men marched into the office.

"Who's in charge here!" they demanded.

"He is!" the three friends said in unison, pointing to the customs man, and handed the officer a large file.

"Read that and sort it out, with Major Borzman's compliments." John said.

"Then you must be the missing officers. I congratulate you on returning safely. Major Borzman has given me most of the details of your, shall we say, involvement up at the bridge." the officer said and both officers saluted each friend in turn.

"Now lets not get too carried away with all this saluting and all that, we're Merchant Officers not ruddy tin soldiers." Sinclair said, but with a large grin on his face.

"You have a hut full of other men behind this office to arrest. Two of them were our kidnappers, but you will need to take them out gently." Sinclair advised.

The senior officer asked why, but soon found the answer when he saw the skull sitting on the custom officers desk. He picked it up and looked at it, as the eyes started to move.

"This your work?" He asked Sinclair, who simply nodded as he sucked on another cigarette.

"A certain Boer army man taught me this trick some while ago, and you?" he asked.

"From similar sources shall we say. But works every time on black people, and even on some yellow or white ones too, don't you think?" Sinclair responded.

"Very much so. It's not so much the severed head, it's the terror of the eyes and the dick poking out." the officer said, nodding his approval at Sinclair's work.

"Still! Mustn't keep you men from joining your ship. I'll take all this away and get a firing squad together for our friends, for when they're paraded down the mile of shame."

The friends thanked the officer and watched as the customs men were shackled, ball and chained to each other, and literally thrown into a large steel lined lorry and driven off.

"Phase 2 and 3 complete. We might as well go ashore and collect on these calling cards as our ship sailed out yesterday. Look!" John suggested, showing the others the daily shipping report, telling which ship was arriving or leaving, where it came from and where it was going.

"I see the *Inverary* had her sailing delayed, bound for Belfast via Southampton. The *Inverkirk* is due in later on today from Perth to Belfast. I think she' one of our new cargo liners." Larter said excitedly, then spotted a few more.

"Even the old *Meadowlea* is due in the day after tomorrow. She's arriving from Southampton and going onto Hong Kong via Ceylon and Singapore. Now that's a good trip to be on. The *Invermoray* is arriving today from Singapore but is sailing tomorrow for Liverpool, via Rio and Gibraltar."

"Oh well, we must leave now. But we might as well help ourselves to some of this confiscated stuff here. We deserve to have something for our troubles even if it's just our own personal documents and belongings. It starts the pay day, or pay back time if you like to put it." John suggested.

They got hold of some suitcases and filled them with whatever took their fancy.

John found a set of fishing rods; a matching pair of twin-barrelled shotguns still in their leather valise; bottles of his favourite whiskey, some very expensive jewellery, and perfumes, several cartons of his favourite tobacco and cigars. They found a huge stash of money in many national currencies, but mostly in bundles of U.S and British bank notes, which they shared out equally.

When all three were satisfied and loaded up with 'extra presents for home' they locked the building with its own keys and threw them away, then left the dock through the side gate again into the still empty streets.

"Now which way to the shipping agents office, Bruce?" John asked.

"Sod him. Lets find a hotel for the day, I'm ruddy starving again!" Sinclair said, spotting and hailed down a passing taxi.

Chapter XXII
Lazy Days

The friends arrived at a luxury hotel and checked in, in time for breakfast.

They ate well, savouring every mouthful and afterwards enjoyed a large cigar while they read the local newspapers before moving off to their respective rooms. Their newly acquired wealth making them act the part of rich tourists out to enjoy themselves.

"This is the life our lordships enjoy, and at our expense too!" Sinclair whooped, looking distinctly pleased with himself.

"Ah yes dear friend. But in this case it's at the expense and kind courtesy of the South African Government." Larter retorted.

"Don't forget our Xmgongo friends, or whatever they were called, and the customs man." John piped up, as all three chuckled at the spectacle of the customs man with the three severed heads swirling around him.

A knock on the adjoining door woke John up from his slumber and he saw his friends come in fully dressed in their 'borrowed' clothing.

"C'mon 2nd! Time we got some food down us and a bloody good run ashore before we show our faces to our shipping agent." Larter announced.

"That's the thing though! We've got the pick of two company ships, but which one are we going for?" John asked sleepily.

"We have to go back on the *Inverary* and start again from Belfast, John. Don't forget, our gear is still on board her." Sinclair advised.

"I suppose you're right!" John conceded.

"Besides, look at the papers. Our major has arrived back to a hero's welcome. And our customs man and his cronies are lined up for the firing squad. In another report, it seems there's been yet another robbery at the customs house and the place had been cleaned out. Xmgongo activists claim responsibility." Larter said, tossing the paper over for John to read.

John read the article carefully, then tossed the paper into the wastepaper bin.

"Oh well! That covers us. Anyhow, if anybody asks, we locked the place after us when we left." John said, washing himself then got dressed for the rest of the day.

"We'll pack our things up into cardboard boxes and leave them in the foyer. We'll have them marked as 'Sea mail by SS *Inverary*' if she's still in port, and delivered to us once we get on board. Save from carrying them around with us. Then we'll go and see the agent and get us a passage back home on it. The *Inverkirk* is a converted freighter converted into a liner, so they might be glad of the extra staff for the trip anyway." Sinclair suggested.

They waited until John was ready, then left the locked rooms and eventually the hotel for the docks.

"Good afternoon gentlemen! What can I do for you?" the agent asked civilly, then looked up to see the three friends standing before him.

He almost had an apoplectic fit when he saw who they were.

"But where the hell have you three come from?" He stammered.

"Lord Belverely was right after all. You are alive and well! He said that nothing would stop you, especially after the headline news you three received for your efforts in helping the survivors of the *Inverlaggan*." he said aloud and gave a cheer that brought other agency workers in to see what the hubbub was.

They too were ecstatic when they saw the friends standing large as life before them.

The agent made a lengthy phone call as the other office workers fussed around the men, and they were given press cuttings of the Shipping Board of Enquiry into the sinking of the *Chantral* and *Inverlaggan*. Mentioning especially, their part in the heroic epic escape from the jaws of death in the Namib Desert.

John read through the articles whilst Larter and Sinclair who both towered over John, looked over his shoulders.

"Well, well! It looks as if Belverley and co are still deeply in debt to us. They still owe us compo and lots of it too." Larter said with glee.

"Maybe that's why this lot here gave gone crazy and can't do enough for us." Sinclair said with a grin.

"I have special instructions for you lot in the event of you turning up. But that was Lord Invergarron on the phone from Pretoria. He has instructed that you are to board our liner the *Inverkirk* now, or the *Fernlea* in a weeks' time. As 'De Lux' class passengers naturally, and still have two weeks leave when you arrive back in Belfast. You sail tonight but I will give you some back pay now and you'll receive the rest on arrival at Belfast. Congratulations gentlemen!" the agent said expansively.

"Please make it the *Inverkirk*, as we're expecting some gifts from the local military." Sinclair said quickly.

"Yes, I've got the good vessel 'Denise' to be winched aboard, just as soon as it arrives on the jetty." John said to the awe-struck agent.

They stood for a while receiving their welcome home pats on their backs and handshakes from the agent and his workers before they left to pick their things up from the hotel and board ship.

The taxi ride back to the hotel was euphoric for the friends at the thought of a proper 2-week cruise without doing a thing to help.

Soon they were walking over the gangway where the ships captain was there to meet them.

"Welcome on board gentlemen! I'm captain Ward, and this is my purser Mr Roberts. He will show you to your cabins and settle you in." Ward said pleasantly when the introductions were completed.

"Come with me gentlemen." Roberts said, leading the way to his office, for the friends to enter their particulars onto the ships passenger list.

"You must be the three missing, presumed dead officers off the *Inverary*." Roberts observed, as Sinclair was the last to sign.

"Pretty much alive and kicking, purser. By the way, we have boxes of personal belongings arriving as forwarded luggage, and a launch that we picked up on the way. Kindly make sure our boxes are delivered to our cabins." John asked the admiring purser.

"No problem 2nd. Here are your cabin keys. You have a free slate whilst on board, but own consumption and personal use only, if you get my drift."

"Thank you purser, but there's no need to worry. We hope to keep within our normal budgets just in case we overstay our welcome or prove too expensive to keep." Larter said, and chuckled at the purser, who led them to their cabins.

"Blimey! Is this deluxe class or is this deluxe class?" Sinclair asked, stepping into a large double cabin.

"This one has been specially set aside for the three of you to share. You must appreciate that many of our top paying passengers usually get the better ones before staff, but on this occasion, it's the company that has the pleasure of seeing that you get the best there is on board." Roberts apologised

"Not at all purser, its just fine. Makes a change from living up jungle, and even in the desert." John said, walking into the luxuriously decorated cabin.

"I'll have your baggage brought along, but if you care to get yourselves organised, dinner will be served in one hour." Roberts said, and left them to explore their new home for the next two weeks.

"Could be worse I suppose Andy. Better than sausage shaped hammocks in the fore ends." John smiled as Sinclair was trying out his chosen bunk.

"Silk sheets and all! Here's me hob-knobbing with the rich passengers instead of the grotty steerage ones I always seem to meet."

"Lets hope you don't get too used to it Andy, it might spoil you for the real world when we arrive back in Belfast." Larter chuckled, opening the cabins mini cocktail bar.

"I like the mod cons too!" he added, showing them the contents.

"Hooray! Stocking fillers!" Sinclair greeted, and opening a miniature bottle of brandy and gulped it down, then licked his lips.

"Real Napolean brandy too!" he said appreciatively.

They got themselves washed and freshened up before they left for their evening meal.

"Mr Grey, Mr Larter and Mr Sinclair! Your table is right over here. This will be your table for the voyage, here is the wine list and the menu." the immaculately dressed steward directed and ushered them to their table.

There were several passengers already dining and enjoying themselves, which made the friends feel a little more at ease.

"A little different than before John! We're passengers this time, so let's keep out of the way of the rest of the crew. Stay together and just enjoy ourselves." Larter whispered, as a few of the other passengers looked over at the three newcomers, staring with curiosity.

They enjoyed their meal and wine, before going out onto the promenade deck for a breather. The harbour was basking in the multi-coloured lights illuminating different features, and the moon was starting to shine its yellowy glow over it all.

"Let's hope our trip home is a peaceful one. I've had a real guts full of it so far." John said glumly, but was quickly cheered up by a voice that came from behind them.

"Hello Mr Grey! And you Mr Larter. Goodness, and you too Bosun!"

They turned round to see steward Burns carrying a tray of drinks with him.

"Burns! Why you old scoundrel. How the bloody hell are you. I always knew you were THE top steward in the shipping line!" John said, shaking Burns outstretched hand.

They all shook hands and with Burns who then offered them the entire tray of drinks saying he'd go and get another one.

"You're in my cabin area gentlemen, and I have put your forwarded luggage there for you. If there's anything I can get you, just call me." Burns said with a large grin, looking at his old shipmates.

"Yes steward. There is something you can do for us. All our belongings were left on the *Inverary* and we've no change of clobber. Any chance of you fixing us up with something? No uniforms though, we're strictly passengers this time." Larter asked.

"Why certainly. I'll have something ready for you later on." Burns replied.

"Then you'd better have our key." John said, handing the cabin key over.

"For shame on you 2nd! You know I have my own set, or have you forgotten." Burns grinned, jangling a massive bunch of keys in front of them.

"Ho hum! Silly me!" John laughed as Burns left them to drink up.

"Wonder who else we'll bump into before we sail?" Larter asked, looking around the deserted deck.

The friends decided it was time to return to their cabins, and found that Burns had deposited several piles of clothes on their bunks. They looked at each garment and tried on a few to see if they fitted.

"Pretty good eye on old Burns!" He's even got a packet of fags stuffed into our pockets, John laughed, pulling out yet another packet from his jacket.

"Better make sure our boxes are full too! You can't trust these thieving dockyard mateys." Sinclair said, opening his treasure chest to check it.

"Yep! All there!" he said after a while.

"But of course Andy. This is a Royal Mail Ship, and our boxes were marked as such too. Nobody, not even our bent customs officer would dare to open them." Larter said with a grin, as he and John found theirs in good order too.

"We'll be able to give Burns a few bob for his troubles now." John suggested and the other two nodded their consent.

They woke up early and had their breakfast in the cool of the morning, before most of the other passengers arrived. They were greeted by some of the other ship's officers as they came in for their breakfast then went about their business.

"Ordinarily I'd be in my shack by now, tuning my transmitter or whatever." Larter said, relishing this unaccustomed free time.

"Aye, and I'd probably be on my deck rounds by now too. What about you Andy?"

"Me! I'd probably still be in my bunk. I'm not needed until about an hour before we sail." Sinclair smiled at his two friends.

"So just who's got the cushiest job then, Bruce? Certainly not us officers!" John chuckled, and tossed a cigarette over to Sinclair.

The friends were standing on the promenade deck when they observed a large black saloon car arrive alongside the gangway. The captain stepped out of it smartly followed by another man in a military uniform.

"Bloody hell! It's the major, hope he's not coming to get us." Sinclair muttered, and flicked his cigarette butt over the side of the ship.

"Better get into the lounge where we can be found. Don't want him poking his nose in our cabin." John whispered as the friends moved swiftly towards the passengers lounge.

"Hello Mr Grey. Mr Larter, Mr Sinclair." Borzman greeted as Ward and he met up with them.

"Glad you're now on your way home I suppose?" he asked politely.

"Hello Major. How did your trip up-country go? We got a bit worried about you being as we've never heard nor seen you since." Sinclair asked.

"Nice of you to ask! Yes, all went swimmingly well. My commander has filled me in on your affair with the rogue customs officer. I managed to get the truth out of him before he was shot.

He was one of the terrorists 'go betweens', and apparently one of their paymasters. Pity we couldn't grab his supply route too." Borzman said in a buoyant mood.

"I have had a special agent follow you three since leaving the bridge, and yes I know everything you have been up to. And thanks to my commander, all about your escapade up north in the desert." Borzman said as he glowered menacingly at the three friends.

They looked at each other uneasily, but John stood firm to the challenge.

"And what have you deduced major?"

"The taxi you caught yesterday was one of our special agents, and apart from giving the game away, you three can keep, shall we say, your souvenirs you found in the customs house." Borzman said with a large grin on his face, then added.

"They can easily be explained away with the reported break in, but I am really here to give the three of you a special present. It is one that very few receive. I will give it to you now, but you must not open it until you are out into international waters. You will understand what I mean later. But suffice to say, it's from a grateful government. In view of governmental security reasons, I apologise I cannot offer you the full ceremonial usual on these occasions, never- the-less, it is just as potent this way." Borzman said and handed each of them a small black box with a yellow and green ribbon tied around it.

The friends looked at their gifts curiously then thanked the major for them before they slipped them into their borrowed clothes.

"We have a gift for you major. Here is a piece of paper that will authorise you, under my license, to make as many as you wish. The object itself is on board awaiting your collection. I refer to our other friend, Denise."

Borzman looked at the paper and the drawing, and smiled.

"Mr Grey. It will be a pleasure to make a whole host of them. But mine will be much bigger and with outboard motors too." Borzman said gratefully.

"Then we have a deal major!" John said and all three shook Borzman's hand to seal the bargain.

"I bid you goodbye gentlemen. If ever you visit Cape Town again, just call the local garrison commander and get me." Borzman said, and saluted before leaving them.

"It seems as if you three have caused quite a stir since arriving here. You've got some explaining to do when you get back. But don't worry it's only to keep the ships records straight and your personnel files up to date. Mind you, Freeman's in for a hammering when he gets back." Ward stated with a grin, then walked into the lounge to be greeted by some friendly passengers.

The ship sailed for the wide-open spaces of the Atlantic and three weeks of mind numbing inactivity not only for the three friends.

The ship settled into a dual work pattern, which for most of the crew was an easy living until they got back into port again. But for the stewards, the ships hospitality staff and all those involved with the passengers, it was the usual hectic time of trying to please them no matter what they had asked for.

It was a time for deck skittles; lounging around the big rubber paddling pool; who would win the daily tombola prize; or the daily tote on how far the ship had sailed in one day, or who was to dance with whom in the dance hall.

Then the guessing just who was next to have the privilege of sitting at the captain's table, or if the cabaret singer would get her kit off rather than show more of her ample bosom, than a decent cleavage would allow.

The list was almost endless, including the crew's betting on which cockroach crawled to the top of the steam pipe in the galley before it got flattened by a mop and added to the ships 'soup of the day'.

On the third day out and after yet another dull anonymous

afternoon quaffing drinks in the luxury saloon, the friends decided to try to find some way of relieving their boredom.

"I don't know about you two, this life is wonderful but totally boring. I'm bored out of my skull, yet we have a perfect opportunity to learn about this new vessel of ours. What say we have a bit of fun with the crew when we go on the next guided tour around the ship." John suggested.

"I'll drink to that one. Even old Burns can't understand why we haven't shown our faces there before now. According to him, they are beginning to wonder if we really are 'company' and not the usual uneducated passengers." Sinclair said glumly.

"I have the feeling I know the Radio Officer, but I would like to look at their supposedly modern set-up on here, as opposed to the antiquated equipment I used on the *Inverary.*" Larter added.

"That settles is then. We'll stick together and take a special behind the scenes trip around the ship. But we must get Burns to take us, otherwise it will be deemed as poking our nose into things." John stated, and got the nod of agreement from the others.

The following morning after breakfast, when Burns cleared their table, he told them the ship was only a few hours away from a severe gale coming their way, and that their little excursion around the ship had to be cancelled.

"Never mind Burns. We'll manage. But I'll bet you a pound to a penny, at least one of us will be required to help out, even though we're not on the ship's payroll." John suggested.

"We were supposed to provide the extra man power to replace you three when the *Inverary* sailed, but we were too late. When they took off several of our crew needed as replacements, we ourselves are now are undermanned, and have been since leaving Colombo.

So in the end Mr Grey, your statement stands true, and I'll not take your bet on it either. You will realise that there are several senior shipping line owners and family on board as free loaders, so you would be asked for your help long before them." Burns said, placing a fresh ashtray in front of them.

"Oh! And by the way, some of the passengers are complaining about the cigars you are smoking getting to them. Not so much the smoking, but jealous that they haven't or can't get the same quality brand to enjoy themselves."

"All their money and can't afford a decent Cuban cigar?" Sinclair asked with disdain.

"You can't have everything can you Burns!" Larter said, and gave him a fat cigar for his troubles.

"No you can't, and I'll enjoy this later. Thanks gentlemen!" Burns said, smuggling the cigar into his starched uniform pocket, and left.

'All passengers are not to use the main weather or promenade deck until further notice. All passengers are requested that they shut all side windows and any other cabin portholes. Your cabin stewards will be coming round to check they are shut and safe. All passengers are also requested to carry their personal life jackets as issued. During the period that we are in the storm area, should any passenger require medical treatment, please contact your cabin steward. We apologise for any inconvenience, but then we are on a ship in the middle of the Atlantic after all.' the anonymous voice advised over the ships tannoy system.

The ship entered the violent storm that created waves almost as tall as her, as they crashed and beat themselves in an attempt to rid themselves of this man made structure that dared to sail amongst them.

The ship heaved and pitched and struggled her way through these natural phenomena, suffering internal damage as she went. Man is no match for the natural elements, and all he can do is ensure his ships are of sturdy countenance to survive such natural powers.

"Excuse me gentlemen. But who among you is a Mr Grey?" a man asked, approaching the men as they were eating their dinner.

"What can I do for you?" John asked, eating his dinner in company of his two friends.

"I'm the chief engineer, and I understand that you hold the rank of 2nd Engineer. If so then I need you to assist me, if you will!" the man hinted in an anxious voice.

"I do. But what can I do for you that your men cannot!" John responded, taking the man by surprise.

"I'm undermanned by two qualified engineers, and below the strength of officers needed for this type of vessel. I need your expertise to help out in the department if this ship is to survive this storm!"

"I've been there myself chief and know exactly what it's like. For your information, I was told quite specifically by the captain and by the company agent in Cape Town that I, and my two friends here, must not interfere with, nor bother the running of the ship." John said with a dead-pan face.

"Yes chief! We are not allowed to be engaged in any shape or form due to the company's rules and regulations governing passengers involved with ship husbandry!" Larter said, and started to rattle off previous cases and incidents.

"Never mind the rules and regulations. I'm telling you to get yourself down this engine room as of now and take charge!" The engineer shouted irately.

"He can't do that chief! It would take a direct and written request from one of the passengers that's on board. Besides, I don't suppose the captain would back your orders either!" Larter said calmly, finishing his coffee.

Their conversation was overheard by just such a group of people, who got uppity and indignant at John's refusal to help out.

"Now look here you lot of snooty bastards. If you're so uptight about it, why don't you go and help the man! Put up or fuckin' shut up!" Sinclair shouted vehemently at them, which silenced them immediately.

"Just as I thought! A shower of shit, and a load of lily livered spongers, living off the backs of the men who sail these bloody steel coffins, and you lot only get to moan about whether your food is hot or your bed is not made in time for your afternoon nap!" Larter said witheringly to the crowd of people who were looking down their noses at the friends.

"You're paid to do these jobs, and we are the ones that pay you. Unless you do as the engineer asks then we'll see you get the sack!" said a weedy little man who stood up to confront John and his friends.

Sinclair had left the party earlier when the beginnings of the confrontation began, but arrived back carrying a leather holdall. He shoved his hand into it and when he pulled out a skull and threw it at the weedy man, the man fainted.

"Talking about sacks! Unless you lot back off and leave us alone, each one of you will end up like that skull. For the last time, we're not allowed to get involved, and that includes the writings from the Lloyds Insurance. So if any of you decide to beg to differ, then start with that skull and then with Lloyds." Sinclair shouted angrily, then went and collected the skull that was rolling over the deck in rhythm of the ships movement.

There was no sound, or objection from the indignant people as they just sat mesmerized at the skull as it rolled between their feet.

"Please 2nd! Its for all our sakes." the chief pleaded, appealing to John's better nature.

"Very well chief! I cannot see a fellow engineer in trouble." John said softly, and patted the engineer's shoulder.

"If anything should happen to that man, I will see to it that each and every one of you will be personally responsible, and cough up very handsomely for any liabilities or misfortune that may befall him. You for a start, you little overstuffed over pompous self-centred ass!" Larter snarled into the little mans ashen face.

Sinclair got hold of the skull and forced it into the faces of these people, with some of the women fainting into the process.

"That's what happened to our last lot of over indulged, self-appointed, bastards such as you lot! Left to rot in the desert they were.

Or can't you lot remember that far back?" Sinclair chuckled, and relished the effect he had over them.

"You, you wouldn't dare!" said another in the crowd.

"Just you watch!" Sinclair laughed, taking out two more skulls and lobbing them into the already panicky crowd. They scattered and fled from the lounge, screaming and shouting in sheer terror as Sinclair and then Larter started to laugh at their plight.

"Tut tut! Gentlemen. You might not only just upset their stomachs, but later on when we arrive in Southampton! Better put those souvenirs away. By the way, only a qualified taxidermist is allowed to bring such items aboard, or have a chit from the Natural History Museum to cover such luggage." Burns advised with a grin, as he witnessed the entire scene.

"Mind you though! You've certainly put a few of them in their places. I don't think they'll bother you for using free travel for quite a while now." he added.

Larter threw the last skull back into the holdall as Sinclair tried to control his laughter.

"We've certainly let the cat out of the bag! And yes, my cousin in Edinburgh will be claiming these items when we arrive." Sinclair laughed.

"I think we'd better take a new head count!" Larter quipped, which brought a few chuckles from the stewards.

"You'd better stow that Bosun, only I think you'll be needed very soon too. And you, Mr Larter! As I've said, we're seriously undermanned." Bond said.

"But what about these shipping company workers pretending to be passengers?" Sinclair asked with annoyance.

"That's just it. They are only shareholders, or pen-pushers and the like. Whereas we're the real crew on board." Bond replied.

"In that case, they should be involved too!" Larter said flatly, looking around at the now empty lounge.

"See they've all scarpered to their luxury cabins, relying on others to save their precious hides. So much for company policy!" he said, with outstretched arms.

"C'mon Bruce. Lets go and see if we can help our fellow crewmen." Sinclair suggested and slung the bag over his shoulders leaving the lounge to the stewards.

John had already arrived in the engine room and was helping the chief engineer to tackle the several problems the ship was developing.

"I will try and sort out your stablizer gear for you but I need a couple of your stokers to lend a hand to do the heavy lifting or handling. If you have electrical problems too then I suggest you get your electrical engineers onto it. Failing that then Radio Officer Larter will help them on that account. If you just have watch-keeping problems, then that's all up to you." John stated to the nervous chief as the ship butted her way through yet another liquid mountain that was as solid as the terrestrial rock kind.

"Fair enough 2nd! But I do need a competent senior officer to supplement the engine room duties, even though we are on passage." the engineer sighed.

John looked at the chief for a moment, and decided that although the man was not much older than him, he had only just been made up to chief, probably just for this voyage.

"Your first voyage as chief then?" John asked with concern.

"Yes! I was the 2nd engineer arriving into Cape Town." the man said meekly.

"That's a bit of bad luck chief. But from where I stand, you're senior to me. I'm still only an acting 2nd. If it's any worth to you, just let your officers have their head and only rein them in if something goes wrong. I operate on the principle that I report to my chief only when or if there's something wrong. In other words, don't tell me all is fine, but scream if something is wrong." John advised.

"Sounds a good idea 2nd! When this storm is over, I just might give it a try."

"Lets face it chief. You've got two engines spinning one single shaft. If one engine cuts out, you've always got the other one to keep the ship moving. Just worry when you've got none." John said, and left the chief with some stokers to see to the stabilizers.

He worked long and hard on the defective machinery until it was working to his satisfaction, before he dismissed the stokers.

"Your gear is working to design chief, and I have prepared my report for you." John stated as he found the chief scurrying around the engine room.

"Thank you 2nd! Would you be good enough to look at my for'ard bulkhead's automatic watertight door control for me. If we can't shut it then we'll get flooded right through."

"On my way chief!" John nodded then turned about and made his way up the steep ladders and out of the engine room. John took several minutes to assess the problem before making a simple adjustment on the telemotor valves and testing them to see if they worked as required.

He returned after a little while and handed another repair report to the chief, who took it with gratitude.

"Many thanks 2nd! I can handle the rest from here on!" He said, and shook John's hand.

"No problem chief. If you need me for any watch-keeping just tell steward Burns. He'll let me know, rather than have the same spectacle we endured in the lounge!"

"That's kind of you, Grey!" The chief said as he left John to see to some other crises.

John arrived into the lounge after his wash and brush up, to find Larter sitting in a comfortable armchair and sipping a large drink.

"All right for some!" John quipped.

"Hello John. What kept you? I saw you down the engine room over an hour ago!"

"A slight problem with the natives." John teased and received an equally large drink from the attending steward.

"It seems as Andy is still otherwise engaged. Hope he's okay! Anyway, some poor ship hit one of our ice-mountains and had to be rescued by the Falkland tugs. It must have been just as hairy as our own narrow escape, John. I listened to the wireless traffic and deduced that the ice-mountain was one of ours, as it had a radar beacon on it which Lovatt planted just before we left it. By all accounts, they have been designated as 'hazardous to shipping' for the next twenty degrees north or so." Larter said tersely.

"Hope everybody survives. Its very poor weather down there at the best of times, as you know Bruce."

"They should be in good hands with those powerful tugs. Anyway never mind them, Andy is definitely taking his time."

"No doubt he likes to steer these cattle barges over the ocean from time to time, Bruce. It somehow gets rid of his tension when he travels over on the Glasgow ferry." John smiled as he finally sat down next to Larter.

The lounge was almost empty, and the dining room even emptier when they ate their meal.

"Fair-weather friends and all that! Cheers Bruce!" John said, raising his glass of wine in a little toast to their well-being.

"Oh yes. Its all right for some!" Sinclair said loudly arriving at their table.

"So what's this about the best job then Andy? And here's us thinking that its only the officers are the put upon." Larter chuckled, beckoning Sinclair to sit down and fill his glass with some of the wine.

"I know Andy. They couldn't sail a wee ship in a bath tub!" John laughed as Sinclair drank with gusto.

"He's reading my mind now!" Sinclair laughed, replenishing his glass.

They continued to wine and dine in the luxurious dining room until deciding it was time for a well-earned sleep.

"I wonder what ships letters will be sent out by the Sparker, about our, shall we say, head count!" Sinclair slurred and all three laughed at the incident as they struggled to keep their feet while the ship writhed and shuddered under their alcoholic induced staggering.

* * *

The ship staggered and wrestled her way through the severe storm over the next few very uncomfortable days, before she emerged into a calm and gloriously sunny day.

It took the ships company a few hours to restore the calm and tranquillity, and for the ship to enjoy itself, as she sailed in almost millpond conditions.

The vicious storm had delayed the ship, forcing her to call into the Ascension Islands to re-fuel, instead of their scheduled stop at the Canary Islands. This angered the 'de-lux' passengers, who caused a furore with their tantrums, and bitchiness, helping to fuel the resentment against them, already felt by the rest of the passengers. John, Andy and Bruce were openly laughing at them.

"Gentlemen, you're requested to attend the captain in his day cabin forthwith." Burns informed them.

"Oh steward! Pray tell us, who among these lily-livered cowards do we owe special honour to?" Sinclair asked aloud and looked around the lounge accusingly.

"It's something to do with protocol. Can't tell you other than that gentlemen." Burns said in a non-committal voice.

"Oh well. It seems that our illustrious captain has a spot of bother for us to sort out again. Better we leave our 'reserved' card on the table in case some fool decides to take it over." Sinclair announced and reached into his infamous holdall.

As he began to pull something out, the horrified onlookers, many of who were hiding their faces gasped, some ladies fainted. Then they realised it was in fact, a small white sign with 'RESERVED' on it. Adding to the merriment of the three friends who also blew raspberries.

This proved to be the last straw for the irate passengers and they stormed past the men and got to the captain's cabin to complain about their behaviour, before the friends had actually arrived.

They arrived to hear the irate and vociferous voices of the

complainants before they were finally fobbed off with some excuse from the captain.

"Come in gentlemen. It appears that you have upset most of my passengers by your actions and your demeanour. I have to inform you that if you continue with your excesses, you will be downgraded to the tourist area of the ship. If you still continue in your manner on board, then I will have to place you three under ships crew management. Do I make myself clear?" Ward shouted.

"I don't know if you are fully aware of it captain. But we three were in the thick of it helping the survivors of not one but two sunken ships, and have been helping your ship to survive that storm we just sailed through. Without our help then none of these ingrates, so called passengers of yours, or in fact, your entire ship, would have survived. It would have joined the other two in Davey Jones' locker. From now on, we refuse to help out in any shape or form. If you should need specialist help in future, we suggest you look to your passengers.

Come on, let's get out of this stinking hole. We know when we're not wanted." John shouted, throwing a newspaper cutting and one of his repair reports onto Ward's table and marshalled his friends out of the cabin.

They were promptly removed from their cabins and placed with the tourist class, or steerage class passengers, much to the cat-calls and derision from the luxury class passengers.

Sinclair was ready to set about one of those passengers, but John told him not to waste his breath, and that he was much better off further down the ships pecking order.

They arrived in their new cabins that had no upper deck windows or portholes to look out of, and were much stuffier because they were almost above the main galley of the ship.

"Suits me fine here. At least we can get a decent pint at the bar, instead of the vinegar they call wine." Sinclair said grumpily.

"Take no heed Andy. We now have the chance to sue the company for breach of contract. They promised us a red carpet voyage back home, yet we are now in less than suitable accommodation. We have them bang to rights now, let alone the insurance money they still owe us." Larter said, and started to recall previous court cases regarding their plight.

"As far as I'm concerned. The ship can go to hell now. When Ward reads my report and weighs it against what he has done to us, it will be his neck on the line, not ours.

His so called deluxe class passengers, and especially those belonging to the shipping company will realise that they have just cut their snooty noses off to spite their faces." John said vehemently.

"Besides, we have the rest of the crew to think of. But what would our legal stance Bruce?"

"I think that the captain is caught between a rock and a hard place. We appear to be his reserve team and will be needed every time the ship is in difficulty. But those idiots up top are only freeloaders who set the tone and pace for the shipping company. Either Ward panders to them or he can forget his pension." Larter said knowingly.

"Well I know what I'm going to do for the next week or so. I shall make those snotty nosed bastards life sheer hell." Sinclair swore, picking up his holdall to leave the cabin.

"Now Andy! Lets do this in a diplomatic and orderly fashion. One in, all in." John said soothingly and catching hold of Sinclair, spun him round before he reached the door.

"Fair enough. But I bagsy I get first crack!" Sinclair conceded and sat down again.

"Actually, it will be me. Because the Radio officer is ill and cannot handle the outgoing telegrams, there are so many of them from our erstwhile travellers that he could not keep up. Just watch me bugger up their stock quotes and other stock exchange dealings." Larter said, then went on to explain the involvement of such dealings and the instant replies needed to keep up with the stock markets.

"As for me, I will inform the chief engineer that due to the imposition and intolerable position placed upon us, we are obliged not to help any further. In fact, ON STRIKE! That will include any emergency that the ship may find herself in. The captain has his hands tied, but we will eventually make those idiots eat their words. And offer us unlimited rewards if we did help the ship." John added.

The friends decided that was their way, and settled down to a less affluent style of travel, but still a little more than their usual way of life on board.

The die was set for the friends to exact their retribution, and it started with mutterings about the missed stock quotes, or the sudden loss of vast fortunes. One such set of passengers had to move down to the same passenger level as the friends.

"What are you doing slumming down with us cretins?" Sinclair asked, leaning over them when they sat down to dinner.
Sinclair pulled the table cloth from under their food, and said

"Whoops! Funny this sort of trick never works every time. Oh! Did you spill your soup all over you? You poor little bastard." Sinclair growled, as he 'accidentally' spilt more soup over the man's lap, making him howl in pain.

"Oh sorry! The ship must have moved when you didn't. Funny about these ships without working stablizers today."

"You! You sent our quotes. Why didn't you wait for the results!" an elderly man among them shouted to Larter.

"Me? I'm only a passenger. What have I got to do with your business? If you have any complaints I suggest you take them up with the Radio Officer who is confined to the sickbay. Speak to the Doctor if I was you." Larter shouted back

"But it was you who sent the signal!" the man protested.

"What me? Not on your life. It's against the Board of Governors of the shipping line, for another officer to do any duty whilst he is on passage. In case you didn't know but it's the Lloyds insurance policy and all that." Larter said innocently.

"But I saw you. I gave you my signal!" the man persisted.

Larter got up and went over to the man and whispered in his ear.

"Commonly known as tough shit! I heard the reply, but you will never know what it was."

"You can't do that! It lost me several thousand pounds." the man groaned at his loss.

"Never mind. Just think of the next several thousands you make every time one of the ships make it into port on time. This one will be at least two days late on current form. The questions we want answering are many. For a start, what about the *Inverlaggan* and the *Chantral* that didn't arrive back? How much compensation did you get from the rescued survivors? You lot owe us three officers plenty and we intend getting all of it, not just a half-baked ride back on this poxy ship of yours." Sinclair answered, adding to the wails and moans of these people.

The ship had enjoyed a few days of peace as she passed over the lazy and balmy area of the equator but was heading for yet another storm to add to the daily misery.

John and Larter were enjoying a leisurely smoke on the promenade deck when the 1st mate approached them.

"Captain's compliments but he asked if you would attend his cabin." He stressed.

"No thank you. We're passengers enjoying a bracing afternoon on deck." John replied.

The 1st mate merely nodded his head and retreated back to where he came from.

The night was a wild one, as the ship heaved and corkscrewed through the heavy seas. Sinclair was on the prowl in among the deluxe cabins, with some help from Burns.

He placed a sack of cockroaches in the bed of one of the group of passengers that were responsible for the friends' displacement. Then left the rotting penis from one of the skulls in another, and the bug filled eyeballs that always rolled around.

The screams from the terrified passengers were heard in the

saloon class area, and even way above the wailing winds and crashing waves.

"Ahah!" Sinclair chuckled and asked his friends to listen to the screams.

"Noise passes through metal quickly, so it must be our ship owners passengers. What have you done to them this time Andy!" John laughed, as the screams got louder.

"Me John? Don't look at me!" Sinclair asked in an air of innocence.

"This is the night of the long knives, if you pardon my expression." Larter said with a grin.

"Here's to our night of pay back time!" Larter said as the three toasted their revenge.

They finished their meal and drank their fill then made their way back to their cabin, totally uncaring what would happen to the ship.

During the night, a rogue wave smashed into the side of the ship, which flooded most of the de- lux cabin area on that side. The sudden inrush of water momentarily unbalanced the ship so that it received yet another freak wave which smashed into the for'ard cargo hold, almost flooding it too.

This made the ship too heavy for'ard and to one side, forcing the captain to turn the ship around and go slowly back down their track, with the wind and tide behind them

As the ship wallowed momentarily, beam on to the walls of water, yet another wave smashed into her and causing more damage.

The ship was now fighting for her life against the tormenting wind and waves, but managed to bob up in time as if to gasp a life saving breath, before yet another wave created another dent into its side.

John heard a persistent knock on the cabin door and told whomever it was to go away. But the captain barged through the door and demanded that they help save the ship.

"We are only steerage class passengers. You had better go and see your friends on the deluxe deck. They are the ones who own the ship, and they are the ones who pay your wages. They are the ones who know best, after all they do own the bloody thing." John shouted and slammed the door in Ward's face.

The friends sat up and helped themselves to a hot cup of coffee from the in cabin supply cupboard, and started to smoke one of their rich Cuban cigars.

But their peace was shattered when an angry mob slammed open their cabin door and demanded that they got out of bed and helped the crew.

"But we're just passengers, remember? We were supposed to be enjoying a luxury cruise home, all expenses paid by the board of Governors and the Government of South Africa. That was until certain people objected to us being there. We've already helped out once on this voyage and this is how you lot paid us. Now fuck off and leave us alone." Sinclair shouted, throwing his holdall at them.

"You are paid by us to do your job. Unless you do it then we have no compunction in sacking you three as of now."

"Well then do so! Sack us right now. But we'll sue the entire company for loss of earnings, let alone the thousands belonging to us as paid to the company by the Lloyds insurance company." Larter said, and thumping one man on the nose, breaking it.

"Now see what you made us do. We are now sacked, yes?" John asked.

"Yes! And you'll be made to pay for your voyage home."

"In that case, we demand to be paid our insurance money right now. Pay up what you owe us now and sort the ship on your own. We cease to exist as your employees!" Larter snarled venomously and slammed the door into their faces.

"Lock the door Bruce. They can do what they like, but we're not moving from this cabin."
Sinclair said angrily.

The noise of the crowd died down for a while until there was a heavy banging on the door again. This time it was steel on steel.

"It sounds as if the cockroaches have their boots on this time." Larter joked as he got hold of a piece of furniture, ready to hit anybody coming into their cabin.

The door slammed open and Ward stood there glaring at the friends.

"You three come out now or sink with this bloody ship." Ward said, trying to contain his anger.

"Hello captain! Nice of you to drop by! Care for a coffee?" John said civilly but sarcastically.

"Let's not play games here. You three are officers of this line!" Ward started to say.

"On the contrary dear captain. Those lily-livered cowards behind you have already sacked us, not half-an-hour ago. We are only passengers on this ship. You cannot touch us. Even Lloyds Insurance and the Admiralty would vouch for our immunity from your orders, let alone the money the company owes us.

Unless you are telling us to abandon ship, which is a different matter, but if that is the case, then why are passengers standing behind you and not up on the boat deck? Better make sure we're not off the Namib Desert again." Larter said, pointing to the sea of faces behind him.

Ward and the passengers behind him were totally speechless and perplexed at the simple logic of what Larter said.

"Captain! If it means anything to you, you are in a no-win situation. These so-called ship owners and self-opinionated members of the board of governors standing behind you, have only themselves to blame. They make the rules, therefore be it on their heads, not yours, nor ours. Between you and me, we've got them bang-to-rights. To put it bluntly, all those standing behind you have sacked us from the company. Therefore we are now classed as Displaced British Seamen. That means we are only passengers on this ship until you arrive at some British port for us to disembark. Rules of this kind come from the Admiralty and not these strap-hangers you seem to pander to." John said quietly, shutting the door on Ward's face again.

The ship managed to survive the night and into the following day, before the storm finally relented and left the ship to lick her wounds again. At sea, the wind and water are the masters, no matter what man tries to do to outwit them.

They emerged from their cabin and went to the saloon for their food before going on deck for a stroll.

"Morning 2nd! Understand you had your own 'Alamo' last night?" a steward asked, whilst he served the three hungry men.

A passenger, whom they recognised as being one of the ones outside their cabin, came rushing over and tried to grab the plates of food off their table.

"You are not to serve these men. They are classed as persona-non-grata. Take their food away." He screamed.

The steward simply pushed the fop away and carried on talking to the friends as if nothing had happened. But the fop was now joined by some of the others.

"What's all this? Deluxe class passengers dining in the steerage class? How come they are down here disturbing us steward?" Larter asked civilly, and unperturbed by the angry shouting from the other diners.

"Their accommodation was flooded last night, and they've taken over the cabins from the Saloon class passengers, who have taken over the steerage, and so on down to us. Unfortunately some of the deluxe passengers had to be transferred direct, their tables are over there." the steward said apologetically.

"No need for apologies steward. It appears that the pecking order on this ship will always be maintained, especially when most of them are from the shipping company offices. I wonder how they'd fare on a crab infested beach." Larter said, and started to eat his meal.

A man tried to grab Larter's plate, but Larter stabbed the man's hand with his sharp knife, pinning it to the wooden table.

The owner of the hand howled in agony as he tried to struggle free.

"I suggest that you leave now while you've still got your hands." Larter hissed at the man, pulling the knife away to free him.

"I suggest you lot order your own breakfast. These are already paid for!" Sinclair said, fishing out a banknote from his pockets and gave it to the steward.

"We are probably the only fee paying passengers in here at the moment steward. I object to having these parasites in this saloon if they haven't paid for their meals." John said as the other diners looked at their empty dishes.

"In fact steward. We wish to buy all the food, victuals, comforts and any other item of value within this saloon. It will then become ours. Anybody wishing to eat will have to come and see us. Mind you it will cost them ten times as much." Larter announced.

"In case some of them question this, all they've got to do is look in their own rule books, that they always seem to quote, every time you go near them. Am I right steward?" he asked aloud, for the steward to nod his head in agreement.

Sinclair stood up and ordered all of the other diners out of the saloon, and even threw several of them out onto the main deck before he locked the door behind them.

"Now we can have some peace!" Sinclair said with satisfaction written over his face, rubbing his hands together.

"Steward. Let the original steerage class passengers in, its their part of ship. Feed them as normal, but we're only paying for our own. Don't forget to keep a tally for us." Larter ordered, and gave the steward a cigar and a £5 note as his tip.

This state of affairs remained on the ship for several days until the deluxe passengers were finally allowed back into their cabins again.

Ward was in a state of siege on his bridge, with the complaints and bickering coming from the ship owners circle, whilst at the same time he was faced with the objections made by the other class of passengers as those ship owners took or demanded just what they liked from them.

The ship was in a terrible state from the mauling she received from the last storm, and as it was undermanned, the crew were almost at mutiny point, which caused Ward to have a nervous breakdown. The 1st mate didn't fare much better, as the ship was nearing British shores again.

The friends had caused such misery on board because of the way they had been treated by the free loaders, which fact was finally realised by the other passengers.

Several of the richest of them lost heavily in the stock market thanks to Larter's signal handling.

The ship was still full of water, thanks to the ill-equipped men and bad leadership from the engineering officers unable to cope. The sailors were worked to a standstill and could not be relied upon to keep their bridge watches

When the ship finally docked in Southampton, there were news cameramen and reporters waiting for them. Including the Lordships and their staff.

Belverley and Invergarron were beside themselves when the deluxe passengers started to point an accusing finger to the three friends.

The press had a field day, even more so than in the Falklands. They somehow managed to open old wounds and items that those passengers on the *Inverkirk* had tried to forget.

"It seems that whenever we three are together, we survive a maelstrom of controversy and confusion!" Larter whispered, seeing that Ward being questioned angrily by Belverley.

"We were promised a red carpet treatment all the way home, but it seems that our lordships gang of friends spoiled it all for them. There will be many resignations from the board before long I'll wager." John replied.

"I don't give a shit about them, it's us I'm worried about. But then there're plenty of other ships around the world run by different companies. Don't forget, we've been sacked, so they can't do much to us!" Sinclair said angrily.

"All they've got to do is re-hire us then slaughter us. But it would cost them dearly if the press was to find out the truth!" John rejoined, which received a nod from the other two.

"Yes John! We were sacked. They reneged on their deal, and we've still got those boxes the Major gave us. Just show them to the press and Lord Invergarron and company will not ever trade south of the river Thames again. And don't forget your ice mountain piggy back from the Falklands!" Larter stated, as he rehashed their recent escapades.

Belverley came striding and gesticulating angrily over to the friends, ahead of a swarm of other ship owners. Unbeknown to them they were being watched and filmed by the batteries of film cameras.

"What have we ever done to you that should wreck our company fortunes!" Belverley exploded as he poked John hard into his chest.

"Putting it that way Mr Belverley, you get no answer!" John said angrily, rubbing his painful chest.

"We demand an explanation! I want it now!" Invergarron bellowed when he too arrived on the scene.

"Just ask your company of free-loader passengers that were on board." Sinclair responded with equal ferocity, and shoved Belverley away from John.

"In case you lot forget, we were sacked by your mob. Now is seems, if that is the case then we can discuss a whole raft of items with the press, pertaining to how your cronies run your affairs, whether you like it or not! Remember the *Inverlaggan*? Well before you start getting uppity with us, you owe we 3 officers, thousands of pounds that the Board of enquiry recommended we got as our reward. And on top of that, we can sue your lot for unfair dismissal, let alone getting the National Union of Seamen onto you. It would be strike after strike until you sue for peace, which will cost you a good ten times more." Larter threatened loudly, and beckoned the gaggle of pressmen over.

Invergarron and Belverley looked at each other in terror.

"What are you going to say? Why are you doing this to us?" Belverley begged desperately.

"You had better ask your passengers. But I fail to see why you didn't know we were sacked over a week ago. And we were forced to pay for a steerage class voyage despite all your promise of a deluxe one. We earned it but your company reneged on it. The publicity of that won't go down with the great cruise travellers of the world, let alone the Union brethren. And especially the insurance companies who get wind of you not compensating us for the *Inverlaggan*." Larter said in a loud voice, which silenced most of the complaining ex-passengers.

A top television journalist leant over and asked a leading question that John responded immediately and candidly to. This started a barrage of questions from the others, which were answered by the friends who embellished certain details making them graphic enough for the pressmen to write down as what they wanted to hear.

In turn, Belverley and Invergarron started to visibly shrink into their rich clothing.

"If you cause a strike, you'll be sorry for all this! " Belverley hissed, but was immediately pounced upon by one of the leading questioners.

"If these men who are the saviours of several passengers, were sacked by your governing body who had a free ride whilst they had to pay, and even by the rules which you plainly use to your advantage, how can they be sorry or held accountable to you? What compensation can you offer these men for unfair dismissal? What are you going to say to the National Union Federation that would prevent an all out strike?"

Belverley huffed and puffed and waffled as best he could, but it was patently obvious that he couldn't answer any simple question put to him, the others, or even Invergarron.

"What's in the boxes Mr Grey?" came a request.

"We were told it was from the grateful Government of South Africa." Sinclair replied, for the friends to take their boxes out and opened them in front of the cameramen.

They looked down at a gold key encrusted with fabulous jewels that sparkled in the sunlight. Under it was a piece of parchment written in highlighted writing.

As they read the ornate writing, it was discovered that all three were given the accolade of Freemen of all cities and townships in the State of South Africa. Duly signed by the President and countersigned by the British High Commissioner.

The flashlights flickered and the TV cameras whirred when they focussed onto these expensive pieces.

Belverley and Invergarron gaped at these three matching accolades, causing a reporter to ask them to comment upon why these obviously brave men were ignominiously sacked by a bunch of 'strap-hangers' and free-loaders that the British leading shipping companies seem to wallow in all the time.

They were not able to answer that or many other leading questions and the friends somehow got shoved out of the way in favour of questioning the lords.

"Oh well. I looks as if we're going by ferry from Heysham if we want to get home." Larter whispered quietly, and then quickly left the scene of turmoil.

They returned to their cabins and collected their gear, but were met by Roberts.

"You still have to remain on board for your passage over to Belfast, and your pay to pick up. I've seen to that, so that nobody can ever accuse me of reneging on my deals. And here is your passage money back. The rules state that once a 'De-Lux' passenger is given their cabin, so they stay, irrespective what those pompous asses say or think!" he said, handing over the money they had spent during their voyage.

"Mr Roberts. It proves that not all people in this shipping conglomerate are fools. We might be at times, but then we know our job, and that's why we do what we do on board." Larter said gently, flicking through the wad of notes.

"Yes Mr Roberts. Here is a gesture of our gratitude for your honesty. We hope you enjoy spending it." Sinclair said, peeling off a few of £5 pound notes, that was matched by the other two, and thrusted them into the man's hand. Roberts got angry saying that he refused to take the money, on the grounds that it could be considered as bribery.

"Nonsense Mr Roberts! Let us say that it's a donation to your favourite charity, and you can take your pick which one. It's our way of returning hospitality. We shall be making our own way back via other travel arrangements." John chuckled, gathering the bunch of fivers up and stuffing them into Robert's top pocket.

"Cheerio Roberts! We'd rather get back home under our own steam, it's much safer that way." Sinclair joined in and left.

"Don't forget you've got 10 days leave! Report back to your own ship after that." Roberts shouted after the departing men.

"We're sacked officially but you heard the man! Lets get out of here." Larter prompted and they jumped into a waiting taxi that sped away from the melee around the dockside.

Arriving at the main train station, they caught the train taking them north.

During their several hours on the train they had managed to get and keep a table in the buffet bar.

"We can have a little farewell party here before we all change at Crewe." Larter suggested, ordering a meal and several cans of ale to wash down the standard fare offered by British Rail. It took them many hours to reach Crewe where John and Larter said goodbye to Sinclair.

"Keep in touch Andy! Scotland is only another 5 hours away." they shouted as the train huffed and puffed on its way, taking Sinclair further from them.

"Well Bruce. Your train is due in shortly, I've got to wait a couple of hours for the Euston Boat train before I get to Heysham and the Belfast ferry."

"It looks as if you're last man off then. Don't forget to switch off the lights!" Larter responded shaking the hand of his smaller friend.

"Keep in touch!   Scouse land here you come!" John said cheerfully, waving Larter goodbye.

Chapter XXIII
Honoured

The green and cream bus chugged its way westward through the morning traffic of the streets of Belfast and out towards John's village of Dunmurry, and Rathmore cottage.

He stepped off the bus and carried his heavy bags down the little pathway of his home.

"Hello Mam!" John greeted, stepping into the hallway of the cottage.

"Hello son! Shut the door and come in." his mother smiled, pecking him on the cheek.

"Got some lovely presents for you all. Where's everybody, where's Dad?"

"He's gone up the loney to get us some vegetables from the big house, he won't be long! The girls are off to your cousins wedding in Belfast, and your brother has gone to Banbridge!"

"Well here's Dad's box of tobacco., a lovely necklace for you, and some perfume for the girls. But this is something we need to put somewhere safe!" John said, placing the gold and green box onto the table.

"What is it John? It looks very expensive." his mother asked curiously gazing at the box

"Something for a rainy day. If ever you need money again, and I mean lots of it, just take it to the bank, they'll know what to do with it."

"Here, sit yourself down by the oven, and have some breakfast!" His mother invited, kissing her son on the forehead.

"I'm home for a few days now Mam. But I've a feeling its going to be more than that. Probably a change of company too." John said as he finished his big plate of fried food.

"What's the matter with the one you've got, son? Gone to the wall like some of the others?"

"Not quite, but maybe it's time for a change to see how the other shipping companies live. But that can wait until after my leave."

"Well whatever it is, as long as you know what you're doing."
John just nodded his head and stayed silent while finished
smoking his cigarette.

"I'm off to bed now. I have a few things to sort out, but
they'll wait until I get up." John announced, kissing his mother's
cheek, and climbed up the winding stairs to his own little room at
the back of the rambling old cottage.

John was up early the following morning, taking his new shotguns
across the fields to bag a few rabbits and hares for supper. He
found the guns much better than his old and trusted one, but put it
down to being able to shoot much better, because of the extra
target practice he had up the jungle. He picked up his dead
animals and walked slowly home again, having a smoke as he went.

He felt at peace now and safe at home with his family, his
hobbies of fishing and hunting helped him unwind and settle
himself back down to his usual unruffled state of mind.

"There're two large buff envelopes on the table for you, John.
They look very official." His mother greeted, as he handed her
the dead rabbits and hares.

"Here! We'll have rabbit stew tonight Mam!" he responded,
swapping the dead animals for the mail.

John looked at the biggest envelope, which declared it was
from the shipping company, and one from some foreign concern,
but remembering the ISDM logo he decided to open it first:

Dear Mr Grey,

You have been nominated as one of our newest
recipients to our International Scientific Fellowship.

Please find an RSVP invitation to our annual prize
giving and following dinner. We look forward to
receiving you as shown on the invitation.

Yours sincerely,
Professor Lovatt (Chairman)

John read the invitation and noted it was only a few days away but at least the event was to be held local.

'*Better get my best suit ready.*' he thought to himself, and grabbed the bigger envelope to rip it open:

Acting 2nd Engineer J Grey, SS Inverary

> This is to inform you that the SS Inverary has now docked in Belfast and you should collect your personal belongings from it. You are to do on the date and time as shown.
>
> You are also notified that on that date you will be allocated another ship and a separate voyage contract must be signed accordingly.
>
> In the meantime, we have enclosed a separate envelope containing the balance of your pay entitlement, which includes any other emoluments due to you whilst you were on board the SS Inverary and Inverkirk.
>
> Yours faithfully,
> Mr Lowther

John examined the brown envelope that contained his 'settlement' money, and decided that it was to remain unopened until he got to his next ship.

'*If I know anything, I'll bet Bruce and Andy got the same letter.*' he muttered, throwing the letter across the room, in distaste.

He went into the scullery and spoke to his mother who was preparing the dead animals for the pot.

"I have good news and probably some bad. But I won't know about the bad until I go to HQ!" he announced quietly.

"Is that big envelope something to do with it?" she asked, pointing to the red seal on the buff envelope.

"Yes, but the small one is a special invitation sent to me. Anyway, must go and make a phone call. Back soon!" John said, and putting his coat on made his way out the door.

John went up the hill to where the red phone box stood next to the bus stop, and phoned Bruce about the ISDM letter that Lovatt had sent. Then discussed the letter from HQ and the move from the *Inverary*.

"I have had the same letter from HQ, so hope to see you on the morning. I'll contact Andy to see if he had the same, for us to meet at the usual place and at the usual time."

"Needless to say, if you need an overnight stay, you know where I live Bruce."

"Yes! I'll tell Andy in case he needs it as well. Thanks for the offer John."

"See you there then." John acknowledged, hanging up the receiver and collecting his unused penny coins.

The next day, John carried an empty case up the hill, and caught his bus to his well-trodden path towards the docks.

"Morning Andy! How was your trip?" John asked, watching Andy stride towards him.

"Hello John. Everything went pear shaped when I received the same letter as you. Only what's puzzling me is this bloody envelope stuffed with money." Sinclair said, and showed his still unopened brown envelope.

"Search me Andy! Maybe Bruce can tell us, but in the meantime, I think it's your turn to buy the bacon rolls and tea." John said with a grin, showing his own still unopened envelope.

Sinclair went over to the café and brought their early morning breakfast back.

"This is the first time I've come to go on board to collect my suitcase, John. Strange that!" Sinclair said, wolfing down his large bacon sandwich and drinking his large mug of tea noisily.

John just nodded and completed his own meal before handing the customary cigarette packet out.

"I have a special invitation sent by Professor Lovatt." John announced, then went on to describe what it was and what he thought was to happen.

Sinclair listened intently at this information and expressed his satisfaction on what was said.

"And that's not all!" Larter said aloud, surprising the other two.

"Bruce! You made it. We've just had our meal!" John said, standing up to greet his other friend.

"That's okay. I've just had my breakfast, and she's just left in that car you see over there." Larter stated, pointing to an expensive looking car pulling away from the ferry.

"We might as well take our time to gather up our gear. The ship is only two berths down and we've got until 1100 hours to get over to the HQ." Sinclair advised, as they strolled leisurely down the docks, picking their way through the hustle and bustle of the stevedores and porters.

It was a brief visit as they went on board to retrieve their belongings, but they managed to grab a brief cuppa in the lounge, before leaving for the HQ.

"Well that was that, as they say! Don't forget to tune into next weeks gripping episode folks! This is Brucey and friends signing off!" Larter quipped, when they tramped over the gangway and back onto the cobble-stoned jetty.

They arrived into the large building where the duty reception clerk met them and directed them to a room saying there were people waiting to see them.

The foyer and reception hall was bustling with people, but when they got to the floor and the entrance to the room it was totally silent and empty.

"Here we go again! What ship are we getting this time?" John asked, opening the door saw the room was empty save for the same weedy, bespectacled clerk, writing furiously into a large book.

"Engineer Grey! Radio Officer Larter and Chief Bosun Sinclair. Glad you came early. I have a special note for the three of you." he announced in a squeaky voice.

"But come in and take a seat over there for a moment until I get the instructions." the man commanded, pointing to an empty row of seats facing him.

"What's all this then! We're being sent to all points of the compass?" Sinclair asked aloud.

"Please be patient." the clerk pleaded, struggling with a large brown envelope.

"That looks very officious and if I didn't know better, we are about to go on another hair-raising jaunt." Larter said knowingly, pointing to the red seals on the envelope.

"One seal from each Ship-Owner. See! 3 owners, 3 seals." Larter added.

The clerk finally opened and unfolded the papers on his desk and started to read them aloud:

"Radio Officer Larter, you will join the SS *Cloverlea* today when it docks here for its annual hull scrape and maintenance. Chief Bosun Sinclair, you will be joining the *Inverath* tomorrow when it docks in Southampton. As for you Acting 2nd Engineer Grey, you will be joining your next ship as its 3rd Engineer, in one weeks time. Your ship will be the *Inverdrum* currently undergoing ship upgrading and acceptance trials in Glasgow." Then he took off his reading glasses and placed them neatly onto his desk.

"It seems we've been demoted and split up in such a way that none of us will meet in any port again, is that it Scribes?" Larter asked angrily.

"Yes it does look that way, but then I'm only a mere scribe, so what do I know." the man said defensively.

"I for one refuse to accept. I'm a 2nd Engineer not a 3rd. If they think that I will accept a lesser berth then they have another think coming!" John said indignantly and got up to leave.

"I have nothing against Jock Wallace, he's a good man, but only the Marconi Organisation can relieve me of my watch on the *Inverary*!" Larter added with equal vehemence.

"Now don't get on to me! I'm only the messenger. Tell their lordships not me!" the clerk said, writhing uncomfortably in his wooden seat.

"No scribes! We do not blame you. All you have to do is enter the words 'Not acceptable' across where we're supposed to sign as our agreement. We can get our trade elsewhere if those ungrateful bastards wish it." Larter said calmly, and started to walk out of the room with the other two.

"You can tell them we're going straight to the Seamans Union to demand a strike!" Sinclair shouted as they left.

The word 'Strike' echoed around the almost empty hallway, which caused a catastrophic chain of events.

Someone blew a whistle making several men look around, down tools or whatever they were carrying, and walk out of the building shouting 'Strike! Strike! Everybody out!

The word 'STRIKE' is an electrifying word that usually causes total fear and panic from the company's management team. Whereby the workers would gather outside the building, shouting and creating mayhem to anybody trying to enter or leave it, who they deemed not to be one of the strikers. The words 'SCAB!' 'BLACKLEG!' or 'SCUM' usually follow on and before you know it, there are fights, riots and civil unrest, and scrums of the press brigade giving their so-called 'unbiased and true' news coverage of the situation, with the riot police arrive and try to bring order to the angry strikers.

John turned to his two friends and signalled that the best place to see it all was in the usual place they saw the last lot of bother. They fought their way through the angry barrier of workers and found their way back to the old pub they had frequented some time ago, and commenced drinking pints of double XX Guinness.

"What happened there Bruce?" Andy asked, trying to make out some of the men on the television screen.

"It was you that used the word 'Strike', Andy" John chuckled,

"By the looks of it, you've caused one anyway!" Larter observed.

"Na! Not me. I wouldn't do a thing like that!" Sinclair denied innocently, quaffing another pint.

"Oh well. It looks as if their lordships are going to reconsider their offer to you John, so its you they'll put the blame onto for all this." Larter said with a smile, offering them a cigarette.

"Me? But I'm the one they tried to see off!" John said with equal innocence, watching a spokesman from the building came out and talk to a reporter.

"It appears that the Union are wild-cat strike happy, and will down tools at the slightest opportunity. We have no idea to who started all this, but we shall not be giving in to their demands, Unions or not!" the man said in a plummy voice, and was howled down by the strikers.

"There's another fine mess you've got them into John. If you carry on like this, you'll end up as the most experienced and knowledgeable 5th engineer in the entire Merchantile Marine, let alone the rising star of a chief." Larter chuckled.

"Well, never mind them. They can please themselves. I'm not taking a demotion nor a pay cut for nobody. I'll go foreign and get my exam papers instead." John avowed strongly.

"That's the ticket. Somehow we knew you'd say that John. Cheers!" Sinclair said, raising his glass to toast the scene shown on the screen.

Someone in the bar overheard them talking and started to whisper and point to them.

"Shouldn't you three be out there with those men instead of in here? Or are you scabs too?" a fat bellied lout, shouted over to them.

"Nah mate! Nothing to do with us, we don't work there anymore, 'cause we got sacked two weeks ago." Larter responded, which seemed to appease their would be belligerent attackers.

They finished their drinks, picked up their suitcases and left the bar to the other customers shouting and swearing at the pictures on the TV screen.

They walked quickly away from the area and headed to the city centre where the large magnificent city hall stood. They watched and listened to the whizzing noise of the trolley buses and the clanking of the trams as they passed noisily, creating a typical city scene.

"That was another close one Andy. But the way I see it is that we are free men, and can leave the line at any time, if we have the mind to. So if any of the lordship cronies start to back us into a corner, we can tell them to stuff it. Just like we did this morning." Larter said knowingly, putting his suitcase down to have a breather.

"Back there, I was only speaking for myself. There was no need for you two to suffer on my account." John said meekly, taking his turn to offer the cigarettes.

"No John. You spoke for the three of us. And Bruce is right. We can go absolutely anywhere." Sinclair admitted, looking around aimlessly at the passing shoppers, but somehow was not convincing enough for his friends.

"I have got that special do on tonight. If you like, you can come and spend the rest of the day at home and stay overnight if you wish. You are welcome to accompany me to the do, who knows what could be on offer." John offered cheerfully, which the other two accepted gratefully.

All three boarded the number 23 Ulster Bus, and sat quietly as it sped out towards Rathmore Cottage and Dunmurry.

"Hello Mrs Grey." Larter and Sinclair greeted, when they arrived into the large cottage.

"How nice to see you both again. We have some rabbit stew for supper, if you want some?" she asked politely, ushering the men into the kitchen.

"That's just great. Rabbit stew is my favourite." Sinclair said with a large grin and gave her a pack of cigarettes.

"Here, your favourites I understand."

"Why thank you Andy! I'll have one now in a minute." she said, going down into the scullery to prepare the men's food.

"I have that do on tonight Mam, and the lads are coming with me, but can you ask dad to pick us up from there afterwards?" John asked.

"He'll be home shortly, ask him yourself." she replied simply.

"Seeing as you're a guest and a recipient of something, we'll probably be given a free ride home anyway, John. Least that's what Marconi does." Larter opined.

"Oh well. Let's hope it's a good night for walking otherwise." John conceded.

They had their supper and got ready for going out when John's father came through the door.

"Hello John! Hello Bruce and you Andy. Off somewhere nice?"

"We're going to that do I told you about dad. Any chance of a lift to the place, as we've just missed our bus?" John asked politely.

"Come on then, but don't ask for a lift back. I'm shattered and want my supper." he said, and turning around, went out to the garage to get the car back out again.

"You've still got your Humber Pullman, Richard! I thought you were going to have a change?" Larter asked with amazement as he stepped into the spacious back of the vehicle, and sat down in the thick leather bound seats.

"No Bruce, this one will do me just fine. It takes me to where I want. Besides, can't afford a new one just yet." Richard Grey said quietly, driving the large car down the lane and onto the main road then headed for Belfast.

"Thanks for the lift dad. Will be home on the last trolley bus, hopefully. If not then we'll probably stay at the hotel overnight." John said as his father waved to them and drove away from the hotel.

"Welcome to the Balmoral conference suite, gentlemen. May I see your invitations please!" a smartly dressed usher asked, taking John's invitation card.

"May I assume that these gentlemen are with you Mr Grey?"

"Yes, they're my quota of allowed guests."

"Will you be staying overnight or will you require transport to take you home, later on?" the usher asked politely again.

"Depends on how the night progresses. However, all three of us will be leaving together for the same destination, when the time comes. Kindly arrange it if you would." John responded with a nod and a little smile to the man.

"Then follow me if you please." the usher said and led the way up a wide and winding staircase to the next floor, where they were met by another usher, complete with top hat and a flower in his lapel buttonhole.

They entered a large room that was decorated with gilt pictures and mirrors, with people sitting down at round tables but facing a stage, which itself had a lectern and an equally smartly dressed man standing by it. The stage had a cloth-covered table, which was full of objects.

The usher showed them to their own 'reserved for Mr John Grey and party' table, which was neatly laid out for a meal, with several bottles of wine in a wine cooler in the middle of the table.

"Blimey John! What have you done to deserve this life. Spent all that Cape Town money or what?" Sinclair drawled, looking around at the decadence and opulence of the place and the other people present.

"Hello John, glad you could make it. We thought you may have been caught up with the strike!"

John stood up and faced the familiar Scottish voice.

"Hello Fergus! It's nice to see you again. Did you get my latest batch of drawings?" John said, and standing up, shook hands with McPhee then introduced the other two to him.

"Yes I did John! Pleased to meet you again Sinclair! How are you Larter?" McPhee said politely but warmly.

"We take it in turns to act as President and as I am he for the current term, I get the privilege to recommend to the ISDM someone with talents befitting the organisation. I am your sponsor for this year's award ceremony, backed by my old friend

Professor Van Heyden, whom you already know, I believe." McPhee said with a beaming smile.

"They have been impressed with your STAN project for automated steering, but the Iceberg Docking Theory was the top hat if you like. Mind you, the work you have done in the past has also been recognised, so it seems that you're in with a good shout to get a top award, John. In case your modesty has forgotten, I refer to your electric circuit tester, and ring main circuitry, which are looking very promising and now your inflatable dinghies are but the latest chapter towards your cause. Just sit tight and enjoy the evening, but I'm over there with the rest of the so called 'chain gang' as you put it last time we met." McPhee concluded, nodding his head to a much larger table closer to the stage platform.

"Thank you Fergus, we'll do just that, and hope to see you later on." John said happily, waving to the departing McPhee.

"Here John, have a glass of bubbly. Its absolutely delicious!" Larter said, handing over a frothing glass of champagne.

"It looks as if the cream of the shipbuilding world is in this room. I'd bet it would cost a good £200 a table. Look, there's Mr Ling from the Taikoo yards in Hong Kong. Next to him is Whately from Thorneys of Newcastle with Deakins sitting next to him who's from the Evans yard in Brisbane." Sinclair observed.

"Good evening gentlemen, I see you managed to get Mr Grey here on time. How are you all?"

John stood up and greeted Lovatt and Van Heyden as they stopped by their table.

"Hello professors! I'm not sure that I should be here, I feel out of my depth judging by all these fur clad gentlemen and their ladies adorning the place." John said humbly.

"Nonsense John! You are just as capable as the rest of them in this room. Its just that they have the capital behind them to back their ideas, whereas the real stars are people like yourself who need to have their light brought out from under the proverbial bush. You enjoy yourself, and hope to see you later. All the best!" Van Heyden said, and left to make their way over to where McPhee was sitting.

They sat and had their food delivered by a series of waitresses carrying silver salvers and all sorts of delicate dishes. They had already drunk two bottles of wine and champagne and were into the cigar and port stage when the MC stood up and took over the proceedings.

Whilst the MC was making the opening announcements, the tables were cleared and fresh bottles of drink were placed on them for the guests.

The evening was full of comings and goings with a procession of people walking onto the stage and making speeches or short presentations, all of whom had their photo's taken by a small crowd of photographers.

McPhee stood up and announced the categories of awards and prizes then handed the microphone over to Lovatt who called out the winning nominee for each award.

"Captain Joe Tomlinson! Winner of the Deep Sea Navigational Aids design!" came the announcement, which took John by surprise. But he was first on his feet to clap and cheer Tomlinson as he mounted the stage and collected his award from McPhee.

As he made his small acceptance speech, he saw John and mentioned his name in his speech, and nodded towards John.

"That was decent of him John!" Larter whispered as everybody clapped and cheered every winner.

The proceedings came to a natural pause while people charged their glasses and had a breather, whilst a troupe of singers warbled a few pop songs for the benefit of those who just might be listening. When the singers had finished the stage re-manned by the prize givers.

"The next category is for the Innovative Design and Ideas Award. The recipient will receive a Fellowship and a bursary to the

ISDM. Academy in Southampton." Came the announcement.

"And the winner is…." Lovatt said as he ripped open the silver envelope.

"Good luck John!" his two friends whispered.

"2nd Engineer John Grey, formerly off the Triple Coronet Line." came the verdict. Sinclair and Larter stood up cheer and clap for their bemused looking friend.

"It seems that news travels fast around these people. But it's you John! Get up there and sock it to them!" Larter whispered as the friends urged and helped John to his feet.

John felt his mouth go dry, his knees shake, and his hands all atremble as he mounted the short but steep stairs onto the stage, to be blinded by the flashing cameras and feel the hearty back slaps from Van Heyden and Lovatt,.

"Congratulations John! It gives me the greatest of pleasures to give this to you! Maybe you'll show some of these silly old dodderers a few things or two." McPhee said with great delight, as John took the scroll and cheque off him.

The catcalls demanding a speech made John feel inadequate for this auspicious audience, but he managed to control his emotions long enough to pull off his unrehearsed sentences.

"It is a great pleasure and honour to receive such an illustrious award. I feel unworthy of it because there are others who would deserve it more. I thank my sponsors and well-wishers for their support. Before I leave the stage, I wish to reciprocate Captain Joe Tomlinson's gesture, and I wish him well at the ISDM Academy.

However, it is only fair that I should hand these back as I feel that I'm not quite ready to quit doing a job at sea that I have worked long and hard to master. By that I mean, I would request that my sponsors delay my entry to the Academy until I have reached my next rank."

This last sentence drew gasps of surprise from the rest of the audience.

"You see I'm just a marine engineer. But like you, I want to be at my best for the ISDM Academy, as it deserves the best, and only the best!" John concluded apologetically.

The room was silent until he finished, then erupted in a standing ovation with cheers from every corner of the room, as John was surrounded by some of the panel of judges, who clapped and shouted even louder.

This went on for a few minutes until the noise died down for McPhee to speak.

"It appears that our engineer protégé is too modest. But I think we can wait just a little longer don't you gentlemen?" he asked, looking over to the judges panel and the sponsors table, who responded with emphatic nods.

"There you are John! Even the judges agree. Thank you for your honesty and we look forward to seeing you again." McPhee said as John was escorted back to his seat by well-wishers thus ending the prize ceremony.

The MC made a few more announcements, before the cabaret artists started to perform and get the real party under way. This went on for some time, with people coming and going to each table.

"That was some speech you made John! You had us going there for a moment!" Tomlinson said, approaching them and shaking hands with the three of them.

"Joe! Its good to see you again! What ship are you on now?" John asked with great delight on meeting yet another of his old friends.

"Yes isn't it! And no white overalls yet!" came another familiar voice.

"Happy Day!" John said in total surprise.

"Hello gentlemen. I've heard of your escapade up the jungle. You must tell me how you sorted out the rivets on the *Inverary* though!" Day said with a big smile on his face.

John looked at the four men beside him and felt a warm glow inside. He put it down to the amounts of alcohol he had drunk, but also realised that it was the pleasure of having so many good friends around him.

They sat around the small table talking and renewing acquaintances for a while before Day and Tomlinson took their leave from the three. They vowed to keep in touch, and were told not to worry about Belverley and his mob.

A large fat man still clad in a rich fur coat and smoking a diamond studded cigar, came waddling over to the friends and introduced himself to them and his reasons for approaching them.

"My name is Whately, and I'm one of the Vice Presidents of the ISDM. I have a large ship-building and repair company, with bases other than at Glasgow. I also have a growing fleet of my own, mostly tankers and bulk carriers. I am in joint partnership with my friends Mr Ling and company, sitting at the table, who express their wish to meet you. The thing is, I need a good engineer of your calibre to train up my engine crews. You are currently an acting 2nd, but without your papers. My friend Mr McPhee knows you can do the job, so I'm prepared to take you on as a proper 2nd, and with the usual career structure for you to get to the ISDM Academy as you put it so dramatically. What do you say?" he asked jovially.

John looked at his friends, around at Day and at Tomlinson, realising that if he left his present shipping line, he wouldn't see them for quite some time if not at all.

This was a defining moment for him and he was thankful to be surrounded by his well-wishers to help him decide.

"We are also free from Belverley and company, so why not John?" Tomlinson asked gently

"If you are worrying of what we're thinking John! Then forget us and take this offer. We told you that we're all free men and we'd have to split up and go our own separate ways again someday. Its part of our life." Larter said quietly, looking into John's face.

"Yes John! That's the way of life at sea and well you know it." Sinclair added sombrely.

"It appears that the three of you have been around the world a few times together. I tell you what. As it happens, I need a good Radio Officer and a good Chief Bosun to help me set up a Training consortium so your friends could join you.

I can guarantee all three of you get promoted up the ladder just as soon as you sign our papers. That's where all the perks start coming in, so now what do you say?" Whately asked quietly. John looked around the circle of friends with uncertainty, before Larter asked the man if they could think it over, and give him their answer tomorrow.

"Why certainly you can. I would have been disappointed if you accepted me right here and now. By the way, my wages for good officers are almost double what the skinflints Invergarron or Belverley are paying you, and without their swinging claw-back penalties. I'm staying here for the next two days or so before I sail on my own ship. Come on board tomorrow sometime and we'll discuss terms then. Here's my card." Whateley man beamed, and rising up from the table, shook the three friends hands farewell.

"Don't forget, don't be adrift John!" Day said with a smile, as he and Tomlinson left the table

"See John. Everything is just as I had thought. We've got our transport home, and we've been offered a job from a different company." Larter said, and they raised their glasses in yet another toast.

"Here's to pastures new." they toasted, then enjoyed the end of the cabaret before they were informed that their transport was ready to take them home.

The limousine ride was all too brief for the three friends as the vehicle arrived onto the gravel driveway of the cottage. Larter gave the driver some money as a personal tip, despite the mild objections raised by the chauffeur, before the driver waved and drove off.

They walked quietly into the house again and sat at the big wooden table, as Sinclair produced one of the unopened bottles of wine that was last seen at their table.

Larter produced three fancy fluted glasses, then asked John

what did he bring back as rabbits.

John smiled and said.

"Contraband glass and silver ashtrays. Shame about the Balmoral name on it."

"Quite apt too considering we were treated like royals." Larter quipped as they sat and completed their night by the warm embers in the fire grate.

Before long they climbed wearily up the stairs and to bed to sleep away what was left of the night.

They slept well into the following morning, before John's mother called them to come and have their breakfast.

"Morning Mrs Grey!" Sinclair and Larter greeted, stumbling into the kitchen, and saw John dressed and busying himself with his newly acquired shotguns.

"Just bagged us some duck and quail for supper." John stated quietly, and finishing his chore of cleaning his guns, came over to sit by his friends.

"Right then gentlemen, we each have a decision to make, starting with Mr Whately. Who will start the debate?" John asked, tossing the business card onto the table.

Author's Note

A special novel called **WE COME UNSEEN** which is currently being written and is a separate novel from my 'Adventure' series, will be published around May 2010 with a special price of **£10.99**. The proceeds of which will be donated to charity to help support our armed forces. The more readers who will subscribe to this book this will obviously determine a bigger amount being donated, but hopefully it will be around £5 per copy.

This will cause a short break in my series for those of you wishing to catch up on your reading, therefore Book 7 *The Repulse Bay* will now be scheduled for publication around October 2010, and at its usual price.

Frederick A Read

Ice Mountains is the sixth book within the epic
Adventures of John Grey series, which comprises of:

A Fatal Encounter
The Black Rose
The Lost Legion
Fresh Water
A Beach Party
Ice Mountains
Perfumed Dragons
The Repulse Bay
Silver Oak leaves
Future Homes

All published by www.guaranteedbooks.net

Also by the same author
Moreland and Other Stories